"CARS COMING. MANY."

Chianda hadn't shouted, but his voice cut across everything. Immediately, every man froze. Crates of ammunition half-loaded into the truck, weapons poised.

There was no sound. The vast silence of the desert held everything in suspension. Two men grinned nervously when they could hear nothing, but Chianda stood perfectly still facing the south-west.

"Seven," he said, as if he could see them.

Disbelief showed on the men's faces. Donovan snapped into action: "If he says he hears them he bloody well hears them!" he shouted. "Get the stuff on the truck and covered. Move it!"

AUTUMN HEROES

OLIVER JACKS

A BERKLEY BOOK
published by
BERKLEY PUBLISHING CORPORATION

Published by arrangement with St. Martin's Press, Inc.

St. Martin's Press, Inc.
175 Fifth Avenue
New York, New York 10010

SBN 425-04037-2

BERKLEY MEDALLION BOOKS are published by
Berkley Publishing Corporation
200 Madison Avenue
New York, N.Y. 10016

BERKLEY MEDALLION BOOK ® TM 757,375

Printed in the United States of America

Berkley Edition, APRIL, 1979

To
Charles Rodgers
Tony Marlin
Roger Hawkins
Tom Swinnerton
Lofty Hayward
Ginger Gray
Sergeant Chianda
Tenente Rocco

And, of course, to Col. Lynn Allen.
Also to the memory of Leonard Bagley
killed in Burma.

AND TO VETERANS EVERYWHERE

None of the above bear any relation to any of the characters in this book in any way.

The tree of liberty must be refreshed from time to time with the blood of patriots and tyrants. It is its natural manure.

THOMAS JEFFERSON

AUTUMN HEROES

Prologue

THE GERMANS WERE the first to print a claim that Princess Anne had been kidnapped. The British were the first to deny it. Confusion set in from that point.

In the middle of claim and counter claim was one solid fact. Princess Anne and her husband Captain Mark Phillips were on safari in Kenya. As it was a private visit press coverage had been stripped to a minimum by Royal request, although security was high.

It was by no means the first time a foreign newspaper had printed articles about the Royal Family that British news editors had baulked at publishing. Particularly one like this.

A guarded Government statement asserted that there was no official knowledge of a kidnap but urgent enquiries were being made through the Kenya Government in Nairobi. This was at least partly false. The Kenya press was playing it down. Within hours of the original release the Germans, and also the French, claimed that the kidnappers were demanding a ransom of £10,000,000 from the British. That news was to create a bitter side issue with enormous complications.

Meanwhile it was impossible to get a seat on any scheduled flight to Nairobi by any route. Quantas were running in from Australia via Johannesburg and Pan American suddenly found that they could fill their seats from New York to Nairobi without relying on European touchdowns. Airlines enjoyed a bonanza of overbooking as newsmen and camera crews jostled for reservations. The Kenya Government let them in. Beneath the frantic activity lay a gnawing fear that stretched the six thousand miles between London and Nairobi like an exposed nerve.

Once in Nairobi the newsmen got little further. The exact whereabouts of the Royal safari were kept secret. Whilst small planes were chartered out, official guidance was deliberately misleading. In an area so vast, speculative searches were a waste of time, particularly with the limited number of airstrips. Rumours of the party's location were varied and numerous; guides who claimed knowledge of the Royal whereabouts were suddenly many and ridiculously expensive. Then came an official clamp-down and transport was difficult to find. The best prospect for the newsmen was to keep an ear to the ground and to badger officials.

One fact emerged. Radio contact had broken down between the Royal party and the central security source. There was no direct contact. In spite of this, in the modest heat of the five-thousand-feet-high Kenya capital the first positive news was released. It came from a spokesman for Captain Mark Phillips in the form of a prepared statement.

Whilst concern by the gentlemen of the press was appreciated, it was regretted that unfounded rumour had caused them so much inconvenience. The problem had been caused by a technical breakdown of communications. Both Princess Anne and Mark Phillips were well and saw no reason to interrupt their safari. Respect for their privacy should be maintained. They would return to Nairobi as planned in four days' time.

Who had issued the statement? An unnamed aide

sufficiently acceptable to the Kenyan Minister of Home Affairs for him to submit on the Minister's behalf.

A communal sense of acute expectation was reduced to suspicious disillusion. No one really believed it but no one was prepared to call a representative of Royalty a liar.

The statement had little effect on the world news media. It took second place to the rumour that the £10,000,000 demand was from a group called the Somali Independence Army. Journalists did their stuff and dug up what they could in a matter of hours.

Enquiry revealed that the hub of the problem was Djibouti, the capital of the French Territory of Afars and Issas which was cradled in the Horn of Africa between the Gulf of Aden and the Red Sea. Because Djibouti is a port, factions in both Ethiopia and Somali saw considerable advantages in possessing it. To complicate matters a rail link connected Djibouti with Ethiopia, a fact that did not deter the Somalis, who considered their ethnic links a stronger bond than steel rails, from making prior claim. Sections of them were willing to fight for it and, with proper backing, they could no doubt succeed, unless France was willing to set its military weight against them.

This was unlikely for many reasons, not least of which was the fact that the Somalia Democratic Republic is not democratic at all. It is a one-party state controlled by the Russians. The desert Somalis lived an extremely arduous life and it was not surprising that they saw Djibouti, gateway to the Red Sea and the Suez Canal, as part answer to their salvation.

The claim that the S.I.A. was behind the persistently rumoured kidnap put a new and harrowing slant on things. For a start it presupposed that the Princess was now over the Somali border, which could only worsen matters. Some claimed that the S.I.A. was backed by the Russians. It would certainly have suited the Russians to possess Djibouti and control the Gulf of Aden. £10,000,000 could effectively finance a small, efficient army, all that was needed to take the port. There was irony in that it involved neither the French nor the Russians.

That, however, was the least of the British Government's

problems. In spite of official denial the public sensed a cover-up and in any event preferred to believe the worst. The press, quick to respond to public reaction, now played upon it. *They remembered Peggy McKenzie*.

Peggy McKenzie had been a young social worker operating in Central Africa at the time she had been seized by terrorists. A demand for half a million pounds had been demanded of the British Government if they wanted Peggy back alive. Strengthened by the result of the Spaghetti House affair in Knightsbridge, which was quickly followed by the success of the Irish over Dr. Herrema, the Government prevaricated. They played for time; but what did they hope to gain by it?

Five days after the original demand, Peggy McKenzie's much raped and mutilated body was found by tribesmen on the outskirts of their village. The Government retaliated to the hostile accusations of "This Week" on Independent Television by claiming that, in any event, the ransom money was required by the terrorists to provide arms to be used against an African state that was wholly friendly towards Britain.

Peggy McKenzie briefly became a martyr. A young, innocent girl, who had wanted nothing more from life than to help others, had been brutally murdered and ravaged. Her ghost was raised within twelve hours of the first published demand of £10,000,000 for Princess Anne. Who was going to suggest that the ransom be paid when Peggy had been hacked to death for the absence of a mere half million?

The principle, then, surely still applied whether it be Peggy McKenzie or Princess Anne. Half a million or ten million? Communists, Marxists, Maoists and Anarchists wallowed in it. Cautious Government disclaimers were brushed aside. Even the moderate press posed the Government's dilemma; was indeed Her Royal Highness in any danger at all? One way or the other it could only be a matter of days before the truth emerged, when the couple were due back in Nairobi.

Arguments flared in pubs, homes, factories and offices. Was a blatant distinction to be drawn? In the midst of public and political conflict, claims and denials, questions in the House of Commons, duplicity, humbug and downright

Machiavellism, a drama of another kind was taking place. But it was evolving against an unhealthy background of procrastination, pressure and an impossible deadline. And amidst all this clamour action was in fact being taken *before* the first German announcement. Its roots were pathetic, its growth unbelievably variant and brittle; its substance blood, some of it tired, some of it much too young. Yet it was to flow across the barren rock of the Somali Plateau to be baked and browned by an unsparing sun until it was indistinguishable from the grinding sand. Only the dung beetles were to know the difference as they scuttled from their shallow holes to feast.

1

The Prime Minister shook his head. "Gentlemen, there will be repercussions whatever we do. If, as Field Marshal Waverly suggests, we sent in a task force, there would be a very serious risk of escalation. If we pay up we have a problem of another kind, and it would be folly to underestimate its potential at a time of political crisis." He glanced at the Foreign Secretary and slowly removed his pipe. "This is no time for humbug. We're in trouble."

The Field Marshal misguidedly took him at his word.

"So it *is* Princess Anne, Sir."

The Prime Minister looked bleak, raising his eyebrows slightly.

"Did I say that?" He lowered his gaze. "Let me make it clear. The situation is confused mainly because the Royal party are well off the beaten track. Out there that means precisely that." He glanced at his notes. "They are up in the Northern Frontier District of Kenya near the Tana River. As I understand it, the growth following the banks of the river at that point precludes a nearby landing, but a search party has been flown to the nearest airstrip and onward transport arranged. I think we must take the worst view. A demand has certainly been made but there is, as yet, no hard evidence of a kidnap." Suddenly he removed his pipe again irritably. "Their bloody radio has either broken down or there's a more ominous reason for the lack of communication. We cannot take a chance. What we're here for now is to prepare for the worst."

"Pay the money."

The Prime Minister glanced across the mahogany table at his friend, the Foreign Secretary. "I'm surprised at you; you've forgotten your narrow majority. If we pay it could be political suicide." He waved his pipe at the netted Georgian windows. "Out there, they'll remember Peggy McKenzie. She was heaven-sent for some of them." Quickly he recognised his own callousness. "Poor girl."

The Field Marshal said, "A task force or the money."

"It's not so simple." Sir Murray Field always spoke quietly. His city broker image was totally misleading; his air of ease a camouflage for the inner turmoil, the mental energy somehow kept tight under a narrow, balding cranium. "If the Princess has been taken I have an idea who might be behind it. If I'm right I wouldn't bank too much on her safe return."

The unease was slow to begin, silence growing from it.

"The message so far is that it's the Somali Independence Army making the demand." The Prime Minister was unsettled.

"Quite so. It's the person at its head who worries me." The M.I.6. chief remained on low key. "A man who has not forgotten a defeat in World War II, who would dearly love to humiliate us for the pleasure of it. Ten million pounds will be the asking price. That will be the beginning of a sadistic protraction that will make us appear both weak and fools. The money will provide the power he wants and will certainly give the French problems. But that's only part of it. I wouldn't like to predict the outcome. The man will not be influenced one iota by world opinion."

"I must accept that you know what you're saying."

"I agree with the Field Marshal. We need a task force and we need it quickly."

"We dare not use troops. The Kenyan Government would never sanction passage, nor the Ethiopians. It would take too long by sea and we can hardly fly them directly into Somalia. Whichever way, it would be considered open invasion. It's not as if the Middle East can stand more pot-boiling."

Sir Murray Field smiled thinly. "My mind doesn't work so overtly. I have an idea. I confess it's a desperate one but with luck something might grow from it."

"You're not thinking of asking the French to let us go in by Djibouti?"

"It had crossed my mind, sir. But the French have their own problems with the Somalis; they're not likely to want to exacerbate them. Apart from that I'm sure the Field Marshal will agree that, in a military sense, Djibouti is too far north. My guess is that any group pulling off such a kidnap would keep well away from the main coastal towns on the one side and from the Ethiopian border on the other. As a wild surmise I'd suggest that they'd take to the Somali Plateau for isolation and protection, not impossibly far from the Kenya border in the south. I have ears to the ground in both Kismayu and Mogadishu. So have the Kenyans; remember the proximity of the Russians to their border."

When the Prime Minister was called away to take a telephone call there was little else said by the few men round the table. The Foreign Secretary rose to look out of the windows. As the Prime Minister re-entered all eyes turned towards him. His added grimness told them much. "From Nairobi," he said, fingertips kneading one brow. "It's still obscure but it looks as bad as it could be. An air search has found what would seem to be the camp. Tents have been burnt, trucks and jeeps destroyed. A small area of bush was on fire, and some survivors were still trying to douse the blaze."

"*Some* survivors?"

The Prime Minister gripped the back of a chair. "There are some dead. We don't know who. The land party has not yet arrived."

"Any sign of—"

"No. The reconnaissance leaves much to be desired but the terrain is difficult. They're doing their best. Gentlemen, we have a problem."

The understatement silenced them for some seconds.

"Can we be sure it's the right party?" The Foreign Secretary was clutching at straws.

The Prime Minister shrugged without replying and then looked his M.I.6. chief in the eye. "I've informed Her Majesty. I think it's time to listen to your scheme, whatever it is. We can stall for four days at the most. Gentlemen, it would be prudent if Sir Murray and I finished this alone."

When the others had gone Sir Murray said, "I have to find expendable volunteers."

"How expendable?"

"Fifty per cent. Seventy-five. Perhaps all of them. There can be no guarantees, and there's no time for planning. In any other circumstances such a scheme would be unacceptable."

"I can give you no official sanction."

"I understand that, Prime Minister."

"Nor may you have the use of recognisable personnel or arms."

"I've already accepted that too. Should Her Majesty be consulted?"

The Prime Minister gave it brooding consideration. "No. I doubt that she would agree and, anyway, you don't seem too clear of the details yourself."

"It's best that I don't give them to you. It could save you embarrassment."

The Prime Minister looked thoughtfully at his Intelligence Chief. "Don't crack too many eggs."

"I doubt I can avoid it. We have to make up our minds whether we go ahead or not."

The Prime Minister nodded. "Do what you think best and spare me the details."

"I have most of their addresses, telephone numbers. Some of us still keep in touch. Reunions, y'know. Why on earth do you want them? Yes. I think I understand. All right, Bill, hold on while I get my little black book." Afterwards, Colonel 'Jumbo' Hamilton stared at the phone for a long time. Through the open door he could hear his wife in the kitchen.

On the window sill, having flown from the folds of the Dorset countryside, a robin eyed him, impatiently awaiting its overdue breadcrumbs. Jumbo Hamilton, in his late sixties, a big man with a mane of hair still dark, straightened. "Christ," he said fiercely, "If I'm reading it right, they're raving mad. They're over the hill. Anyway, they wouldn't go." He growled to himself, suddenly annoyed that only names and addresses had been asked of him.

Jumbo Hamilton threw some bits to the robin, chin out, eyes bright with reminiscence. Memory surged back. About to stomp into the kitchen to tell his wife his suspicions, the telephone rang again. He stiffened noticeably when he answered. "Yes, sir. Yes, indeed, Field Marshal. Of course."

When he went reflectively into the kitchen his wife was chopping onions with the nimbleness of experience. "Two calls in one morning? There's solitude for you."

"One was from Bill Chandler. You remember him. He wanted the address of one of the lads." Lads? God Almighty. Yet he still thought of them as such. "The other was a wrong number."

Jumbo Hamilton had received the second call at ten thirty a.m. At ten to eleven Pat Donovan was stepping from his car, having driven the short distance from Amersham to Hazelmere in Buckinghamshire to ask his typist to retype some manuscript. The severe-faced Miss Jones opened the front door before he reached it. She was never called anything else and he'd never discovered her Christian name.

"You're wanted on the telephone."

"Me? Here? Only Stella knows I'm here."

"It's not your wife."

Puzzled, Donovan stepped into the small bright hall and picked up the receiver. The discreet Miss Jones disappeared like a fading shadow.

"Who is it?" Aggressively, jawline not dissimilar to Jumbo Hamilton's.

"The Ministry of Defence, Mr. Donovan. Your wife said you'd be there."

"Ministry of Defence?"

"We have a problem. We think you can help us solve it. We wondered if we might have a word or two with you."

"Go ahead."

"Up here in London."

"Well, yes, all right. I won't be up until next week."

"We were rather thinking of this morning."

"How the hell—You've had that."

"There's a helicopter on its way. We'd be most grateful."

"*A helicopter?* Jesus! What are you on about?"

"Your wife promised to lay an old sheet out on your lawn. It will be easier for the pilot to pick out."

Donovan held the phone away from his ear, looked quickly towards the door Miss Jones had gone through and, satisfied she couldn't hear, said, "That's you, Brian, you bastard. Having me on. You let your voice slip there."

"No, sir, it is not Brian and I'm certainly not having you on. The copter should be there in twenty minutes. It *is* rather urgent."

The police car drew up in front of the terraced house in one of the quieter streets of Northampton. The neighbours knew the man living alone there to be something of a recluse. He was sometimes seen shopping in the local supermarket which seemed to cover all his needs. A tall, bespectacled, slightly stooped, thin character who always wore dark, shabby clothes and a hat to cover his bald head. He had a strong, pleasant face, but the dark brown eyes were constantly reflective behind the steel frames.

Curtains along the short street were plucked as the car stopped outside, flasher off, siren stilled. A police inspector went to the door and hid his surprise as it was opened. A trained glance took in the scuffed carpet slippers, concertina'd trousers, tieless shirt. "Reverend Vale?" Difficult to keep disbelief from his voice. Intelligent face, though; surprisingly strong. So what conveyed the impression of adversity?

Colin Vale hesitated. It had been a long time since he'd been called Reverend. "Yes."

"May I come in, sir?"

Vale stood aside reluctantly, suddenly aware of the smell of late breakfast cooking from the tiny kitchen. Cheap fat always smelled rancid. They went into the living room. The inspector tried not to look around. It was like a Victorian transplant. Browns and fawns and a clock that had stopped one day at ten past two. The air was stale.

"Please sit down." Vale removed some ancient magazines from a chair. Library books were neatly stacked on a cheap table as if ready to go back.

"No, thank you, sir. I won't be here long enough." The inspector smiled, wanting to break through the barrier Vale quietly transmitted. "The Ministry of Defence have been on to us. Apparently you are not on the phone otherwise they would have contacted you direct. They're asking for your help in a matter."

"Help from me? The Ministry of Defence? There's been a mistake."

"No, sir. It's you all right. They want you to go to London now, sir."

"That's impossible."

"We're to run you to the Thurbridge Sports Ground. There'll be a helicopter waiting. All expenses will be met, sir."

The Inspector had been told nothing of expenses. His instinct had prompted him to embroider.

"Really?" Vale gazed round critically at the near squalor. What must the inspector think? Suddenly it mattered. "Well, we'd better not keep the Ministry waiting. Give me five minutes to change." There must be less crumpled trousers somewhere.

"The Ministry of Defence can get stuffed. I'm busy. Anyway, what sort of con do you think you're pulling?" Jimmy King held on to hear the answer. A good con intrigued him. He stroked the pencil moustache; it had been there for over thirty years, grey now when he forgot to touch it up with that special stuff. Like his sideburns.

"I'm serious. sir. We can send round a car at once."

Jimmy King liked being called 'sir'. Especially by a plum-in-mouth, upper-crust son of a bitch like this treacle-treated yes-man on the phone. "So you want my advice?"

"We think you can help. Yes, sir."

"It'll cost you. I don't come cheap. And there's an import clearance I want fixed."

"I'm sure we can help, sir. I'll send a car now."

"Stick your car. I'll come in one of my own. Where are you? Okay, cocker. I'm on my way."

King flicked the intercom and gazed across the room, through the windows to the Thames. The sun shone on the moving water. "Charlie? Bring the Bentley. And put a Union Jack on the bloody standard. We'll arrive in style." He pulled out a mirror, smoothed his hair. Some day he'd have the fringe transplanted. Like Frank Sinatra.

"The Guv'nor wants you."

Thompson switched off the lathe, finger-combing a mane of white hair as the pitch of the hum dropped. "Doesn't he realise I'm busy?"

"Cut the bull, Thompson. It's important."

Thompson preceded the warder through the workshop, meeting enquiring expressions from some of the cons. He gave no thought to the summons—he had learned to blank his mind to everything except his cell, the workshop, the exercise yard and a few of those around him. There was nothing beyond the external security of the prison.

He'd been in the Governor's office twice. As he stepped in for the third time he was as indifferent as before. There was the desk, the window, the dullness and a soldierly man standing beside the Governor who himself, surprisingly, rose. It sparked the first faint interest in Thompson.

The Governor said, "This gentleman is from the Ministry of Defence, Thompson. He wants a word with you. I'll leave you alone."

After the Governor left Thompson turned to see the warder, too, had gone. His interest rose but he was suspicious. He eyed the stranger by the desk. "Ministry of Defence?" It was a rough, uncaring challenge.

"We think you can help us." The man came round the desk, not too far, held back by the agate bleakness of Thompson's stare. The prisoner was a rock, harshly moulded, ready for trouble. Although the hair was white, the face was still young, the body spring-loaded. Eyes hard and penetrating, full of distrust and aggression. Ideal. "I would like you to come to London with me."

Just like that. Thompson's quick mind darted round for

snags. He didn't trust the smoothie in front of him. "You've got the wrong man."

"No, Mr. Thompson. All we're asking is that you come and listen to us. Whether you return here afterwards is up to you."

It was the right bait yet there was something wrong. "Are you saying I can step out've here?"

"With me, yes. Doesn't the prospect of being away from here, if only for a day, appeal to you?"

He dared not think about it. That had all been shut out. Yet common sense told him this was something special. He didn't understand and he could see he'd get little more from this slicker, but special just the same. "Do you know I'm in for murder? They'll never let me out."

"I understand it was reduced to manslaughter."

"What's the odds? I killed the bitch."

"It makes no difference. I have Home Office authority in my pocket."

"But you won't tell me what it's about?"

"Not here. In London. There's a car ready to take us to Speke airport." The Ministry man hesitated. "There is a possibility that this could lead to parole."

Thompson stiffened. His impulse was to squeeze the lie from the white collared throat in front of him. His powerful fingers coiled even as he checked himself. That was how he'd got here. It wouldn't get him out. He studied the Civil Service image. The man would say what he'd been told to say.

"It's not something I'd mislead you about, Mr. Thompson. But it's up to you. It will depend on events."

Mister. The Governor should have heard that. "There's a catch. There's gotta be. But I'd be a mug not to listen."

"Indeed. We've really no time to spare."

It was like getting up after being sick for some time. His legs were weak like the struggling sun behind patchwork cloud. It was unreal. He left without a prison escort; he felt strangely insecure. The Ministry man was hardly a guard. Perhaps the driver, then? Nothing felt right, not even his suit after the weight he'd lost in prison. He could have run for it but he didn't want to run. Not yet. He sat back in the comfort of the car suspicious and reflective.

Then the craziest part of that crazy day happened in an unbelievable way. Police cars took up front and rear to siren and flash their way through the increasing traffic to the airport. Suddenly he felt important.

There were six men in the room off Whitehall and they were reacting as old comrades do on meeting after some time. They had a bond. Nor would they forget it. Ever. Even Thompson suspended his suspicion on meeting old friends who had known his problem. And the Reverend Colin Vale found a safer outlet for his emotions and, for the moment, could forget.

At one end of the room was a covered table with canapés and drinks. The men laughed and leg-pulled in an increasingly relaxed atmosphere; they could have been waiting for a briefing in their younger days.

"Gentlemen. Your attention please."

Glasses in hand they turned to face a stocky, middle-aged, soldierly man who spoke with quiet authority. None of them recognised him. Later they were to realise that none of their contacts were visually identifiable. None were known to any of them. Nor were they to see more than one individual at a time, as if corroboration of the meeting from their hosts might be difficult to obtain.

"I'm called Smithy." He smiled at them, accepting that they weren't convinced. "Before we go further it will be necessary for each one of you to swear the Official Secrets Act."

The group of men stirred, eyed each other. They all well knew about commitment.

Smithy smiled. "Old hands, I see. Gentlemen, no one can force you. It is merely that certain details cannot be divulged until you have sworn in. Your only obligation then will be to maintain silence. Anyone not wishing to stay will be taken back the same way as they were brought here."

A note of sobriety crept into the room.

"This way, gentlemen." An inner door was opened and they filed through. There were more than enough chairs. They spaced themselves out as they sat down, a habit that had not died with the years. All were men who had experienced isolation to some degree. The surprise of seeing a huge map of the Horn of Africa draped over a blackboard came in varying degrees.

Each man in turn took his vow of secrecy on the Bible and Vale's hand trembled very slightly as he held the book. But he uttered the oath in a steady, slow voice. A venetian blind was dropped over the window and the map was spotlighted.

"Gentlemen, I don't have to tell you of the rumours about Princess Anne." If Smithy wanted silence he had effected it with one sentence. "News is gradually filtering through; much of it is obscure. There is only one certainty we accept. *Two women* are missing. The princess and a lady in waiting. Some male members of the party are also missing."

A pointer cast a low finger of shadow as it prodded through the light. "Our information is that they are not far over the Somali border." He let it sink in, knowing that it would register and, with it, the purpose of their being here.

"Now as you well know, Somaliland is one of those countries where few Europeans have been. In the interior, on the plateau we're talking about, you can count the white visitors over the years in dozens. Men who have intimate knowledge of the interior, as you have, almost don't exist at all. Most of them are in this room."

It was only a slight exaggeration. They understood that he meant men who were immediately available. There were a few in South Africa, others in Rhodesia.

"You mean we *used* to have intimate knowledge." Donovan was wary. "It was a long time ago."

"Yes, it was. But places like that don't change. The towns, yes. Progress in parts. But where we're talking about it will never change in our life time. Even a mosquito needs water. It's not the type of place one could ever forget, wouldn't you say?"

The men were suddenly uneasy.

The pointed tapped the map low down. "Gentlemen, from the research I've had the time to do, it comes over clearly that your operation, though small, was unique. With your African askari you went where white troops couldn't go. You endured insufferable water, when you could find it, you learned a good deal about the Somalis, not the easiest people to know. You learned to operate in virgin country without tracks and your trucks did impossible feats by the sheer skill of your handling. You learned to survive in almost impossible conditions in a heat of," he referred to a note which spoiled the effect he had been building up, "124 degrees fahrenheit in the shade and sometimes higher than that. It is unfortunate that your mopping up exercise was obscured by the main advance of the Ethiopian campaign, still the fastest in military history. But to anyone who has fought in these conditions, the suffering and danger of winkling out Banda born to the environment, the knowledge and experience built up must surely remain for all time."

It was a speech that might have stirred youngsters. It even stirred the men in the room, for different reasons: it revived memory, in some quite vividly.

"So what do you want of us?" The rest were content to let Donovan act as spokesman.

"Whilst we aren't clear at this precise moment who has been kidnapped we believe that the person behind it is Hassan Kilewe." Again a calculated pause.

"Twinkletoes?" Thompson remembered. "If it's him you'll be lucky to get anyone back. He's a vicious bastard."

The appraisal hung in the air. King voiced their recollection. "The first thing he did with prisoners was to hand them over to the women who cut off their balls." He gazed round at the others. "You remember. The last thing was to hold their heads up on the end of spears. So no one got him? If the Princess is with him God help her."

"We haven't got God, gentlemen. At least not in recognisable form. We do have you."

"You want us as advisors?" Donovan again, trying to force out the truth.

"We want a task force. We believe it's the only way we'll get them back. World opinion won't touch men like these, if it ever reaches them. They're on primitive ground with primitive requirement. *In and out in four days*."

No one moved. The sound of the pointed butt touching the carpet was amplified against the total silence. Disbelief filled the room in a growing atmosphere that finally had Smithy fidgeting uneasily; he had to sell the idea.

"Just what do you want of us?"

"I thought it obvious, Mr. Donovan. We want you to

form the nucleus of the task force. Your experience would be invaluable."

"For Chrissake." Donovan gazed round at the others. "You must be raving mad. We're over the hill. Look at us, for God's sake."

"You know the form, gentlemen. What you may have lost physically you more than make up for in experience."

"It's gone. It's over, long ago. Our experience isn't worth a light."

"I suggest to you that confronted with the same conditions, problems, dangers, as you encountered before, you would not only respond in the same way as you did but you would remember your old mistakes and avoid them. *In short you would know exactly how to cope, gentlemen.* A man never forgets how to swim, however old he is. What he will have learned is how to conserve himself. How to survive. Putting in men half your age without experience of the terrain, the heat, the conditions and the Somalis, would be suicidal. We don't want recklessness, we want success."

"You mean just us?"

"No, Mr. Donovan. Your group would be in command, dictating the moves. You would have younger men available to do the running around, the main physical work."

"Troops?"

"We dare not use troops. But experienced men, nevertheless."

"*Mercenaries*, then?"

"Most of them have served with various armies at some time. All will be young, tough and willing."

"My God. Us, out of the ark, and a bunch of trigger-happy youngsters. Nothing official. Just a bunch of—" He searched for the word; "patriots?"

"Isn't that exactly what you are? If we are to believe the worst, wouldn't you be directly helping the Royal family?"

"And would the Royal family know of this little caper?"

"Perhaps not initially. Success would ensure that they would. You would command the highest respect and show that the British still have guts."

"You're a good con man, Smithy." King was grinning. "We're all too old for a lark like this."

"So you won't offer to go?"

"No. Not me."

"Anyone else?" Donovan was reflective. "We couldn't stand up to it. Not now."

"You would merely control the rest. Tell them what to do, where to go. You'd have three days there at the most." Smithy was beginning to despise himself. The very least they needed was a small arms refresher course. It couldn't be squeezed in.

"Why the time limit?"

"Princess Anne and Mark Phillips are due back in Nairobi in four days' time."

"So you can only cover up that long?" Donovan did not expect a reply and didn't receive one. He was excited but cautious. There's no fool like an old fool. Well, they weren't old but middle age had been with them some time. Once on this sort of venture there could be no turning back. *Stella*. For God's sake, just what was he thinking of? "Count me out," he said, suddenly angry at himself.

Smithy remained upright, unsmiling, expecting a breakthrough and not surprised when it came. He was both satisfied and unhappy.

"I'll go," said Thompson. Anything was better than going back to prison.

"I will be delighted to help," said Vale. If he couldn't escape from himself he could at least perform a useful function. Help someone. He hadn't done that for some time.

2

"You'll need at least half a dozen of us. Some might not make the grade and mercenaries will need controlling."

"Am I to understand you've changed your mind, Mr. Donovan?"

"Not quite. How many would we be up against?"

"Perhaps thirty. You'd have the element of surprise. You'd need about sixty men."

"If you believe we'd have the element of surprise in Somaliland you'll believe anything. The word will spread like a bush fire. We'd need arms and equipment. If we can remember how to use them."

"We'll supply arms with which you were familiar. I agree that half a dozen of you would be ideal to control a force of sixty, particularly if you split into small groups. It would also allow alternative command among you if conservation of energy is required." Smithy knew that it sounded much better than saying that with a high casualty rate one or two of you might see it through.

"I know a man who would most probably come if I can speak to him."

"Who have we missed out, Mr. Donovan?"

"Pietro Frascelli. He was a lieutenant in the Carbinieri when we first met. He was there much longer than any of us. Certainly a long time before us. After the war he went back until the Russians made their grab."

"We couldn't use an Italian."

"Why not? Wouldn't it add to your spontaneity spiel? He was an explosive expert. Still is. Demolition."

"What's your association with him?"

"It's a long story. We met near Gelib. I took him prisoner. We maintained contact after the war."

"It's too dangerous. We must maintain secrecy."

"I'd trust my life to him."

"You're trying to pressure me, Mr. Donovan."

"But I'm not employing the same humbug that you are, Smithy. We all know the score. We know what you're leaving out. We know damn fine there'll be no official backing, that you'll pull the plug if things go wrong. We know who'll take the credit if it works. So cut the crap. It's occurred to me that there might be useful material for a book. Do I contact him or not?"

"As long as you realise that any leak of information from him leaves you liable to prosecution under the Secrets Act."

"You're beginning to annoy me. Where's a phone?"

"You'll have to wait until this session is over."

"I'll need one too, cocker."

"Am I to take it you want one for the same reason, Mr. King?"

"Yeah. They all know 'im. A South African banker named Gerry Steinberg. He gets bored from time to time. I see him about every three or four years. What that bloke could do with trucks and armoured cars up rock faces and in the desert had to be seen to be believed. Should've been a mechanic but made more money banking. He also did some medical training. He'd go for Princess Anne. And for me."

While Smithy considered it, Donovan whispered to King, "What made you change your mind?"

King grinned wickedly. "I just remembered my yacht's out on charter. I might as well fill in the time. Anyway, it's a last fling." His eyes were reflective, gazing back over the years.

Of the six men in the room four had agreed to go. The other two were politely shown out after being reminded of their obligation and thanked for coming.

In the map room the four volunteers had reached the stage of demanding an African guide. Although they all stored knowledge, when it came down to reading the signs in virgin country there was no one as proficient as a bush African. They were unanimous in who they wanted if he was to be found. A young sergeant, who had been called Chianda when he had served with them. No one, unfortunately, knew where Chianda might be. The last heard of him was when he had finally left the battalion a few years after the war and had returned to his village near N'dola in what was then Northern Rhodesia.

There was no time. Everyone knew it. It was difficult for them to absorb that they were flying out that night to Nairobi. There was the matter of arms, transport, the other two men somewhere in Africa and Pietro Frascelli in Rome, all to link up if they agreed to come. There was clothing, general equipment, and families and wives to be fobbed off with placating lies. The mercenaries had to be contacted and organised. It seemed totally impossible to achieve so much in just a few hours. It was under this beginning of utter hopelessness that the character of the four men soon proved the faith of official judgment. It was evident from the moment that Jimmy King, the man who refused to grow up, gave the V salute to the others. It was to be their symbol as it had been once before.

Officialdom, too, under the clandestine direction of Sir Murray Field, and of a subordinate of Field Marshal Waverly, was pulling its weight with some electrifying manoeuvres.

"World War II stuff. Bren guns, mark 4. Short Lee Enfields, Sten guns, pistols and automatics, No. 36 grenades.

Plenty of .303 and 9mm ammunition. Anything you can find to arm a force of sixty men. In good working order. For delivery Nairobi midday tomorrow latest."

"Impossible."

"We'll give you an extra fifteen minutes for the impossible. We're hiring back arms you've already had from us cheap, so what have you got to complain about?"

"Rico? Where's that shipment for Southern Abyssinia? Yeah, that's the one; the Ethiopian Liberation Movement. They're all liberation, boy. That's what they want the arms for, so they can liberate themselves and enslave the rest. Negelli? Where the . . . wait a minute, I've found it." A stubby finger traced the map. "There's a road leading into Somaliland. Any way of making contact? Through Addis Ababa. That'll take too long, Rico. I want the stuff diverted to Nairobi by midday tomorrow. I know I'm crazy but the buyer is solid and it makes me respectable. I might even get a knighthood out of it. Yeah, it's like that. So you can't help? Who else is supplying these monkeys? Oscar Haslam. Yeah. Uganda. That sounds hopeful. Hope the Bermuda sun is up by now. Don't let it burn the back off you, Rico. Ciao."

"Stella, I'm sorry love but I won't be back for a few days. Can't explain. Top secret and all that. You shouldn't have put the sheet out on the lawn." Donovan could feel her concern creeping over the line. He felt a heel suddenly and then something stronger. Supposing he didn't see her again?

"What are you trying to say, darling?" She was worried sick his bantering tone coming from the past. It meant he was playing something down.

"They're hanging on to us a bit. Nothing to worry about."

"You can't tell me about it but there's nothing to worry about?"

He heard the dog barking in the background. The little devil. He began to churn. Stella's voice had driven home what he was leaving behind. Oh, Christ, what had he done? "It's hush hush. We'll make it up. Really."

"Make up for what?" Her worry shrieked at him. "I can cope with you being away for a few days. What I find difficult is not knowing what you'll be doing. Will you be in danger, Pat?"

What had made her say that? "Danger? At my age?" He laughed and could hear the hollowness of it himself. He had no right to do this to her. There was no way out without letting the rest down. And two young girls suffering in the desert.

"Come back, Pat. I know that tone. Come back. *Please*."

He sweated on the end of the phone thinking he'd better wind it up fast.

With a percipience that cut through him she said, "Are you doing something stupid? Don't try to put the clock back, Pat. And don't leave us like this, without knowing, with nothing but worry. I love you."

"I love you, too, sweetie. And you know it. You just remember that. I'll explain in due course. Chin up." He put the phone down as she started to plead, not hysterically, but with the deep conviction that something was wrong. It made it all so much worse.

He leaned against the wall trying to put it out of his mind but he would never do that. Just what the hell had he done to her? And if he didn't come back would she ever understand?

"You still in bed, you lazy sod? Well, it took me long enough to reach you. Jimmy? Of course it's Jimmy. Who else d'you know who speaks with a bloody Etonian accent? Listen, cocker, can we get together? Have a head-shrinker over a plate of cockles and mussels? I know you don't like them. A pint of Van der Hum then, with an inch of brandy on top. Well, tomorrow. Midday at latest. It's sort of urgent. No, not Jo'burg. Nairobi. If the schedules don't fit, what's wrong with your own plane?

"Well, I'll tell you. There was this bunch of has-beens. Funny blokes who remind me of Pat Donovan, Tommy Thompson and Colin Vale. Then there was the fairy princess who was snatched from her ivory tower. And the bad, bad wolf *twinkletoed* across the desert to his secret lair and demanded her mother's lollipops. So the prince got an army together and all he could get were old-age pensioners armed with pitch forks which they stuffed between their legs and flew all the way to save her.

"You won't forget the great de Knacker, half Somali, half Bantu? You'll have guessed he's in on the act. Thought it might interest you, bearing in mind what he did to your brother.

"Not later than midday. Norfolk Hotel. Right, cocker."

"Oscar, this is Michael. I have this problem. I have to get a small quantity of small arms to Nairobi by midday tomorrow. A very important buyer who'll probably sell them back to us after a few days at half the price they'll pay for them. I'll guarantee the money myself. Oscar, listen. The buyer has sold us plenty of surplus before. We don't want the source to dry up, do we? I hear you're dealing with some death-wishers in Uganda. If I give you the list you'll know who I'm handling, okay?

"What can you do for me? Twenty-five Stens, five Brens, thirty Short Lee's, a dozen assorted automatics and a three-inch mortar. Oscar, that's very nice, but it's not enough. Fifty No. 36 grenades. Okay, but we need more Stens. I know you're doing me a favour but I'm doing you a bigger one. Believe me.

"Plenty of ammo to go with the stuff. Twenty per cent on normal price. That's acceptable. I take it your latest list is unchanged? I'll pass it on. And that's the best you can do? Where's the stuff now? Somewhere between Mombasa and Nairobi? Can you make contact for the switch? You'll stop it in Nairobi before it continues on to Lake Victoria. Great. Now listen carefully while I tell you exactly where. Then call it back. Thanks Oscar."

Michael Harkill put down the phone, made a note and blew out his cheeks. It was his best break so far. What he needed now was a miracle. One of the best intermediaries in the arms game, he was known to dealers throughout the world, both big and small. And he was trusted. With wars escalating practically everywhere, the arms runs were increasing almost daily. Where wars weren't actually taking place arms were being cached for one reason or another, even if only for defensive purposes. In Britain, too.

He well knew that the arms now travelling between Mombasa and Nairobi for rebel Ugandans might now be doing so with the full knowledge and the blind eye of the Kenya Government; or they might be travelling as agricultural equipment. It would depend on their feelings towards General Amin.

The problem of the arms dealers was not in getting orders but supplies. And in that they had their own private war. The last call Harkill had made was to Belgium. Now he dialled an English number. He would respond verbally according to whom he spoke, his method differing with each one. Only his integrity remained unchanged.

"For Chrissake, Jeannie, what would I be doing with a woman at this time of day? The same as at night. All right, but you're wrong. I know it's a bit late to trust me but you've got to try. Four days at most. I can't tell you, sweetheart. Cross my heart. Look, if I was hiding something I'd be spinning you a better load of rubbish than this. This is the truth, Jeannie. Straight up. No, I haven't run out of excuses. I've still got a few tucked away but this ain't one of them. Look, you're not short of money or anything, so what's the beef? I know you need me. I'm coming back."

Silence and distrust hung on the line then, more softly.

"Jeannie, if something happens, if I have a road accident or anything, I've left everything to you. Okay? You can sort it out with the kids. Anyway, they're old enough to look after themselves. You'll never want, old love. No, I'm not drunk and I'm not expecting anything to happen. Just in case. All right? And Jeannie; those others, they didn't mean a thing. None of 'em. You're the only one I really love. Always have been. I know I'm a right bastard but I sometimes have to prove I've still got the knack. I don't know why; it's the way I am. But it's just you, Jeannie. Trust me just this once. All the way. Okay? See you."

When Jimmy King put down the telephone he could not understand why his wife had finished up crying. She'd never done that before. Clouted him when he'd got home, stormed at him unmercifully, locked him out. But never had she cried before. He sat there stroking his pencil moustache wondering where he'd gone wrong and why he had a lump in his throat. Poor old Jeannie. He hadn't intended to do that to her. He'd miss her; it came as a shock to him as he realised just how much. For the first time he seriously considered whether he would get back safely.

"Hello, Pietro. I'm glad you are back from the States. Listen carefully and try to read between the lines. You remember where we met? How would you like to go back there? At our expense. We could meet in Nairobi tomorrow morning." Donovan let it hang for a while.

"I can't tell you on the open line what for. The motive is much stronger this end than yours. Although I seem to remember that the Carbinieri were Royalists. Take your time. Let it sink in. You can always return direct from Nairobi where I can brief you better. I believe you can contribute very much to what I have in mind." Then, pushing it as far as he dared, "It would be marvellous to be on the same side."

"Would you prefer to ring me back? Or would you rather we talked about it over lunch at five thousand feet? All costs met. It's up to you. You want my number? Here it is. Ah, the penny has dropped. I can't comment on what the newspapers say. You understand? If I don't hear from you I'll take it as negative."

"Major Francis? Michael Harkill. I've had trouble getting you, sir. I've a rather urgent request for small arms. Nairobi by lunchtime tomorrow. I realise it means depleting someone else's delivery but the buyer is not entirely unconcerned with your own dealer's licence. Yes, sir, I'm well aware of your reputation. You would not have your licence without it nor would I be ringing you now. I want thirty or forty Short Lee's, five Brens and twenty Stens. Grenades and pistols. I realise you deal with more modern arms but it's a matter of gravity and well in keeping with your own high principles, sir. I cannot divulge the buyer. I can only say that the request is not for any form of subversive group but for a subject close to your own heart. I cannot add to that.

"Where's your nearest point? Mozambique. Say twelve hundred miles away from our pick-up point. Rhodesia's no better, Zambia only marginally. Unless they can be flown in. Risky. I can understand. Anything in Tanzania? A difficult market right now. Yes. Uganda? Tied up with Oscar Haslam?

Really! Southern Abyssinia? We might be able to arrange our own transport from there. No? Damn. So we're back to Mozambique and no air transport. We might be able to get a light plane down to Beria. You don't advise it in the political climate? Might be shot down. Yes, I suppose they are still a bit trigger-happy. Will you hold on a second?"

Michael Harkill covered the mouthpiece with one hand and chewed on a knuckle. It wasn't going too well. The luck he required was enormous; to find the right quantity of arms at the right place at the right time. Once arms were in the possession of buyers there was no way of retrieving them. So an additional difficulty was to find a batch in transit or at a pick up or delivery point before actual collection. Even the batch promised by Oscar Haslam was in doubt. The quantity on arrival might vary from the promised amount, unless Oscar was on the spot to arrange fair play. But Oscar was in Belgium. And fair play depended on a point of view and on who was being deceived.

Harkill was temped to tell Major Francis what the arms were required for. Officially he didn't know himself, but he wasn't a fool. None of them were. The trouble with Francis was that he saw himself as a pillar of respectability and he bent over backwards to be straight in all his dealings; perhaps a compensatory factor to a man who dealt in weapons of death. Perhaps, too, a conscience. Meanwhile it meant that he wouldn't stretch the rules. Harkill sensed an answer under his nose yet they had covered all the nearest points. It was the time factor that was beating him. It was ridiculous. Wearily he raised the phone again.

"No. I'm sorry but it looks as if we've covered everywhere. You can think of nothing else, Major? No." A last try. "Where exactly in the Mozambique is your supply? Near Lorenço Marques." Harkill made a quick calculation. "Could you get it to Jo'burg? Less than three hundred miles as the crow flies? You can't?" It meant he wouldn't. Harkill accepted it. Taking it into the Union of South Africa would contravene the major's codes. He would consider it to be dirtying his fingers. "Can you get it to the Swaziland border? You could. If there were no delays getting through to Lorenço Marques. I'll be back, Major. I'll be back."

Harkill left the small office in a hurry. He glanced at his

watch. Ten minutes to three o'clock. Time was running away. He was left with twenty-one hours in which to make the drop. Twenty-one hours to find transport, load, beat border patrols of two countries, possibly more if touchdowns were necessary, and the last mad dash by road. Say a distance of two thousand five hundred miles as the crow flies. And there were no straight lines in Africa. I'm off my rocker, he thought, and was spurred to run down the short corridor.

"Harkill's got one small uncertain consignment. Something should come from it. However the main hope lies in Francis' parcel at present tied up in Mozambique. Without fully revealing our hand he won't risk taking it in to South Africa. In fairness he's probably not got the time to get it properly organised. We can't be open about it so that's where it stays unless we can get it out ourselves."

"You're the Africa expert. Can we?" Sir Murray Field could pressure in the softest of tones.

"I think you know the answer as well as I do, sir. It means putting men at risk. Two at least. We'll need a chopper but that's not our main problem. You'll have to ring 'you-know-who' in Mbabne to smooth things out in Swaziland. Perhaps it might come better from the Foreign Secretary if you can get him to do it. As it will bust a communication gut to put through two calls to Swaziland at the same time I'll deal through Schwartz in Jo'burg. It's important that the Swaziland end is cleared otherwise there'll be considerable extra mileage for deviations, evasions and risk-cutting and that means time we simply cannot afford. Is that a fair appraisal, sir?"

"Very fair," Sir Murray reached for the scrambler. "Get me the Foreign Secretary."

"He was a sergeant called Chianda. He left the NRR in 1959. I know it's seventeen years ago but please do your best. *Joseph* Chianda?" The caller turned to Donovan who was standing in on the call. "Was that his name?"

Donovan nodded. "That was it." Biblical Christian names were common among the Africans, a tribute to the missionaries.

The caller turned back to the phone. "That's the

name . . . Oh, Jesus Christ, that's all we wanted." He turned to Donovan again. "The name's well known in Lusaka. A Joseph Chianda is operating a guerrilla force over the Zambian border."

"That sounds like him. Good. It means he's in trim."

"He's a rebel, for God's sake. He has a big reputation out there."

"I always thought he'd make it. Get him out from wherever he is and fly him up to Nairobi. Tell him to wait for me there at Eastleigh Airport."

"Mr. Donovan, you don't understand. We couldn't use such a man. Anyway, a rebel is hardly likely to respond to a call to the British flag."

"And you don't understand that we can't operate without him. We must have a tracker and Chianda reads the bush like a book. He may not respond to the flag but he'll answer to personal loyalty. Get a message to him that Bwana Menya and Bwana M'futi want him there. Tell him that they need him life or death. Tell him that his family will be looked after and that he'll be returned to wherever he wants to go without strings. Now it's not going to take long to get a plane down to Livingstone from Lusaka and get the bush telegraph working from there. If I know Chianda he'll have radio. He was always fascinated by it. Try him on the old army wavelength. This is how you spell the names."

The more they delved into the problem, the more contacts they made, the more the years concertina'd together and memory came back in strong, thrusting spasms as time closed.

"Mr. King. Amongst other things I believe you own a travel agency?"

"That's right. Look, I'm starving, when do we chop-chop?"

"I'll get sandwiches and coffee up. You have safari flights to East Africa?"

"Right again, but the seats are sub-let. That is to say several agents have blocks of seats on the same plane."

"When is your next flight?"

Jimmy King considered it. He was not too familiar with

the detail. "The day after tomorrow, so far as I remember."

"It will leave tonight."

"We can't inform all the passengers in that time. It's impossible."

"*Those* passengers aren't going. Ring up the other agents and cancel the flight. Tell them that the Kenya Government won't allow the plane in due to the unsettled conditions arising from the kidnap. Inform them that the Kenyans refuse to accept responsibility for the safety of the passengers and that all entry permits have been revoked as from now. That gives them adequate time to telephone all concerned to tell them the trip is off."

"I do have a reputation, you know. I'm not losing it on a cheap stunt like that. Besides, they'll wonder why it's only me that's been informed."

"Whose office deals with the charter company?"

"Mine, you bastard."

"Well, then. It's enough to hang your hat on."

"A plane-load of people are expecting a holiday, some of 'em the holiday of their lives, and you want me to squash them flat with forty-eight hours' notice or less?"

"Let me put it this way." Sleek hands folded across an immaculate waistcoat. "We can't use military planes. That would be much too obvious and they wouldn't be allowed in. So we have to use civilian aircraft. All right. The scheduled flights are full. We could use our influence to offload passengers but it's a much more public way of doing it than the way I'm suggesting. No other charter planes are available at such short notice. We've already tried."

"The travel boys will be glued to the phone trying to answer awkward questions. Some of them will ring the Kenyan Embassy and get the truth."

"They'll merely get a contradiction. They can leave a week later. Will that satisfy you?"

Jimmy King wasn't influenced by the sop. A near-millionaire, he hadn't made his money by being taken in by a convincing lie. "All you want, matey, is for the blame to go elsewhere. Anywhere away from conniving officialdom. Let the agents take the blame. Another travel cock up. Has it occurred to you that the hotels will have to be compensated, that they may not be able to take the guests a week later, that the safaris may not be bookable then, either?"

"If that happens we will make full compensation. Under your auspices, of course."

"Cancelling the plane two days ahead does not make it available tonight."

"It *is* available."

"You've checked."

"We wouldn't be discussing it now, Mr. King, if I wasn't certain that plane would be available. We would have clandestinely chartered it ourselves for tonight but it had to be back in time to take your tourist party out. With servicing it made too tight a schedule of it."

"It means a booking clerk dropping everything and starting again." King was reflective. "The charter boys won't believe me. Out tonight with a fraction of the load and a rebooking for the real batch next week. My name'll be mud. You find another way. With a mind as bent as yours it shouldn't be difficult." King rose, then added, "There goes my bloody knighthood." He gave an inverted V sign and left the room.

At half past three the four volunteers were given a belated lunch of assorted sandwiches and poor coffee. Even this scratch meal was full of interruptions. A tailor was running round them, taking measurements, making notes. When he had gone they had to pose full face for a photographer for passport photos. They filled in forms and were told to leave the date blank. Jimmy King, perched on the edge of a table, looked down at the seated Donovan. "You really going because you need material?"

Donovan put down his coffee, pushed back dark hair barely greying at the sides. He finished munching. "Partly. Partly from vanity. I don't like accepting I'm beyond it. That and to get the Princess away from Kilewe. If it's not too late."

"Remember the old rope climbing with full equipment and the log throwing, eh? Christ, it'd kill us now. It's got to be vanity with me, too! Sure, I'd like to think we could save the lasses but the old Beau Brummel of Rocco Littorio isn't dead yet. Where there's fertility there's hope."

Vale was abstractedly fingering a gold crucifix at his throat. A desk lamp spun a faint halo around the natural tonsure on the crown of his head. He had always been a religious man but full of life, capable of lifting people with his belief and energy. He still showed odd signs of vitality but it was subdued, as if he was holding it back. Or holding something in.

Thompson was relaxed. He was staring at his crossed feet. There was a sense of relief about him that communicated. King said, "What you thinking about, Tommy? That it'll be better than nick?" They'd always understood one another.

Thompson looked up, smiled lopsidedly. "No," he said evenly. "I was just thinking about loading a Bren gun. Due to the curve of the magazine the rim of each round has to be inside the rim of the preceding one. Right? 'Look at the target. Get the tip of the foresight in the centre of the target. Contact thus made being in the centre of the field of view through the aperture, aim. Fire.'"

Two offices away Sir Murray Field was consulting with his subordinate again. He listened attentively.

"Harkill confirms that Major Francis will make a delivery to Gobo, just his side of the border. Before I get through to Schwartz I'd like a report on the Foreign Secretary's call, sir. I must know if we're clear. Apart from that, supposing Schwartz has a problem getting an aircraft for Nairobi?"

Sir Murray rose from his desk; it was his only outward concession to inner tension. The wheels were beginning to creak into action but the road was pitted, fraught with hidden traps. It was the most unlikely exercise that he'd ever mounted. He had all the advice he could need close to hand and his own considerable experience to disseminate and to evaluate it. He was also attuned to intonation. "You say that as if you have an ace up your sleeve."

"A joker, actually. King's banker friend, Gerald Steinberg. I gather he'll be taking his own plane to Nairobi. I can find out from Schwartz the size of the plane; it wouldn't be smaller than a twin-jet executive."

Sir Murray placed his hands slowly in his trousers pockets. He straightened, lifted his head, looked his subordinate straight in the eye. *"Dare we?"* And then with his question unanswered he posed another. "Could it be done without his knowledge, do you think?"

3

"IT'S TIME TO meet the troops." Smithy had poked his head round the door.

Donovan, nominated by the others, left the room and was taken to another. "Take a pew. Smoke? No? I wish I could drop the habit, too. Well now, I'll fill you in as best I can then you can go and meet their leader. Captain Donovan—"

"Mr. Donovan. Let's not play make-believe, Smithy. We stopped being soldiers a long time ago."

"All right. The men you're taking *are* soldiers, however. Their commander has the agreed rank of captain among his men. His name is Stuart Maxwell. He was a warrant officer II in the Parachute Regiment. He is thirty-two, tough and will kill anyone for money. He has a temper but was a fine soldier and as a sergeant major put the fear of God into his men. They respected him Whatever Maxwell lacks it is not courage.

"The rest are the usual assortment of mercenaries. They've been gathered together now for ten days as part of a force that was to invade Southern Africa in small long-range groups. They are financed by Black Africa but the economics of it are diverse and it's difficult to determine if anyone in particular is behind it. The front men are all white. It's as well to know something of the background. They are paid £160 a week and we have had to up that to obtain a temporary diversion of their objectives. In fact, it wasn't too difficult to borrow them from their masters. No one believes they'll go. It's an expensive dream. A bonus is at the end of a successful mission. All expenses, food, clothes, paid by us. Incidentally they have travel permits to Kenya, Tanzania and Zambia to cover any approach to Southern Africa.

"You might be interested to know the kind of mixture you have, to prepare you for possible friction. There are, for instance, some ex-Special Air Service men. A misnomer, some say. The same people also say that these are the men that British Intelligence use as killers. A legacy from the war days. I make no comment but it's as well to know. You are, after all, going to have to control these men. Then strangely, you may feel, there are a few Ulster Loyalist guerrillas who want a change of scene. Odd bedfellows, you see, particularly as there are two renegade I.R.A. men. These have developed a craving for violence that even Ulster failed to satisfy. The rest are all ex-servicemen; some have already fought as mercenaries. Any questions?"

Donovan already felt out of touch. Thompson, Vale, King; these men weren't natural killers. They had fought to a man but their motives had been different from the men they were taking with them. Suddenly he felt his age. Inadequate. "This is the bunch we get? Blood-lust killers?"

Smithy shrugged. "You'll be up against blood-lust killers. The threat you must make will be to annihilate every man if the hostages are harmed. It's all the way, Mr. Donovan, or not at all. Hopefully, with your past experience, you might achieve a quick snatch yourselves with little or no bloodshed."

Donovan stirred uneasily. "I'm beginning to have my doubts about the whole thing. It's ridiculous to be emotionally deceived at my age."

"You wanted to do it. It's too late now. A lot has happened in the short time you've been here."

Donovan smiled wryly. "Don't bust a gut, Smithy. I won't chicken out." He sat back stretching. "'. . . . that reverend vice, that grey iniquity, that father ruffian, that vanity in years,' as Shakespeare had it. How do you know so much about the mercenaries?"

"Does it matter?"

"Look, if you have plants among them it will be helpful to know."

"They'll be withdrawn before you go."

"They bloody well won't be. If there's trouble among them it's useful to have warning of it."

"One's a Southern Rhodesian. We have no jurisdiction over him."

"Well, well. Who's the other?"

"I prefer not to give his name. He'll identify himself to you if the need arises. Otherwise, you'll never know."

"So you'll leave him in?"

"Reluctantly."

Donovan was irritable when he left the room. He had now been in the building for three and a half hours and already it was closing in on him. He was tired of the pushing, of the spontaneous improvisation that seemed to arise at every turn because there had been no proper planning. On the way down the two flights of stairs, having refused the elevator, he was accompanied by yet another nameless official.

Outside, they turned the corner into Northumberland Avenue. The sinking sun was developing into a blood blister behind a faint haze. It was a little cold but fine. Another irritating point was that he was escorted to a chauffeur-driven car almost as if he were a prisoner. And he was worried sick about Stella.

The car took him to King's Cross. When the driver got out to open the door for Donovan, he suffered a sharp pain in the lumbar region as he bent to get out. Rheumatics. Something he had learned to live with. He rubbed his back and entered the Sunbury Hotel and asked for Stuart Maxwell at reception.

The lounge was almost empty. Maxwell was fair and compact. Celtic skin and snub nose. Quick, dark eyes, faintly out of focus through drink. He swayed very slightly as he held out his hand. There was nothing wrong with his grip. There was a modest belly under the thick, white cardigan and his ginger hair spread unmolested over a bullet head and bushed around the face and chin. He smiled with tobacco-stained teeth and there was spirit on his breath.

"So you're Donovan." The lilt was Scottish.

Donovan led the way to a corner. They sat down and Maxwell looked around for someone to bring drinks.

"I don't need one and you look as if you've had enough." Donovan took the bite out with an easy smile.

The dark eyes chilled, then softened slowly. Somewhere under the straggling beard was the movement of a smile. "If that's the way you want it, *dad*."

"Don't ever call me that again."

"Touchy. Do you think you can make it?"

"Right now I'm more concerned whether you can. For a young man you've put on too much weight and the drink's slurring your words."

"Och, a drink or two never hurt anyone."

"How long have you had the beard?"

Maxwell fingered it thoughtfully. "Do you no' like it?"

"The last man I knew with a beard that colour got shot through the face. The bullet smashed his jaw and lodged in his throat. He choked to death in agony. The sun had reflected on the beard and it'd shone like gold for some sniper's sights to fasten on. We were on half a water bottle a day at the time. We could drink it, shave in it or clean our teeth with it. None of us shaved but he was the only one with a ginger beard. Thought you should know."

Maxwell's eyes were reflective. "So it's the desert we're going to? No one told me."

"No one will until we've landed. I understand you're already decked out with tropical kit."

"Sure. We're ready to move."

"Where are the rest of you?"

"All in nearby doss houses. They're reporting to me at eighteen thirty this evening. I must have word by then."

"You will. Meanwhile, I want a list of names."

Maxwell produced an envelope from his hip pocket. "They're all in there. Fifty-eight including myself."

"Fine. I'll see you get instructions in time."

"Who's behind it? Who's footing the bill?"

"I am. I've got a personal grudge and a lot of money to vent on it."

Sir Murray Field observed, "British Airways won't be too pleased."

"It's the only way, sir. The direction will have to come from someone in the Ministry of Transport. It won't be the first time they've offloaded passengers for V.I.P.s"

"Sixty-two of them? Are you quite certain there's not a charter available?"

"Not without even greater disruption. It has to be cleared the other end and sixty men travelling alone won't go unnoticed. At least on the scheduled flight there will be some women and children, some sort of a smoke-screen."

"So I'd better ask the Minister to insist on as many unaccompanied male passengers to be offloaded as possible."

"Sir, Donovan must instruct Maxwell before six thirty. All transport problems must be finalised by then."

"Get the ticketing under way. Sixty-two. Oh dear. Here goes detente and possibly our own smokescreen."

"Mr. King. I have a more amenable suggestion for you."

Jimmy King was suspicious. He was becoming tired of the seeming confusion and, like Donovan, the restriction. Everything was so disjointed; yet he could sense progress of a kind. There were so many ends to tie. So much to do in so little time.

"Can you get sixty-two air tickets made out for Nairobi for tonight's flight? I have the names."

"When by?"

"Five-thirty at the latest."

"Okay, I'll get it moving."

"You can use the telephone in the next room."

King smiled. He leaned forward to pick up the list on the desk. "I take it our four names are included."

"Of course."

"First class?"

"Tourist, Mr. King."

"I never travel tourist and I'm not starting now. Get six first class. Got it. Six. Four for us and two for a couple of them." Before leaving he gave the V sign again, this time the respectable way round.

Thompson was getting restless. He paced the room. It was much bigger than his cell but the confinement was becoming noticeable. There was activity around them. Footsteps, doors opening and closing, the faint indecipherable murmur of voices and the subdued ringing of telephones. Always the telephones. He looked down at the seated Vale who was abstractedly cleaning his glasses. "You all right, Colin?"

"I'm fine. It's like a dream, dear boy." He'd almost said salvation.

"I wonder what's going on? Pat and Jimmy are buzzing around like blue-arsed flies. I want some action."

"You'll have it soon enough. We all will."

Hesitantly: "I hear you didn't go to the reunions after you were ordained."

"A small parish takes a lot of looking after. There are a lot of calls to make." Oh, yes. One in particular. "Is Sandra all right?"

Sandra? Didn't he know Sandra was dead? Everyone knew. Momentarily he saw her face. Paling, then turning blue. And her eyes. He'd never forget her eyes. Oh, Christ. *Sandra.* Savagely he said, "You don't look fit enough for this caper. You should drop out."

Vale looked up sharply. "I'm as fit as any of you. They're satisfied with me here."

"They're looking for fools, Colin. They'll take anyone who's mug enough." It was still better than jail.

There was a hiatus when nothing happened at all. Connections were pending to Swaziland, Johannesburg, Lusaka, Nairobi. Confirmations of one kind or another were awaited with visible signs of impatience. Even the most languid among them were desk tapping, pacing, fiddling with loose change in their pockets. The short time left passed too quickly for some, slowly for others.

A portable television set had been provided for the volunteers. Drinks had been set out again and there had been time to prepare better canapés. Rich American prawns with hot sauce, smoked salmon, vol-au-vents with hot chicken centres, sausages, garlic sauce.

Thompson could barely stop licking his lips. Prison had not been like this. He poured himself a stiff whisky and toasted all and sundry. To him it was like a doomed man's last request and the analogy wasn't lost on him.

The normal television service was interrupted for a comment on a rumour that the Queen had offered to pay the £10,000,000 ransom herself. It was flatly denied by a Palace spokesman and emphasised that it was not yet known that Princess Anne was missing.

Pat Donovan recalled the visit to his typist that morning. *That morning*. It was impossible. He thought of Stella and tried to black out what he'd done to her. Jimmy King thought of Jeannie with a love that had sprung from the past to surprise and to confuse him. Colin Vale considered redemption and the near squalid home he had left behind. Tommy Thompson intermittently thought of the woman he had loved and of the relief of being out of prison and of never going back. One way or another.

In the nearby Sunbury Hotel Stuart Maxwell considered money, killing and Pat Donovan in that order. Donovan was a has-been who had long since lost his edge. He'd stand no nonsense from him. He had checked that the bank's draft was already being held in trust.

Things started moving again just after five p.m. Sir Murray Field received the message that onward transport from outside Nairobi had been arranged in the form of two three-tonner trucks and four Range Rovers plus a small breakdown truck. They had safari markings which had been a minor work of art by the Nairobi contact. A truck had also been organised to transport the arms to a compass bearing in the Northern Frontier District.

Just after that the seats on Flight BA 011, six first class and fifty-six tourist were guaranteed at the expense of a seething atmosphere between the Ministry of Transport, supported by the Ministry of Aviation, and the British Airways executive. Journalists who had booked seats became involved and a further reshuffle resulted in other passengers being blocked off. What made it worse was that the Ministry had insisted that passengers would only learn that they could not travel at the time of reporting in at the airport. British Airways should only offer the excuse that the plane had been unavoidably overbooked due to the unusual demand and that an expected extra flight, which would have solved the problem, had been taken out of service due to a technical fault. Eventually the Minister himself and the Chairman of British Airways had established an electrifying friction between them. Understandably British Airways bitterly resented accepting the blame. Their airport staff had yet to cope with the problem. Feelings ran high but the cracks were somehow plastered over under the magical cloak of security.

The four men, the unwitting eye of the storm, mentally prepared themselves for the flight ahead and for what lay beyond. Suddenly it was all much too close.

Parcels arrived with large cardboard boxes. Tropical kit hastily sorted out for size. Boots, not army pattern, socks, and floppy hats lined with aluminium foil to reduce the heat inside them by fifteen degrees fahrenheit. The years rolled back as the four men sought clothes that fitted.

Smithy smiled. He was satisfied. They were lost in the emotion of past days, of each other and a genuine desire to help a critical situation. Something they wouldn't admit to caring about. Men still with a passion for life who did not accept age as an excuse for doing nothing. Like himself. Yet the pace had to continue to hold it together. If departure were delayed another day he knew that the whole thing could fall apart, that second thoughts might set in. The flight was still some hours off. He puffed his cheeks reflectively. And he quietly prayed.

"Let's get down to it, gentlemen." Smithy's pointer roamed the map, hovered over the equator north-east of Nairobi. "You must operate from Kenya. We've arranged for two three-tonners, four Range Rovers and a breakdown truck to be at a point between Nairobi and Thika. We don't want you moving out in convoy. It will have to be a jeep at a time, three-tonners interspersed. They will be loaded for stores and spare parts in Nairobi. And they will leave there one at a time with good intervals. We don't want to arouse the interest of Kenya officials. I would suggest to you that you don't link up until you arrive at your arms pick-up point."

The pointer tapped rapidly. "Our advice from Nairobi is to play it absolutely safe. They're understandably touchy about the whole business without something like this. The arms, therefore, will be dropped just north of the equator between Koreh Wells and Garbatula. Thirty-nine degrees longitude, thirty minutes latitude."

"In the middle of nowhere."

"As you say, Mr. Donovan. But not too far from the road linking the two places, which itself intersects the Wajir Road. Our local report is that while it means not following a route which might exactly meet with your own ideas, it does avoid your crossing the lower Tana River. The arms will travel by solitary truck in darkness." If they ever reached Nairobi.

"Are the arms being offloaded there?"

"Yes. The truck will return to Nairobi."

"We'll need the truck. Leave it there."

"I'm not sure we can do that. There's also the matter of the driver and co-driver."

"They'll know damn fine it's not a cargo of skins when they unload however they're packaged. *We need the truck*. Two three-tonners aren't enough. Sixty odd men. Arms. And what about water and reserve fuel? There'll be no replenishing points either coming or going on the routes we'll have to use. The drivers will have to tag along. See if you can make one of them a cook. How big is the breakdown truck?"

"Five hundredweight."

"We'll need spares, tyres, and springs especially. Camp beds, mosquito nets, blankets. It can be cold and wet at night. We've got two or three nights out there in bush or desert. Okay, we'll settle for sleeping bags, but something to make it difficult for snakes, spiders, scorpions and red ants."

Smithy made notes, which worried Donovan and the others.

"Surely your people know what's needed?"

"Mr. Donovan, we're not running a department store out there. So far one man, with help, has worked miracles. Make a list of what you need and I'll see that it gets through. I'm sure it's already been done." Smithy produced some paper.

Donovan said angrily, "It's late to think of it."

They scribbled away thoughtfully. When they'd finished the notes were handed back to Smithy who scanned them slowly. When he reached Vale's it took him all his self-control not to lift his gaze to the clergyman's. *"Bible"* had been inserted boldly, followed by "for funeral *services*." Smithy tapped the notes together. He knew that as from this moment Vale should be excluded. Behind the strong outline of his features the clergyman was carrying his own cross. If it preoccupied him it could endanger the others. Yet if he dropped him it might well start the break up of them all. He looked up expressionless. "Thank you, gentlemen. Are there any questions?"

"Just where the hell are we going? How far in?"

Smithy remained smooth. "We're only getting dribbles of news. We'll give you a target before we leave, based on the latest information, and again in Nairobi on arrival there. We understand that Hassan Kilewe is not too far over the border."

"Which side of the Juba River?"

"At this stage I'm not absolutely sure." It was the nearest he came to losing his men and he knew it. "I believe below the Juba but I'll come back to you in half an hour and give you your answer."

"I hope to God all this stuff is laid on. Ropes, a breakdown truck conveying raft, binoculars, explosives. Look at the list. Christ, sir, I think we're in trouble."

Sir Murray smiled briefly. "You're losing your nerve, Smithy." He looked up. "I take it someone's onto Nairobi again?"

"Yes, but his own phone is burning the wires. There are now constant delays. I think we've bitten off too much."

"All that means is our team is beginning to be perceptive. Giving you a rough time for the right reasons. Isn't that what you want?"

"I suppose so. I think Vale has too much on his mind to be included but I'm afraid to upset the apple cart."

"Let him have his Bible. It might prove useful." Beneath his own calm Sir Murray was seething with unrest. It was so touch and go. But like the rest he was ensnared by the event and the need for it. He couldn't back down. It was far too late.

"They want to know where Kilewe is hiding..."

"I'd rather leave it for a while."

"I've told them he's south of Juba."

"Have you? You'd better leave it at that. Our latest information is that he might be at a place called Ober Uen."

Smithy traced the map behind Sir Murray's head. "Good God. That's at...

"I know it is, Smithy. About three hundred miles over the border. Better that they find out in Nairobi, don't you think? They can do it. Give them time to acclimatise to the idea."

Smithy was shaken. In this office he could release his feelings, brace his nerves for the next encounter. "How many hours of the four days do you give them to get used to the idea?"

"Sarcasm doesn't become you."

"You're not dealing with them. I'm getting to know them. They'll never make it to Ober Uen. I think we should call it off."

Sir Murray rose, looked at the map, then eyed Smithy coolly. "Now why on earth should we do that? Have you forgotten what's at stake?" And then in a conciliatory tone, "We knew at the outset that there would have to be sacrifices. You're too old a hand to go soft, Smithy. Too experienced to become attached to them."

"Yes, sir. About as old and experienced as they are."

"Give me a workable alternative."

Smithy stood by the door, too security-minded to open it yet. He recovered his poise. With Military Intelligence he had co-operated with the M.I.6. chief before. What he didn't like was the fact of operating a military campaign through intelligence channels. He well understood the security involved but it gave the operation an improper balance. The task force needed full military aid. As it was they were being handled like a bunch of saboteurs. With dignity he said, "I can't. But I do believe that it's not just our four volunteers who are playing at war games. There should be some thought for the degree of expendability."

"I'm sure they know the form, Smithy."

"Except where we've deliberately misled them."

4

THE SPRAY HUNG like low cloud over the ragged gash of the Victoria Falls. The thunder of the Zambesi was covered by the twin engines as the plane banked, the narrow drop of the Devil's Cataract falling under the port wing. As Gregg levelled, the foaming cauldron slipped away and the mass of Lake Kariba faced him like an enormous grey slug. He banked again, caught the suspended colour of Rainbow Falls, then slipped in towards Livingstone. The African beside him was spell-bound by the sight. Sensing it Gregg said, "Not seen it from the air before? Don't let the turbulence worry you. Not so much volume of water at the end of the dry season, but there's less spray and you can see much more." He checked the approach. "Twice as high as Niagara and three times as long." As if his companion needed convincing.

Gregg lined her up, concentrated, then said, "You sure this bloke Chianda is this side of the border?"

"Sure, bwana. Right now. He has to come back every now and then for supplies." The African cradled the old thirty-eight set as if it were a baby. He'd refused to let Gregg store it in the back. "I'll find him."

"Don't forget. It's Bwana Menya and Bwana M'futi who want to see him in Nairobi. No trap. You convince him."

"He will listen to me, bwana."

"Let's hope so. Here we go. Hang on to your squawk box."

Gerald Steinberg was almost diminutive. He had a lined, near wizened face with twinkling brown eyes. Greying hair ran back from his forehead, like Cape rollers, deep and straight. Because of his size he had a specially mounted chair which gave an illusion of height behind the huge desk. His impish sense of humour sometimes conflicted with the dignity of his public image of banker. It was not unknown for him to pull off the odd practical joke, particularly at banquets which he had always considered stuffy.

As Jimmy King had intimated, Gerry Steinberg was a mechanic at heart and a banker by natural acumen. At one time he had almost become a doctor but had reverted to engines rather than bodies. He couldn't help making money. He loved to poke fun at his failures but they were so few he had difficulty, these days, in recalling them. He was glad that Jimmy had telephoned; the brash cockney humour had always been the perfect foil for his own. They had enormous respect for each other. He had cancelled his engagements for the next few days. Delegation had never troubled him; the art of it was one of his many attributes. He pulled a crocodile wallet from his pocket. From it he extracted some old snapshots he always carried. They were a little faded now. There they were, socks rolled down over boots, K.D. jackets unbuttoned to reveal bare chests. Bush hats at a variety of angles. Tramps. Or saints. All that could be said of them that was uniform were their grins. And it had been stinking hot at the time.

On the left-hand side of the small group was his older brother; older by only two years. He'd survived for three months after the snap had been taken. Gerry Steinberg put on bifocals and stared at the photograph for some time. Behind the group to one side was the bonnet of 'Sadie,' his Marmom Herington armoured car that had headed the troop which had accompanied the African infantry company. The other side of the background was part of the elaborate water well Mussolini's troops had built; the faggots and axe standing proud in the sun. He wondered what the Somalis or the Russians had done with the stone victory emblem. He well knew what he and his friends had done. Sometimes singly, sometimes all together.

His gaze went back to the small, cheerful blob that had been his brother. And he remembered. Hassan Kilewe. The light died in the lively eyes.

"No, my dearest. I do not know how many days. Perhaps I'll be back the day after tomorrow. *Si?*"

"But, Pietro. Nairobi?"

Frascelli shrugged eloquently. "It is nearer than New York." A handsome man, tall and lean with calliper lines from temple to chin. He bent forward to kiss his wife on the forehead, stroking her cheek. As he straightened he could not avoid her troubled eyes.

"Do not worry, Franca. I take your love with me."

"But why, Pietro? Please, why? You've told me nothing."

He pulled her to her feet, buxom now but still beautiful about the eyes and mouth. He held her loosely.

"We both know, don't we, that were it not for Pat Donovan, we would never even have met."

"He doesn't believe that, Pietro. He has said so often."

"He's a modest man. He is also a fine friend. What's important is that I not only believe it, *I know it*. He is not the kind of man to ask empty favours. So I go. Now pack some tropical clothes for me, dearest Franca, for it can be hot in Nairobi. Do not worry."

"I hate goodbyes, Pietro. Even after so long."

He smiled, kissed her again. "*Because* it's so long. Yet it was only yesterday."

"For God's sake, can't you hear me? What's happened to the line? *Very* pistols and flares, yes. Binoculars. And three old thirty eight sets if you can lay your hands on them. It seems they're the only receivers they can remember. And don't forget the spare petrol. *Petrol, for Christ's sake*. I know you're working your guts out but if you don't work them harder someone's going to spill theirs."

The call had been unjust and cruel. The urgency had not been exaggerated. Nerves were becoming frayed as take-off time became imminent.

Pat Donovan sat in the back of the car restlessly looking at the busy street scene. Rush hour. The newspaper headlines were still blazoning the Queen's rumoured offer. A news vendor stood with empty stall awaiting the next delivery.

A cold sweat started to pour from Donovan. It came suddenly and conversely with a hot flush and a tremendous wave of insecurity. *Stella*. He looked down at his hands, puzzled and momentarily dazed. This was no manuscript he was holding but a packet of air tickets. What the hell was he doing here? Stella would have a fit if she knew only half of what was happening.

Donovan passed a hand over his eyes, bemused and not quite sure of what he'd done. The mind, he told himself. Okay. But what about the body? It's slowed. It creaks at times like old wood. What about a wife left alone who might be widowed not knowing what had happened?

He sat trying to understand how he'd got into such a situation. It was almost as though they had all been hypnotised. By what? The challenge? Or, as he'd said himself, vanity? Or was he really concerned about young women held by a sadistic bastard called Hassan Kilewe somewhere in the Somali desert?

As his mind worked on his motivation it overlapped into a probing search of the actual problem ahead. He pulled himself from the spell of indetermination by sheer application to what had to be done.

At the hotel Donovan noticed that Maxwell's beard had been trimmed short and, catching the glance, Maxwell remarked, "I just don't like crabs in my fungus."

Donovan let it go. "Here are the tickets. Fifty-eight of them. Two first class. How are the men?"

"Leave *me* to worry about the men."

"When do you brief them?"

"The hotel's rented us a room for an hour. Eighteen-thirty. I told you before."

"So you did. Report at Heathrow No. 3 Terminal at not later than twenty-thirty hours."

Maxwell removed a ticket from the envelope and opened the cover. "I can read. We'll be there."

"Don't let the men batch up. I don't want the appearance of a party at the airport."

"Anything else?"

"No. I just hope your men are in better condition than you are, or God help us."

"I can still take the ash of a cigarette at thirty yards. You wouldn't know which end it came out of."

Donovan smiled good-humouredly. "Twenty-thirty hours," he repeated.

"Whose orders?"

"London."

"Look, man, you can't get a tsetse fly's crap on the plane."

"There's something behind it, Jan. Top priority from top men."

"Blast it. Why does it always have to be the cargo that has to be moved? There's important machinery to be freighted, man. How much?"

"Six hundredweight."

"I can't do it. I'll shift three. And that will mean splitting an order."

"Six, Jan."

"Three. Shift your bleddy passengers."

"The plane's loaded from Jo'burg to Nairobi. Overloaded. I can't turf off passengers."

"This freight is more important than your bleddy passengers. Christ, man, I should have joined South African Airways instead of B.A. They get their priorities right. What's so important?"

"Drilling equipment."

"To Nairobi from here? Who're you kidding?"

"That's what they say. It's not here yet but I've been told to make space. Look, I'll split it with you. I'll offload a couple of passengers and you make space for the rest."

"Three passengers. You'll still be winning."

It was already dark, the Jan Smuts airport a lighted oasis of shadowy activity. The air was cooling rapidly, almost chill. The twin beams of a Boeing 737 switched on as it came in to land. At first the plane itself couldn't be seen and only the two huge orbs shone down spectrally from space, probing the beginning of the runway. The gigantic, bat-like shape suddenly detaching itself from the dark velvet backcloth added to the eeriness as the roar of engines transcended all other sound. The plane was then seen side on, its lighted windows gold fluorescent strips.

At another perimeter of the airport, where the private plane hangars formed a mushroom line, a small towing truck trundled through the darkness with two mechanics on board, one European, one African. They pulled up at an intersection separating two hangars.

"This is it?"

"This is it, sir."

"We'll have to hurry. We don't know take-off time. Has it been serviced?"

"Yes, sir. And fuelled."

They slid back the doors after opening the lock with little effort. The European climbed back into the towing truck and drove her as far into the hangar as he dared. He drove without lights. Because they couldn't work in the dark, the men pushed the doors across again and switched on the hangar lights.

An HS 125 Executive Jet preened herself under the fluorescence. The personal colours of Gerry Steinberg stood out in gold and red strips. Blood and sand he always called them. The men trundled a small mobile stairway to the doorway and then offloaded the first double-rope-handled case.

"God, this weighs a ton, Sam."

"This is the easiest one, sir."

"It'll kill us. I'm already ruptured."

The African grinned. The box was heavy but not so bad. "Only three more."

"You know where to put 'em?"

"In the galley. Cover them up."

"Won't he see them?"

"Only if he goes in the galley. But you said he'll probably be travelling alone."

"So?"

"He takes a picnic basket for himself and the pilot when they travel alone."

"Is it all in?"

"No. We could only raise a small chopper out of Swaziland. This is the first batch. We'd better hope the rest turns up in time."

Maxwell cast his eyes over the motley group of men sitting in front of him in the large hotel room. Some were good soldiers, others cold blooded killers to whom death had long since lost meaning, and a few in it simply for the kind of money they could not possibly command elsewhere. Maxwell was afraid of none of them and knew more about soldiering than most of them. He had the qualifications and the reputation and could play the part. But he was constantly on trial. One show of weakness and he would be finished in their eyes. If it happened in the field they'd know exactly what to do with him. He briefed them and stood no nonsense.

"Here are your passports, gentlemen. Sign them inside." Smithy came into the room and handed the passports round. While they opened them he poured himself a modest whisky, added a little water.

The passports were not new, having a used look about them. The dates of issue varied, some going back three years. The official stamps coincided with the date on each one. Inside was a folded white, seemingly official, Kenyan tourist permit.

To forestall questions, Smithy said blandly, "It would look odd if all your passports were new and bore today's date." He raised his glass. "To your success." Better than wishing them a safe return. In the few hours he'd known them he had got to like Donovan and King, formed a respect for Thompson's obvious unrelenting toughness and a sympathy for Vale whose unwavering eagerness showed glimpses of his being plagued by his own personal devils. He felt sorry for them all but kept his feelings wrapped in his stocky frame and masked by his soldier's face.

With feeling he suddenly realised that he didn't expect to see them again. Certainly not all of them, anyway. News had filtered in from African stations. The hostages were well secured by men with a reputation for unbending behaviour and fanatical beliefs; and their leader was Hassan Kilewe.

Smithy accepted the returned toasts from the four

volunteers and remained bland as he sipped his drink. Four days, that was all the time they had. And half a day already gone. He caught Donovan glancing towards the telephone. Deceptively big man. Looked more like a pug than a writer. Laughter lines were crusted round his eyes as if printed there by a postage cancellation stamp. There was no humour there now.

"Time, gentlemen." Smithy lowered his glass. "Are there any last questions?" He waited as they finished their drinks. "Good. You're clear about what you do once you get to Nairobi? Fine. There are two cars outside to allow for the luggage and to give you a comfortable journey." He shook hands with them all. "If you have any last minute thoughts make a note and hand it to the driver of the first car. Please pick up your cases and let's go down."

"Look, miss, I bought these tickets and nine of my party can't go. Where can I get a refund?" Maxwell held the tickets out.

It was the usual late evening show at No. 3 Terminal of London's Heathrow Airport. Talk, loud speakers, people leaning over balconies, moving up stairs and escalators.

Susan Barry flicked open the covers.

"You want me to cancel the seats, sir?"

"Aye. And give me a refund."

She picked up the intercom, called out the names. There would be some relief at reservations. For the last half hour the complaints had been strong from passengers who thought they were to travel to Nairobi that night. When she'd finished she handed the tickets back. "Thank you, sir."

"What about my refund?"

"The tickets were issued by an agent. The refund must come from them."

"How the hell can I see the agent when I'm travelling to Nairobi?"

"You can hand them in at Nairobi, sir. They'll be sent back to London and you can give an address for forwarding the refund on. Or you can wait until you're back here."

"You can't give me credit?"

"No, sir. They are different names. I can have them sent back to your agent if you like."

Maxwell held on to them tight. He'd think of a way to beat

the system later. He checked in and went into the departure lounge and up to the bar.

"My dear young lady, this is disgraceful. I booked weeks ago."

"I'm sorry, sir. An extra flight has a technical fault. The regular flight is overbooked." Susan Barry kept it cool. It was building up to the worst night she could remember.

"I didn't book on the extra flight. Look here, I'm not having it. I'll sue the airline."

"Yes, sir. I'm sorry." A tendril of hair escaped from under the blue uniform cap. Signs of stress were beginning to show on the young, pretty face. The false hauteur had gone, leaving her vulnerable. Over sixty passengers had been offloaded and this was the eighth she had personally confronted. None had been pleasant. The young, well dressed businessman still remained in front of her bay.

"I demand to see whoever's in charge. I simply won't tolerate it."

"No, sir. I'll ring for the duty officer." *He* finished up with most of the complaints. And for all his experience even he was beginning to show signs of wear. The girl picked up the phone.

At the departure lounge bar Jimmy King handed drinks round. "Any sign of the troops?"

His answer came in the form of a fracas near the suspended constantly changing flight departure board. A young man fell backwards over one of the low tables sending crockery flying. A little further away in the loosely-packed departure lounge another man started to sing.

The respectability of the lounge froze. Waiting passengers were both dismayed and disgusted. They reacted as they usually do to a distasteful situation they don't know how to handle. They pretended it wasn't happening: read newspapers, turned their backs, talked, anything to occupy their minds.

Not so Maxwell. He edged towards the singer, grabbed the back of his neck, dug his strong fingers in and whispered vehemently. "Close your mouth or I'll stick my fucking fist in it." He was red in the face, angry at what was happening.

He'd been drinking heavily but, by God, he'd never fallen down because of it in his life.

Thompson read the signs quickly. "Jesus Christ! *Not them.*"

"The ginger mop belongs to their leader, Stuart Maxwell. Take a good look, all of you."

Thompson couldn't believe it. He put his hands on his hips and drew his shoulders back. He eyed Maxwell speculatively, his gaze hardening. The mercenary was some distance away but Thompson recognised a tough nut when he saw one. He was still one himself. He turned to Donovan. "That the best they could do?"

"He's an ex W.O.II in the Paras. The mantle of officer doesn't exactly ride easily on him. But he knows his stuff, I'd say."

"If he's not too pissed to remember."

"He can hold it. See if you can pick them out. There should be around sixty of them."

"That's easy, old cocker. Bead in on the youngsters and if they stagger they're ours." King saw the funny side. He was the only one who did.

At the check-in bays some truth of what King had said was evident in the late arrivals who intermingled with the growing bunch of irate passengers whom the duty officer was trying to mollify. Some press men, turfed off the plane, were phoning their offices complaining bitterly. Afterwards they refused to budge and squatted with their camera equipment in the main hall to the uneven chorus of "Why are we waiting". They were later joined by the younger members of a group of businessmen who, whilst declining to squat, were all too willing to add vocal protest. There were some women too who did not join in but who were well capable of voicing protest in their own way until Susan Barry burst into tears under the intolerable strain. There was no remorse for the poor girl's breakdown except from her equally harassed colleagues.

From the balcony over the arrival hall Smithy watched with considerable concern. There was a tragi-comedy about the scene although he saw no humour in any of it. Lives were at stake. From what he saw they were more at stake than ever. The thing was becoming a farce. There was no way of stopping it. Not now. Even if he had the authority. They had progressed beyond the point of no return. As he reluctantly reached his personal verdict, matters were made worse by some of the offloaded pressmen seeing news value in their own situation. Cameras flashed. Disgruntled passengers were interviewed. Why? They would ask. What was going on? The pressures would build up. And the dangers. Well that was for politicians to counter. Smithy came away from the rails as voices of protest were raised again. The flashes had hurt his eyes. He rubbed them, glanced at his watch. Forty minutes to take-off.

5

By the time Smithy arrived back at his office the plane carrying the task force was gaining height above the English Channel. Feeling his responsibilities, he first saw Sir Murray Field, who appeared to have retired behind an attitude of near-indifference, as if he had done what he could and the remainder was in the lap of the Gods. Or in the hands of the devil. Smithy detected an impending air of resignation. After the early, really tense efforts to organise a campaign from embryo to birth in a matter of hours the steam had gone from it, as though the actual departure of the men was the signal to ease up. There was unspoken feeling that it was a lost cause, that the difficulties were too many to surmount.

Angrily, Smithy whipped round from person to person. The links with Johannesburg and Nairobi he stirred into follow-up actions with standby reliefs to take over. The lines between London and the two African capitals were almost permanently open. He made them go over the check lists with him to ensure that nothing had been overlooked and, under his constant pressure, discovered that some important, ridiculously obvious items had been missed. He rousted round and decided to stay all night.

Gerry Steinberg sat in the back of his Rolls-Royce, reflecting. It came as a relief to him to do something crazy. It wasn't the first time, much to the embarrassment of his co-directors. There were very few people he would fly two thousand odd miles to meet on so obscure an invitation. He was glad that Jimmy King had made the grade against the odds, and suspected a little piracy along the way. He smiled. It wouldn't be Jimmy otherwise. Yet Jimmy wouldn't harm a fly; officialdom, yes, bureaucracy, but not a fly.

Normally, Steinberg would have driven the car himself. He had been to Rolls-Royce in Derby and had learned to drive the queen of cars there, learned about what was under the bonnet. He hated being chauffeur-driven but he wanted the car to go back after dropping him. *Harriet.* He'd forgotten to tell his wife that he was going away. He reached for the phone then decided against it. He leaned back again grim faced.

She wouldn't even notice that he'd gone. He'd made the mistake of marrying, late, a woman too young for him. He didn't resent her desire for money. He had more than enough. But it hurt him to discover that she despised his tastes, his mechanical hobbies, his resistance to convention and formality. He was what he was and wealth could not change him. Tolerance was one way only. She had lovers. That hurt too. He'd done nothing to deserve that. He hadn't gadded about himself but he wasn't a prude either. A mistake, yes. Flaunting affairs at him was another matter. He could divorce her and one day he might, but it was a dirty game he didn't much care for. At least she wasn't deceiving him. It was the best he could think of her. He hoped that Jimmy had something to keep him busy. It sounded very much like it.

At the Jan Smuts Airport, the cargo manager was restless. A good deal of the precious cargo he had made space for hadn't arrived and all other cargo, apart from normal passenger baggage, was already on board. There was going to be hell to pay over some of the stuff he hadn't loaded and he didn't intend to take the can back when the balloon went up. He would give it another half hour and that would be it.

Pat Donovan had managed to get a seat next to Stuart Maxwell. The fiery ex-sergeant major knew why Donovan had sat next to him. Once they had gained height and the engines had throttled back, Donovan asked, "How many men have we got?"

This was no time for dissent. "There were nine bastards short at roll call. That leaves forty-nine. I won't know until we reach Nairobi how many more went AWOL."

"Nice disciplined bunch."

"There're mercs, not regulars."

"How far can we rely on them?"

"They booze up because they know they won't get any in the field and because they might get killed."

"Does that go for you too?"

"I drink because I like it." Maxwell's reply was acid. "Never too much."

At Jan Smuts Airport, Johannesburg, the cargo manager made his final decision. "That's it, man. Load back those two crates over there on the BA flight to Nairobi. I've held on bleddy long enough. Get them out of here." He picked up the phone to tell Jamie then slammed it down again. Sod Jamie. Sod the lot of them. He wasn't going to hold the flight up for a piddling hundredweight or so of so-called drilling equipment. It should have been here. He'd waited longer than could be expected.

About an hour later Gerry Steinberg was strapping up beside his pilot. Without guests he always travelled in the co-pilot's seat. Qualified to fly light aircraft, he regretted lacking the time to train on jets. He had learned a lot from Dan Vermaak who sat beside him. If Dan was taken ill in mid-air Steinberg was confident that he could get the plane down safely. Dan, an ex-South African Air Force pilot, had taught the sort of emergency procedures that wives of light aircraft pilots can be taught, should their husbands suddenly be taken ill in mid-air.

They got clearance and rolled towards the approach

lanes, port, starboard and tail lights suspended in the darkness. They had already done the check list, Steinberg playing full part. Vermaak trusted him completely; his boss had an instinct, an eye and an ear for anything mechanical from lawn mowers to tanks, Tiger Moths to executive jets. Vermaak put on brakes and full power and the aircraft strained like a terrier on a leash. He throttled back and moved in line.

When they finally got clearance the runway lights traced back like streamers while Steinberg called out the knots. They rotated, whined into the African night, tail-light blinking at a tilted Southern Cross.

Vermaak climbed quickly, turned to port, then headed for the long route north. He half-throttled back before turning to Steinberg. They had developed an easy manner between them.

"You got anything special on board? Something I don't know about?"

Steinberg was surprised. "I wouldn't load anything without telling you, Dan."

"That's what puzzles me."

"It's just the usual. A couple of cases and a picnic basket and your stuff."

"Boss, there's extra weight on board at the stern. When I trimmed her just now it was noticeable."

"Nothing that I know of. I'd better go and look."

"Wait till we've reached height."

"It might be a bomb."

Vermaak grinned. "If it is it's a bleddy big one. Now who'd want to kill you?"

"My whole board of directors. Maybe it's you. Woman trouble."

Vermaak continued to smile. "And maybe we have stowaways. Another ten minutes."

Steinberg unstrapped and went aft, switching on the cabin lights before leaving the flight deck. There were a dozen well spaced seats up to first-class standard and, at the rear, two dickie seats for when they carried cabin staff. He walked between them slowly, crouching now and then, looking under the seats and at the same time checking that the lifebelts were there. He checked the two small toilets and then the galley. A blanket had been thrown over the crates and caught his attention almost immediately. He lifted the blanket tentatively. He studied the crates. Two of the smaller ones seemed familiar. It was the thick rope handles at each end that disturbed him. He went back to Vermaak.

"You're right, Dan. There are crates down there that look as if they might be arms."

Vermaak forgot himself. "Shit, man, do you want me to turn back?"

"I want to be sure first. They're screwed down."

Vermaak checked his route and his instruments then switched on the auto pilot. He opened a side flap at the rear of the flight deck and took out a tool case. He passed a screwdriver to Steinberg. "You drag 'em out, boss, while I re-trim. Then I'll come back to help."

Steinberg pulled all four cases into the aisle. The diminutive banker sweated and cursed. When he finally lifted the lids of the smaller boxes, he wiped his creased forehead, rose and leaned against one of the seats. Vermaak, who had joined him, was not much longer with the larger crates.

Both men were silent for some time, Steinberg breathing quite heavily.

"We'd better turn back, boss."

Steinberg ignored his pilot. "Two Bren guns with spare magazines and barrels and four Short Lee Enfields. Two boxes of .303 ammunition. Hardly enough to start a war."

"Who loaded them?"

"More to the point, Dan, is who knew we were going? I've only discussed it with you."

Vermaak took it the wrong way but Steinberg soothed him down. "No. Not you. Nor me. Someone else."

"What do we do?"

"We *manga* them up, put them back and sit and think over a meal."

"Manga?"

Steinberg smiled self-consciously, his face wrinkling up in an ugly, yet attractive way. "Funny that. Haven't used the word in many years so why should I use it now?" He looked at his pilot still slightly embarrassed. "It's Chinyanja. They call it Chichewa now. Means tie up, secure. Let's get them back, Dan."

When they had finished they went back to the flight deck with Steinberg carrying the hamper. In the subdued light they could see out into the vast blackness of sky and the mass of pale stars like a sander sprinkling over ink.

"Hot soup?"

"Great."

"Followed by chicken in gelatine, and that special salad mixture you like. There's some caviare, Dan. And some pumpernickel to go with your cheese."

"You're slipping, boss. But I'll rough it with you."

They were silent for quite a long time, eating thoughtfully. It wasn't until coffee that Vermaak said, "We'll have to make up our minds. We're still heading north and I don't want to run into a fuel problem if we're going to turn back."

"I know. It's like this, Dan. You've told nobody and nor have I." Steinberg caught the pilot's dubious glance. "No, not even Harriet. I was going to but didn't." He felt no embarrassment in speaking like this to his pilot. Everyone knew how it was between himself and Harriet. "The only other person who knows we are coming is the one responsible for the trip and I trust him implicitly."

Vermaak was interested in the strength of Steinberg's assertion. "You trust him that much?"

"All the way, Dan. He was a friend of my brother, too, you know."

Vermaak kept quiet. The boss's mind was working on a strange wavelength. There was something here he didn't know about and was instinctively reluctant to probe.

Steinberg asked, "Would it be fairly easy to offload this stuff and escape customs at Nairobi?"

"No. It would need proper planning."

"If we're checking in would it be easy for someone else to get on board before customs clearance and offload it?"

Vermaak considered it. The questions were unexpected.

"*Easier*. They'd have to know what they were doing and they'd need to know the airport and its routine very well. It will be dark, which will help."

"Dan, make it as easy as you can for them. Park somewhere remote."

"I have to park where I'm told."

"Do what you can. Don't worry. I'll see that you're not involved if things get out of hand."

"I don't mind being involved for you, boss. I wish I understood, that's all."

Steinberg was touched. "I can't tell you. I'm not sure that I know. I'm gambling, Dan."

"Keep going north?"

"Keep going north. Although I might live to regret it."

At roughly the same time as Gerry Steinberg made his decision the Governor of Wakefield prison was mulling over a statement he was to release to the press. It had to be convincing. The Home Secretary had made that very clear. The best he could come up with was that it happened while Thompson was being transferred to another prison.

Fortunately Tommy Thompson did not rate highly in news value. He had not even been confined to the top security section of the prison. All national papers prepared to print the story but it rated little more than three inches of column space. No pressure was attempted on the press.

From the moment they crossed the French coast Tommy Thompson considered the possibility of not returning to prison. It was like a fantasy. At seven forty-five this very morning he had been slopping out. Now he was sitting next to Colin Vale, drinking champagne and eating Chicken à la King. Afterwards, he'd have a brandy. A miracle. He was afraid to doze off for fear of waking in his cell, the dream becoming a nightmare.

Thompson gazed across the aisle at Jimmy King, who was nodding off after the meal. Jimmy, with whom he'd shared molten bully beef from a hot can. How he remembered. Yet the meal that Jimmy just finished was probably substandard to him now. Times changed. So did some people. Jimmy hadn't basically changed. Nor Pat Donovan. They didn't even look that much older. They had always been easy going but tough when the chips were down.

Apart from himself the one who had changed most was Colin, who sat beside him, hands clasped and eyes closed. He was still solid but had quietened considerably. He had a recollection of an angry young man scudding down an outcrop, bush hat off, blood streaming down one side of his face from high on his forehead—shouting, "He's ruined my hat, dear boy. A bloody new puggaree and he's ruined it." He stood there with a forefinger through a bullet hole in the hat band. The bullet had creased Vale's forehead just as he turned. It had sliced *inside* the hat emerging through the puggaree further along. They'd had a drink that night to the luckiest man alive.

Thompson looked at Vale and wondered whether Colin still considered himself lucky. He looked closer. He could just see the faint white scar of the bullet runnel. After all this time.

Thinking back reminded him also of the present. Escaping on reaching Nairobi had crossed his mind several times.

Donovan felt responsible for the others not because he had been appointed leader, but because he had capitulated over coming. For Tommy it must be better than jail but it was clear that Colin had clutched at the opportunity. If he was running away from himself, Colin was running in vain, in step with his own shadow.

Donovan glanced at King. No one could have forced Jimmy to come. Behind the natural cockney humour was a shrewdness of tungsten toughness. And he certainly wouldn't run away from Jeannie in spite of capers he had tried to disguise with such ineffective guile that he couldn't really have wanted to keep anything from her. For some reason he had to go through life proving his virility. Poor Jeannie.

He himself had been lucky with Stella. During his earlier struggles at writing they had lived almost rough yet, rarely complaining she had helped him all the way. Both self-willed they had hit head on at times, like two colliding storms. When it was over the clouds had rolled back, weakened and stunned, but leaving clear skies and the invigorating freshness of the aftermath coupled with the sadness of remorse. They were as close as any couple could be, closer as the years rolled by. So why had he left her now on such a crazy, dangerous scheme?

Stella, love, I'm sorry. *Really sorry.* Donovan closed his eyes wishing his wife was sitting next to him instead of a man who seemed to have left the pride of the Parachute Regiment with his discharge papers.

* * *

Joseph Chianda was still suspicious. Flying didn't come too often his way and he didn't like it. The first time had been with the captain. He recalled the days when Donovan had taught the askaris to box and he, Chianda, had clouted the young captain round the ear when they were in the ring of shouting askaris. A huge cheer had gone up as the captain had staggered. It wasn't that the askaris disliked him, he was popular, but they supported their own in Chianda. Chianda had made the mistake of lowering his gloves and of grinning round at the adulation of the ninety odd men of the three-inch mortar platoon.

Even to this day he wasn't sure of what had happened next. It seemed that half a dozen men attacked him. He did recall the sweating face of the captain in front of him, of bunched gloves hitting him from every conceivable angle and, strangely, of the silence that suddenly struck the platoon. Then he was flat on his back and the sky was black then blue again and his jaw felt as though it had been hit with a rifle butt.

There was the bwana looking ten feet tall above him and smiling crookedly. The words came like the beat of a drum through his head. "Good punch sergeant. But that'll teach you not to drop your guard in future." Bwana Menya. The askaris had named him well. The bwana who hit. But that was then. He had been waging war against the whites almost ever since. Bitterness tinged his thoughts.

They'd got the mortar technique so sorted out that they could get seven bombs in the air before the first one exploded thirty seconds after firing. When all six mortars were going at once that was a lot of bombs. He remembered them blowing up a road by mistake and loading up and getting out quick; of baboons fleeing from their myriad caves as mortar bombs ricochetted down a perpendicular rock face at Leopard's Hill while the chasm echoed and reverberated with screams and explosions. They'd been together a long time. Had the captain changed too?

Bwana Mfuti had been like the missionaries, religious. Yet he had joined to fight the Maliwongo. The enemy. And he could shoot. Bwana Rifle. There were two reasons why he'd been called that. One was his uncanny accuracy with a rifle but, more importantly, because the askaris considered he looked like one. Tall and thin. Was he still as tall and as straight?

Of all the men Chianda remembered through life, these two, in particular the captain who had taught him to read, filled a very special place. In truth, before he was approached near Livingstone, he had almost forgotten them; they had belonged to some distant legend. The mere mention of their names had thrown back the years to his happiest days when they had all been fighting the same enemy. But he was suspicious, and afraid that he had changed too much to accept them now.

The sun was licking the earth rim with blood red-lips when Chianda looked out of the window. An inverted bush fire crept over the sky like long tongues of flame of varying density, sometimes like an anteater's tongue, flashing forward so quickly. He had never seen dawn from this height. It shadowed the hills with mauves and gold and changing greys and the sky was streaked with colours he had not previously seen with such clarity, as it crept, sometimes spurted, from the very edge of the world.

Pietro Frascelli watched the magic of the same dawn more analytically than Chianda. He found it odd that it should remind him of a blazing hot day in Somaliland. He had been captured with many of his men by the King's African Rifles and herded into a barbed-wire compound. Being cut off from food and water had been the biggest factor of capitulation.

The Italian armies were scattered, surprised by the speed of the British advance. Broken pockets of troops fought fiercely or gave up, depending on circumstances or strength of belief in their cause. Tenente Frascelli had belief in his own skills and a natural desire to be free.

The wire compound in a roasted, scattered Somali town north of the Juba was inadequate and badly manned. The British were moving so fast that they'd left few troops behind for consolidating and garrison troops had yet to arrive. There was ample opportunity to escape but nowhere to go. It was possible to walk out into the desert and die and that was all.

Frascelli's skills prompted him to believe that he could do better. At intervals along the advance route of the British Army were broken-down Italian trucks, almost like kilometre posts. If he could service one he would be mobile and would then head north to find the main area of resistance and rejoin his own forces. As he could interest no one among his tired, disillusioned and dust-caked compatriots, he escaped alone. There was little problem in getting a couple of tins of canned meat, biscuits and a bottle of water. He left at night. The sand was still hot to his touch.

He escaped from the compound with little difficulty. He found his truck just before dawn. With it was a carbine and ammunition tucked down behind the driver's seat. The truck, over-run by the South Africans, had bullet holes through the bodywork but the tyres were sound. It lay canted on the camber of the strada. Frascelli made certain the carbine was loaded, released the bonnet catch stripped off his jacket and started work. There was enough fuel. The radiator was damaged but there was half a drum of water on the back and tools in the driver's cab. If he could patch the radiator, he reasoned he could get her going. He lost himself in his task while the sweat poured over him. He lost sense of time and was reminded of its passing only by the increasing pressure of the heat.

Where the British officer came from he had no idea at the time. Frascelli was on his back under the shaded part of the truck when a voice said, "Come out of there. Hands on your head." He didn't understand English but he needed no interpretation. When he peered from under the engine he saw two dusty boots and gaiters. His carbine was near him and out of sight of the enemy. His hand closed on its slowly and he dragged himself from under the truck but away from the pair of legs. He rose the other side of the bonnet.

The British officer was so young, his fair complexion burned like a fried tomato. His eyes were clear, screwed slightly against the sun, and a bush hat was pushed back on his head. An Italian carbine was slung over one shoulder and a pistol dangled loosely from his right hand.

"Come round this side. Quickly." The pistol movement endorsed the instruction and Frascelli understood. His own carbine hung at his side out of sight. He pushed forward the safety catch with his thumb and started to move round the bonnet. The British officer sensed something wrong and levelled his pistol. Frascelli now accepted that the odds were heavily against him. There *might* be a chance. His finger curled round the trigger and he half raised the carbine which was still well below the bonnet level.

"Drop whatever you're holding or I'll blow your bloody head off." None of the meaning was lost on Frascelli. The whole tone and attitude of the Britisher had hardened. It was no use, he had to admit failure. The pistol followed him all the way round. The hammer clicked as it was cocked. His neck prickled. He came round the bonnet, carbine held out to throw, when he tripped over the wrench he'd been using. He was facing the officer as he fell, hands reaching out to save himself and the carbine roaring thunder as his fingers involuntarily pulled the trigger. The Britisher dropped even as he was falling himself and he waited for a return bullet.

Ludicrously they faced each other across the sand and Frascelli was staring at the black aperture of a .45. His carbine was still in his hand and he tried to push it forward. The young face, just feet away, was sweating, the eyes fastened on a point above his own. The pistol steadied and a second hand shot forward to hold it. Frascelli steeled himself to die knowing he couldn't raise the carbine in time. Then the face so near to his broke into a smile and the voice said,

"You're a lousy shot, Itie. If you don't take your hand off that carbine you're dead. Now up on your feet."

Frascelli always maintained afterwards that only an Englishman would have shown such compassion in the middle of a war. Donovan had not known that the shot was an accident and Frascelli had still been trying to use the carbine. *Donovan should have fired.*

Years later, when they discussed it in English which Frascelli had started to learn in a P.O.W. camp, Donovan explained why he hadn't fired. The company had been one issue pistol short and the company commander had lent Donovan his personal Colt .45 until another issue pistol arrived. Donovan had discovered only that day almost to his cost that the Colt fired only rim-fired cartridges, it was so old. A central firing pin would not detonate. *Had* he fired, Frascelli would have heard the click and taken his chance with the carbine as Donovan's had fallen clear when he dropped. Frascelli had never accepted the story. It was in Donovan's nature to soften the whole affair, make light of it.

Frascelli never forgot the Colt pointing at his head, the complete steadiness of it and those cool, youthful eyes taking focus on his forehead.

During the few seconds they had lain facing each other, something more than fear had communicated: the fallacy of war stripped bare. After the war Frascelli had set up enquiries through the International Red Cross and the War Office in London and had traced Donovan with reasonable ease. He had then invited him to Rome. So two men who had pointed guns at each other under the umbrella of world hostility had become close friends. Now they were to meet again in equally strange circumstances. Frascelli considered emotionally that the Somali bond was to take another turn that might put the clock right back for both of them. He looked forward to the meeting with both pleasure and trepidation as the aircraft began its descent to Nairobi.

6

GERRY STEINBERG WAS the first to arrive at Eastleigh Airport, Nairobi. Dan Vermaak brought the executive jet down as if he were landing on glass. It was dark still as he followed the fluorescent discs guiding him in. He shrugged helplessly at Steinberg as if to say, "Sorry, boss. There's nothing I can do."

Steinberg was no stranger to Nairobi nor to most of the world's capitals. His office had already signalled the Norfolk Hotel on Kenyata Avenue where he had made reservations both for himself and his pilot. After airport clearance he left Vermaak to attend to the formalities and ground costs. He went to the hotel and straight to bed, asking for a call at eight.

A few hours later Joseph Chianda stepped off the Lusaka—Nairobi flight. He had no hotel reservation. He had been told to wait at the airport until Donovan arrived. He went through immigration and customs without difficulty. His Swahili hadn't been used for years but he found it came back readily enough. There were many similarities in the Bantu languages. He went into the lounge and waited for either recognition or a call. He was used to waiting. Crouching for hours on end, patiently, barely moving a muscle, making no sound, had played a fair part in his life.

Pietro Frascelli, arriving an hour later, ran into immigration problems. He had no tourist permit or business visa. In the rush he had forgotten the need for either. His passport was in order. His clearance was delayed but eventually he obtained his permit. He had never met Gerry Steinberg but he chose the Norfolk for the same reason; they had all used it in the old days. He did not go to bed but he shaved and bathed at leisure, then breakfasted two tables from Steinberg.

Flight BA 011 touched down at seven fifty-five, five minutes earlier than scheduled. In the arrival hall Donovan breathed relief. Maxwell's men had split up as they had been told to do but even then they were somehow conspicuous. The numerous journalists were gregarious, joking among themselves, gathering equipment. They all seemed to know each other; they'd probably met in odd places around the globe. The mercenaries looked like men trying to keep apart. Donovan wondered if he was being too sensitive as they collected their baggage.

Finally, however, they were through. The minibuses were well spaced outside the airport and the men climbed into the first three of them, leaving the fourth for Donovan, King, Thompson and Vale. There was no sign of Chianda so Donovan hurried back inside. Could the grey grizzle-headed African asleep in the corner be he? He'd aged a lot if it were; hadn't they all? He sat beside the quietly sleeping form. Cheap European clothes. That wasn't Chianda. Yet there were points he remembered. He said quietly in Chichewa, *"Njoka."*

The head did not move but the lids opened immediately, eyes searching for a snake someone had warned him was there. Direction shifted to the smiling Donovan. "You old sod, Chianda. You were snoring your head off."

Chianda smiled awkwardly. After all these years the word

bwana had reached his lips but it was sliding back again, choking him. He gazed slowly at Donovan, warmth gradually reaching his eyes. "Bwana." It came diffidently yet he could not sell memory short. "Your body is bigger, your face older. But your voice hasn't changed."

Donovan, reading something of Chianda's mind, understood. He kept it to banter. "I'm surprised they let you into Kenya with your reputation."

"I'm not that important. I'm nothing here." It was said with regret.

They stood up and shook hands, their grips lingering, smiles widening.

Donovan said, "There's little time. We're on an impossible schedule. Others are outside and some are at the Norfolk. I'll explain there. Anyway, it's great to see you, you bloody rebel."

Chianda's reservations faded. But his bitterness was there still, aware that dreams could be broken by the stink of reality. Outside, he climbed into the last minibus to join the others he had known and had fought with. He trusted them and trust was something from the past being jostled into recognition by their back-slapping and laughter. A little less cautiously he began to laugh back.

Donovan met up with Maxwell at the front bus. "Forty-six in total," Maxwell reported.

"Forty-six? Christ! Including yourself?"

"Including myself."

"So from your original fifty-eight we've had twelve deserters. Over twenty per cent."

"Some of them didn't like the idea of helping Royalty, in any shape or form."

"Who said anything about Royalty?"

"We're not bloody fools. What we've got will stay."

"Every time I receive reassurances from you, our numbers thin. Still, maybe you're right," Donovan added to avoid a flare up from Maxwell. "The drivers know where to go. I'm sending Tommy Thompson with you. We'll be an hour or so behind you. We have a call to make first." Donovan swung round as he was about to leave. "You're right, Maxwell. There's no point in further secrecy. It's the Princess. We've got three days to get in and out."

Donovan hurried back to the last bus. As he stepped down for Thompson to get out, a voice behind him enquired, "Mr. Donovan?"

Donovan stared at an insipid face. He nodded, guessing that this was their contact.

Handlebar moustaches looked ridiculous on the almost cavernous face. The handshake was wet and limp. "May we go on board? It's a little conspicuous out here."

They sat in the front seats away from the others. "I believe you have a call before going on the Thika Road?"

"The Norfolk Hotel. We hope to pick up two more who know the terrain. Look, can't we talk on the move? We've a lot of distance to cover."

"Quite." A long-fingered hand reached forward to touch the African driver on the shoulder. The bus drew away. "We've got most of what you needed."

"Most?"

"Terribly difficult at short notice. Been up all night. We had to scratch and scrape under the watchful eyes of a very sensitive authority. They really don't know their arse from their elbow over this."

Donovan smiled. The tone was so cultured, the face so impassive that the vulgarity sounded quite out of place. "Have you learned anything more?"

Pale eyes turned to Donovan. "Everyone is being cagey. They're hoping for some miracle. You, evidently, are it. Yet if they knew about you they'd scream blue murder and stop you. It's apparently acceptable that terrorists can invade this country to perform a monstrous act. They can use all the right rhetoric in way of protest. Yet if someone else does it in an attempt to restore a *status quo*, that, sir, is invasion by an imperialist power. It is, I'm afraid, the protracted transitional time in which we live. You learn, too, that public announcement has no bearing on private statement. They don't know what to do for the best and because they don't they'll tolerate no outside interference. They are negotiating."

"If it's Twinkletoes they're wasting their time."

"If that quaint-sounding gentleman is Hassan Kilewe, then I agree with you. You are our only hope, Mr. Donovan, and we have done the very best that we could for you in the time available."

"Have the arms gone to the pick-up point?"

There was a hesitation while fair lashes closed. "Some were late. There has been no time to check the contents. That you will have to do yourselves."

"So you've no idea what we have?"

"No. It's been sheer hell; London's been pressing all the time."

"It's not going to be too good for us either, especially if there's a delivery cock-up."

"Yes, well, I have here comfirmation of the pick-up point for both the arms and the trucks. The minibuses will be brought back tomorrow, by which time you'll be out of reach of Kenyan jurisdiction. Maps and compasses are in the lead Range Rover."

"Any news of the whereabouts of the hostages?"

"It's all in there." A bony finger indicated the envelope just handed to Donovan. "I would accept it as being reliable. It was relayed from Mogadishu only an hour ago."

"Mogadishu is a long way from where these boys are likely to be."

"Indeed. The radio has been a God-send."

Donovan could see that he would get no more. "Any information on the identity of the hostages?"

The moustaches twitched. "Oh, they won't admit that until the last moment. The cover-up is so ludicrous that the press are virtually stifled. I've no doubt in my mind who it is you must rescue."

"Force yourself to say it," said Donovan irritably.

"My dear fellow, I didn't think it was necessary. Princess Anne and another lady."

Donovan tore open the envelope, his fingers tightening on the slip of paper as he read. "'Ober Uen.' Jesus, that's between Bur Acaba and Bulo Burti, about three hundred miles over the border." He had difficulty in keeping his voice down.

"About two seventy-five, actually, if you travel northeast from your pick-up point. You seem to know the place."

"I remember it." Donovan screwed up the paper without realising it. "I understood they were this side of the Juba."

"They've moved fast. Perhaps they expected retaliation. Incidentally, I'm advised that it hasn't rained there for three years."

Donovan quelled his temper, smoothed out the paper again. "We'll never do it in the time." He read on: "'About twenty-five men'. Well, that's not so bad," but he was talking to himself; his mind was on the mileage problem, calculating averages and hours. He shook his head. "It's too much to ask of them."

"You'll probably find the roads better than you remember."

"Roads? For Crissake, we can't use roads."

Soft lips were smiling under handlebar moustaches. Donovan was letting off steam. He would go even if he swore all the way that he wouldn't.

On arrival of flight BA 011 Gichui Luanda of the Kenyan Immigration Authority had noticed the unusual number of men gathered in the baggage hall. Ever since the kidnapping scare that had been sweeping Nairobi from sunup yesterday, foreign journalists had been arriving in droves. Usually they were distinguishable in many ways. Equipment always separated the photographers who were often paired off with the reporter or journalist. There was something about them that demonstrated their experience of travel; they had that general air of resignation that, whatever it was, they'd seen it all before.

Luanda had seen tens of thousands of visitors to Nairobi. Tourists were equally distinguishable. Businessmen generally communicated their purpose. Sometimes hostile if delayed, always in a hurry, some superior in attitude, in a position of power away from their own home. Politicians were usually met by someone, even if only a minor official.

So the number of males that peppered the hall caught his attention after a while. He could pick them out in twos and threes, hardly stirring. They weren't laughing, nor even talking much. There was something quite unnatural about them, as if they were waiting for something to happen. He considered it and decided they were noncommittal in expression and attitude. Almost all, anyway. Another thing struck him very forcibly and began to worry him. They were all young. None of them more than mid-thirties, most younger than that. There had been no group like this on any of the other flights. Yet they weren't a group so why had he thought of them as such? Another thought struck him. Most of them had a similar bearing. A relaxed posture yet upright. It reminded him of his own military service. Soldiers. *Soldiers?* They hung around the same the world over.

Gichui Luanda swallowed awkwardly. He was a very senior official, none higher at the airport. At the moment there was nothing more he could do other than pass his duties to a junior. Having detached himself he wandered into the hall. Luanda was shrewd in his observations.

When the men had all collected their baggage and left the hall, Luanda followed by another exit and watched his surmise proved right. Now they were grouping at last, climbing into the minibuses. There would have been nothing wrong with that if they hadn't taken such great pains to separate in the baggage hall. A few older men he could not really categorise were at the rear bus. He saw Donovan and Maxwell have their brief exchange and noted Donovan's authority. He noticed Chianda. This surprised him. The African wasn't a Kenyan. No tribe he immediately recognised.

What surprised Luanda most, however, was when a figure he did recognise approached Donovan. Peter Hayton-James. A coffee planter at Kiambu just outside Nairobi. He'd been in Kenya since the end of the war. Had even stood unsuccessfully for the Kenyan Parliament. He was well known, accepted in all social circles. That puzzled and unsettled Luanda. He was thwarted from speaking to them by the departure of the planter with the buses.

Luanda went to his office and telephoned the Immigration Office in Nairobi. The official there thought about it and telephoned the Minister for Internal Affairs. He did not get him direct but obtained an under secretary who in turn made a call before reporting to his minister. He was careful what he said: "Sir, Airport Immigration report the arrival of about forty men who left some minutes ago in four minibuses. He thinks they might be soldiers."

The Minister looked up. He noted the nervousness of his under secretary. "Forty men come to invade Kenya? I tremble in my shoes. Were they armed?"

"No, bwana. We can stop them."

"Why, what do you think they're up to?"

"Mr. Peter Hayton-James was with them."

The Minister straightened. Now he had to take it seriously but his under secretary was not supposed to know that. Mr. Peter Hayton-James worked for British Intelligence. He also grew some of the best coffee in Kenya. He was tolerated because he was considered harmless. This was different. Quite different. The Minister was already under enormous pressure due to the Princess Anne scare. More than a scare if he was honest. The British had better play ball. "All right. Leave it to me."

"Would you like me to give instructions—"

"I said leave it to me." The Oxford accent faltered.

"Yes, sir." The under secretary turned to go.

"Leornadi."

"Yes, sir."

"I'm sorry we've no more news of your brother."

Once Donovan's group made contact with Steinberg and Frascelli they went to Steinberg's room where Donovan explained everything. He gave it to them straight with no frills. The Italian and the South African had realised that the purpose of their visit was connected in some way with the kidnapping. They had guessed that their own involvement was due to their one-time knowledge of the Somali Plateau, that Europeans who knew the area were very thin on the ground. And they had known it in a military sense which made it more specialist still. They also recognised the similarity of winkling out a terrorist group to destroying the pockets of Banda at which they had been expert.

Steinberg echoed what the other four had said at the outset.

"Christ, it was a long time ago, man." Neither he nor Frascelli had visualised being part of a task force. Advisers, yes. Hunking a gun around, hell, that was different.

"Okay. Look: Jimmy, Tommy, Colin and I have a certain

loyalty. The daughter of our Queen is stuck out there somewhere with Twinkletoes and we all know that one way or the other she's suffering. We feel we have a duty. Neither of you are under the same flag. We understand. Don't worry about it."

Steinberg smiled his grizzled smile, his whole face taking part. He waved a small hand. "You're as cunning as a banker. You don't fool me by craftily wrong-footing us. Try something more mature."

Frascelli was sitting on the dressing-table stool. "I do not require persuading. I'm with Pat. All the way."

Steinberg looked over at Frascelli with regret. "All right, this is what I'll do." He held his arms wide and they remembered and knew that a large amount of what Donovan had once described as self-deprecating bullshit was coming.

"I'm too old and bent and aching for a job like this. It takes me half an hour to get out of bed each morning. My sight's not good. Can't read a thing without glasses. I only tinker with a Rolls-Royce now and I don't suppose you'll have any of those. And what little I knew of medicine has long gone. But we've all come a good distance. There's a certain fatalism about us meeting like this." Steinberg looked at the ceiling. "As if it was ordained. So I'll come but only as nurse and mechanic. I'm not getting mixed up in any rough stuff. Never could stand it. I also expect you to help me up when I fall over."

With the exception of Frascelli who had yet to understand the South African, they were all clapping, even Vale, who had snapped from a reverie with the close proximity of friends in a room designed for two. Jimmy King rose from the bed and pushed Steinberg's head to one side. "You forgot the bit about you coming from Israel and what a mean bastard you are."

But Steinberg ended seriously, "The mileage is crazy. I'll pass judgment on the feasibility once I've seen the transport. Let's go pick up the trucks."

Stuart Maxwell felt the pent-up power of Tommy Thompson in the seat beside him. He glanced at Thompson; tough but over the hill. He'd deal with him now, no nonsense.

"Och, you look as if you've been in prison, you're so pale."

Thompson turned on the seat, ran one thick arm along the back. "Came out yesterday morning."

Maxwell hadn't expected a blunt confirmation. But it did not worry him. "What did you get up to?"

"Murder." Near enough.

"And they let you out?"

"Just for this job. They thought I'd feel at home amongst other murderers. They were wrong."

"Ye'd better be careful what you say. Some of the boys might not like being called that."

"Murderers? They're cast-offs from the U.V.F., Provos, outcasts of the S.A.S., aren't they? What would you call them?"

"They're bloody fine soldiers. You'd better keep your voice down or I might not be able to control them."

"You couldn't control them if they were chained, sonny boy. I've seen you trying."

Maxwell's eyes flashed. "Looking for trouble, are ye?"

Thompson didn't stir. "I'll tell you what I'm looking for; obedience to Pat Donovan. You try crossing him, Maxwell, and I'll throttle you. I'm good at that." Oh yes, very good. Especially women. The word triggered the vision that seldom left him. Maxwell had disappeared, a nothing. Instead, Sandra was sitting next to him, the colour of her hair not dissimilar to the stocky ex-para. Better cut though, beautifully cropped and wide, wide blue eyes that always latched on to him so innocently. The most beautiful, the most innocent eyes he had ever seen in his life. And the most treacherous. Soft yielding lips that seemed never to let him go and a firm, willing body always eager for him. Shit. For any man she could win away from any other woman.

Those closest see the least. For eleven bloody years he hadn't known. Unbelievable. No one had warned him. Afterwards he had realised they might have been afraid of his reaction to the mere hint. He had worshipped her. Oh, Christ, he still did.

The unearthed diaries she had kept went back long before their marriage. Long enough to show that almost up to their wedding day she was knocking it off with his best friend and *best man*.

The court had decreed that the diaries were a complementary form of perversion to her nymphomania. But how could she have hidden it from him for so long? Accepting that she was a convincing, intuitive liar, there should still have been a sign, if only physical, from her. She had been passionate with him but not excessively so. And she had loved him.

To this day he was convinced of it. During the four years he had spent in prison he had re-lived their life again and again. God, she must have loved him to have married him. He'd had nothing particular to offer. A small import business which he'd started a few years after the war. Nothing like Jimmy King's enterprises.

Yet had he known, had he understood, he could not have lived with her, whatever he'd felt. A lapse or two he could have survived but nothing as nightmarish as this. He still carried the love and the nightmare with him.

It had been totally unexpected that he'd returned home that night. He should have been a thousand miles away but fog conditions the other end had persuaded him to postpone the trip. There appeared no evidence that she had used their own home before. Perhaps, as she had aged, lovers had become just that little more difficult to find and she had taken a risk not normally acceptable.

They weren't even upstairs. Yet he could not have chosen a more damning, more heart-sickening moment to have walked in. They were so intertwined, so straining with passion that they hadn't even heard him. He'd almost thrown up on the spot, almost passed out as the shock hit him again and again. After that he wasn't too clear of anything. A man lay at his feet, a naked stranger, with a terribly mis-shapen face that was blue one side over the ugly swelling of a broken jaw. He recalled Sandra's scream, would never forget that. He could still see the desperate plea for forgiveness in wide eyes that held no physical fear but expressed the sheer terror of losing him.

Some recollection came much later. He still couldn't recall catching her by the throat, though he could remember the eyes fastening on his, trying desperately to convey a message, but the vice-like hand wasn't his. He was never consciously aware of touching her naked body. When the light disappeared from her eyes she fell in front of him. He must have released her in a reflex action which brought him a measure of sanity. It was too late. He never managed to revive her.

Yes, he was expert at throttling. Beside him, Maxwell received a surge of something he didn't understand. He kept quiet.

The light-hearted mood of Donovan's group changed in the minibus. They weren't young men preparing for battle for the first time. There was no weight of an army behind them. From this point on, in official eyes, they no longer existed. Henceforth, every hand would be turned against them. They had no allies. No one to turn to except each other, and the strange belief that they could succeed. London, Rome, Johannesburg were in different worlds. It was ten forty-five a.m. on the second day.

Nairobi fell behind. The bush replaced it. And the dust. At the end of the dry season the ground was parched, the bush grey, the eternal stunted flat-topped trees drooping from lack of water, stretching monotonously for ever. Yet it suited their mood. The sooner they were conditioned back into the harsh reality of barren country the better. This was the civilised stretch, the road good. They had no illusions of what lay ahead. Out here too, the sun was master, brassy, unrelenting. That too would get worse once they were over the equator.

As Donovan looked round the bus, all he saw was a bunch of middle-aged friends. At least two of them were softened by success. One lost in a private hell. Only Chianda had stayed in the fighting business.

It was better to face the truth. They would have to rely on their common sense and their experience. And they would have to lean heavily on the mercenaries. One of them was up ahead now. He was waving them down from the edge of the bush already changed into his tropical kit, floppy hat shielding his eyes. There were no vehicles in sight.

7

THE TRANSPORT WAS well hidden in a shrivelled copse about two hundred yards off the road. Now they were all there the bus drivers were anxious to return to Nairobi and Donovan let them go. All the men had changed and the late arrivals hurriedly followed suit, feeling the cool comfort of shorts and bush shirts. They stored their own clothes in the cases and stacked them forward in one of the three tonners.

They were one Range Rover short. As there was another three-tonner to collect at the arms pick-up point it was not too serious. There was a reasonable supply of petrol drums and water. An assortment of water bottles, British, American, Italian and crates of food. Tinned meat, butter, biscuits, condensed milk and fruit. There were a dozen compasses but no raft equipment which annoyed Donovan because it meant diverting. However, there were more than enough bedrolls.

Steinberg checked the breakdown truck and was fairly satisfied with the spares, ropes and tackle and the medical box. He ran up each engine, listening, shaking his head or nodding depending on his verdict. The tyres were far from new but should see them through. The trucks were old but serviceable. He had seen worse.

The mercenaries, now that they were together as a recognisable force, looked more the part. Faces, personalities began to take shape and Donovan wondered whether he'd been too hasty in his condemnation of them. He included Maxwell in all the deliberations with his own team, introduced him to them in an effort to establish rapport. Maxwell listened attentively but it was clear from odd comments that he considered he was carrying a bunch of oldies who would never stand the pace. The oldies were too experienced to take the bait, most of them privately conceding that Maxwell might have a point. Time would tell.

The men were divided into four platoons of eleven men each, headed by Jimmy King, Tommy Thompson, Colin Vale and Maxwell's second in command, a lank Australian called Digger Williams. From the start Donovan thought of him as a young Chips Rafferty.

Donovan was commanding with Maxwell as two i/c. Pietro Frascelli was needed as a loose head. A demolition expert, his purpose depended on what arms were waiting for them at the pick-up point. No one questioned Gerry Steinberg taking over maintenance and medical.

Due to the need for separation at this point and the desire for each unit to be as self-supporting as possible, one drum each of water, and petrol was loaded on to the other vehicles. An ex-welsh Guardsman named Ossie Jenkins was appointed quartermaster, a concession Donovan found prudent to make to Maxwell. In all they had two three-tonners, three Range Rovers and a fifteen hundred breakdown truck and, as far as could be determined without a detailed calculation, adequate supplies. One important item missing was field glasses; perhaps they would be with the arms. The whole force totalled fifty-three men.

Chianda who, like Frascelli, had his own rôle to play, watched Donovan quickly organise the force and it was as though nothing had ever changed. If only it could stay that way.

The men were divided for travelling purposes, six per Range Rover, two in each cab, four behind, Ossie Jenkins with Steinberg as co-driver, the other thirty-three being divided between the two large trucks. Donovan watched how Maxwell handled the problem. There was some argument as most of the men preferred to ride in the smaller vehicles for speed and comfort. Maxwell bore down like a bull at them and sorted it out. But it was clear that he might have trouble later.

They arranged to move out at fifteen minute intervals. A Range Rover, three-tonner, Range Rover, another three-tonner and the last of the Range Rovers followed by the breakdown truck.

They moved off, one vehicle at a time. Donovan in the lead, followed by Thompson with Chianda, Maxwell and Williams, Vale, King, with Frascelli and Steinberg and Jenkins bringing up the rear. Twenty-six hours after Jumbo Hamilton had received his second telephone call the task force was on the move.

Donovan had not been under so strong a sun for a long time. As he drove with one of Maxwell's men beside him he kept his elbow from the open window of the cab. In an odd way he felt at ease. Almost at home.

He drove at speed, urged on by the knowledge of the huge distance they had to cover. Compass bearings had been checked. They could not stay on the main road for too long and would have to cut across the bush when the vehicles would really be tested. He kept almost north towards Nanyuki, the icing of the giant plum pudding of Mount Kenya brilliant white under the afternoon sun. The arid plains lay ahead, dried, waist-high colourless grass sprinkled by lack-lustre trees. Maxwell's man beside him gave a shout above the engine. He pointed upwards, his head craning out of the cab. "Spotter plane, boss."

Donovan kept his eyes on the road. "How d'you know it's a spotter?"

The soldier grinned, "I've seen enough of them."

Donovan turned his head briefly. "Looking for us, do you think?"

The soldier sank in his seat to get a better view.

"Could be. He's circling. Just as well we broke up the

convoy." He looked at Donovan with a new respect.

"I don't like the idea of a spotter."

"No. Well, that's the way it goes."

"What's your name?"

"Would you believe Bill Brown?"

"You're a Londoner?"

"Essex. You don't sound like a Donovan."

Donovan grinned. "My lot have lived in England for generations. How old are you?"

"Thirty-one. Getting on a bit."

Getting on a bit. Christ. He looked older. "This all you do? Go from war to war?"

"The pay's good. What else is there? Hang about a factory picketing a strike? It's better than holding up banks. I'm satisfied. And don't underrate the boys. Their lives are on the line."

"Mine too."

"They won't let you down."

"Some already have. We're short on numbers."

Brown smiled. "You always get a few hangers-on who chicken out."

Twenty per cent constituted more than a few but Donovan said nothing. He liked Brown's easy way; he was clearly not a man who would panic.

"Plane still there?"

"Yep. Lower. Banking. It's us all right, I'm sure of it."

"All we can do is to drive on. Once over the border they can't touch us. But that's a long way."

They were silent for some minutes. Brown periodically crouched to keep an eye on the plane. The tyres were drumming on the road, the bush a monotonous grey either side of them. The heat in the cab was oppressive. Brown said, "I hope we lift the Princess okay. Tricky business with trigger-happy terrorists. They might knock her off when they see us."

"She's the only bargaining factor they've got. If she's gone they've got nothing except the wrong end of a bullet."

"You'd go all the way?"

"All the way if they harm her."

"You sound as if you care."

Donovan hesitated, suddenly realising that he did but unsure of why. "I care," he said.

Brown eyed Donovan for several seconds, one finger toying with his lip. "There are ways of hurting her other than killing."

Donovan nodded soberly, keeping his eye on the road. "I know. I know the bastard who's holding them."

"You've met him?"

"No. If we'd met, one of us would be dead. I crossed swords with him a long time ago."

Brown picked up the message. "We're up against it. You mentioned *them*. If it's another girl she might come in for more trouble than the Princess. Destroy one to increase the demands on the other."

"It's occurred to me." Donovan briefly took his gaze from the road. "Pretty good reason for going, isn't it?"

Brown shrugged. "I get well paid. That's my reason."

"Who did you serve with?"

"Special Air Service."

"They have a reputation."

"Sure. What kind of reputation depends whether you're friend or foe. Our enemies didn't like us. That meant we did a good job."

Donovan picked up the dust cloud in his mirror a few minutes later. They had made good progress and were near the turn-off point. He checked the tripmeter. Seven miles more. The dust cloud which had started as a suspicion of haze was now clearly indentifiable and had steadied to a constant size about half a mile back. It was too small for the three-tonner. In any event it was unlikely that the big truck could have caught up at the speed they'd been travelling.

Two miles from turn off Donovan slowed. The brush had thickened, growth denser. He was looking for tracks left by the arms truck. Finding them he nursed the vehicle off the road into the bush. There was give in the surface under wheels. He didn't much like it. The long dry season had drained the moisture from the earth, leaving the surface crust hollowed underneath. He went straight over the smaller trees, the sapless branches cracking like tinder, rumbling and screeching under the chassis. Their own dust cloud swelled considerably once they were off the road and there was nothing he could see beyond it. He swung off course deliberately to get a side view and to ease away from the trail of the arms truck. He picked up the other cloud which was not gaining on them. Putting his foot down he kept his eyes open looking for gulleys and potholes. Brown straightened to act as his second eye.

All the mirrors revealed was a huge, swirling plume with the sun playing on it. Donovan kept going as fast as he dared. In this, he knew he was out of practice. The earth could be treacherous, but he was a good driver and the strangeness of what he was doing fell away as two parts of his life converged. When he saw the jeep slightly behind and to his right he was annoyed at not having drawn away.

The jeep gained ground and someone from the passenger side of the cab was waving him down. On the back of it, holding on like grim death, were armed askaris. Donovan thought quickly then braked. "Leave it to me," he shot at Brown. "Just pick up the drift." The jeep, now ahead, was bearing in from the right, its dust eddying untidily, ballooning as it stopped across Donovan's bows. The cloak of dust cocooned the jeep and settled. "While I'm talking to them get out and warn your men to keep their mouths closed."

Brown nodded laconically. "No problem."

An African officer stepped from the jeep tapping a fly switch against one very black knee. His face was caked with the red dust, the eyes two clear oases. Sweat channelled tiny rivulets through the grime. He was smart as African soldiers almost always are. As he drew nearer Donovan recognised the badge of the Kenya Rifles.

"Something wrong, captain?"

The askaris had climbed down, four with rifles, two with submachine guns.

"May I see your identification, sir."

"My passport's already been seen at the airport."

"We've received a report that there are ivory poachers up here. I have to check." The voice was thick but the words quite distinct.

Donovan was blessing the fact that his passport was in the

glove compartment instead of being packed with his discarded clothes on a three-tonner. He produced it, climbed out to give Brown an opportunity the other side. "We'd have a difficult time of it if we are ivory poachers. We have no arms." He would have to break this up before the next truck arrived.

"I was going to ask you about arms." The captain had his head down over the passport but his gaze was wandering elsewhere. He handed the passport back. "What exactly are you doing here, sir?" The streaked ebony face was classic African. Good jaw line, slightly splayed nose.

"Isn't this a free country?"

"Of course, sir, but you're off the tourist routes, away from the game parks. Unarmed, that could be dangerous for you."

"That's the whole point, captain. We want to get away from the normal tourist runs." Donovan curbed his impatience to move on.

"You've certainly done that. There's nothing around here to see."

"Not even elephant?"

The captain grinned, the teeth superbly white. Donovan was wary. The captain, though pressuring, was extremely polite, there was nothing officious about him and Donovan wondered if he'd been instructed to play it cool. That could be ominous.

The captain walked to the rear of the Range Rover where the four mercenaries sat two aside. They smiled and nodded and Donovan guessed that Brown had managed a quick word with them.

"Good afternoon, gentlemen." The captain raised his fly switch. "Have you seen anything worth photographing yet?"

Donovan said. "This isn't a photographic tour. We're simply touring the more untamed parts of Africa. That's all we want to do. That's why we have no women with us."

The captain nodded as if he understood. "I would like to look in the back,"

"By all means." Willing hands helped him up. He poked around, pushing his fly switch into odd corners. He jumped down, clearly puzzled.

"You have no camp beds. Little equipment of any kind except plenty of water and petrol. If you're sleeping out it's wise to sleep off the ground."

"We'll only be a night. Perhaps two. Then we return to Nairobi."

"I must warn you that if you continue the way you're going you'll eventually come to the Chalbi Desert. It's no place to survive."

"Don't we link up with a main road ahead?"

"Eventually. You have maps and compasses?"

Careful. "We have a map. Don't worry about us, captain. We're seasoned travellers. We won't go too far."

The fly switch came up in salute and the captain walked thoughtfully back to his jeep.

Donovan and Brown climbed back in. Brown said sidemouthed, "He's not satisfied, skipper."

"No." Donovan switched on. "He'll be less satisfied if he runs into the others. Keep your eyes peeled." He drove off, waving at the askaris who weren't sure whether they should wave back.

As they pulled away, looking straight ahead Brown said, "He's on the squawk box. There must be others around."

"I know." Donovan half smiled. "You must have eyes in your ears to have spotted that."

Brown didn't reply. He sat with narrowed eyes looking forward, but a long arm came out to adjust the central mirror for Donovan who nodded in understanding. He'd been lucky with Brown.

"Do you think they saw the other tracks?"

"You'd veered a good way from them."

"Yes. But they're Africans." Donovan wasn't convinced.

They drove on, the bush becoming sparser, the earth dustier as they travelled north-east to pick up the tracks again. The seats were sticky, their backs wet, but neither spoke for a long time. Both eyed wing and central mirrors for signs of dust clouds.

Late afternoon Donovan stopped to take compass bearings as the tracks had died out on harder soil, then he let Brown drive. He wasn't tired, would have preferred to keep the wheel but it would break the monotony for Brown and show what sort of driver he was in bush conditions. Donovan need not have worried.

They arrived at what they considered the pick-up point at four p.m. and Donovan took more bearings while the others stretched their legs and swigged at water bottles. Donovan had already fallen into a survival technique of resisting drinking during the day.

The arms had to be somewhere nearby and they had to be found quickly. Somewhere here, there should be a truck and two drivers. He gave a shout and a dik-dik fled from the bush. The men spread out to search but found nothing. Finally he left them in scanty shade to form a central point then, with Brown, drove round in concentric circles, concerned that no one had heard them.

They found the arms but no truck. Crates had been off-loaded half a mile away. Why hadn't the truck remained? Donovan sent Brown back in the Rover to collect the men so they could start unpacking the crates.

The first three-tonner arrived ten minutes later. It sounded like a foraging beast crashing through the bush, the grind of the engine difficult to pinpoint. The canopy reared above the parched growth and one of the mercenaries went forward to guide it in.

Tommy Thompson and Chianda climbed down stiff-legged and the men jumped down from the back to help immediately with the uncrating.

"Any problems?" Donovan came forward.

"No. The mileage was right. We saw your tracks leading off. Chianda noticed a second vehicle had run parallel with you for some distance from the road. The tracks disappeared north."

"North? We were stopped by troops. Weren't you?"

"No. There was a plane panning like a white hawk. Dunno if it was for us. What have we got?" They hurried over to the arms catchment.

"The arms truck has disappeared. The buggers must have got windy."

"Yeah." Thompson cast a keen eye over the arms coming to light. "They don't seem too well cared for." He picked up a rifle. "It hasn't been cleaned in months. Any pull-throughs?"

He looked around critically, then gave the men a hand to open the remaining crates. By the time Maxwell arrived in the second Range Rover the whole area was a mass of boxwood and arms. Some of the crates had been split wide open, as if they'd been pushed off the back of the truck. As the arms were lined up Thompson and Maxwell examined them, both swearing in disgust from time to time. Donovan was considerably worried by the shortage of weapons.

By the time the rest of the convoy had arrived, most of the sorting out had been done. Gerry Steinberg did not even glance at them. With the aid of a hose and lip suction he made sure that all the vehicles were refuelled, and the water and oil checked. He was quietly happy, nursing his convoy, casting an eye over tyres, checking on mechanical problems with the drivers. Jimmy King reported an indifferent foot brake and Steinberg took the Rover into the bush to test it. Two of the mercenaries quickly got three calor gas stoves going to make tea in three open urns.

It was a strange, untidy gathering of men and machines in the middle of a sun-baked wilderness. One of the men started to unload his sleeping bag and Donovan made him put it back.

"It's only an hour to sundown."

"We're moving on."

"Driving in darkness? Through this?" A sweating Maxwell intervened, bad-tempered through the journey and what he saw as suicidal arms.

"We're driving through the night." Donovan knew they couldn't wait for more arms and doubted that any would come.

"You may be."

Donovan barely kept his temper. "We did it through night. This and worse and two thousand feet escarpments *without bloody lights*. Are you afraid of the dark?"

All the men were listening now. Thompson, a faint smile on his face, was thinking the bastard hadn't changed at all, thank Christ. To stir it and because he couldn't stand the brash pretension of Maxwell, he called out, "Of course, we lost the odd few trucks over the edge on the way."

Donovan did not want to alienate the men from himself or from Maxwell. He called them round.

"You can take two-hourly driving shifts through the night. The remainder will get some sort of rest while we're moving. If you feel tired now you'll be shagged out before this is over. We've less than three days. After that you can sleep as long as you like. We'll be travelling *with* lights. Any questions?"

Maxwell was inwardly seething at his own mistake and at misjudging Donovan. "Before we go anywhere let's take a final count of the bows and arrows we've been landed to fight Russian-armed terrorists."

Donovan had been expecting it and dreading it. The last crate had just been emptied. Donovan did not look immediately at the cache but at the faces of his friends. Thompson, King, Chianda, Brown. Vale was ferreting around the trucks where the main force was grouped. Tommy Thompson looked grim. Jimmy King pushed up the brim of his bush hat and blew out his cheeks. He said nothing for Donovan's sake. Maxwell strolled up and down the rows of arms as if inspecting a parade. "This it? This the lot?"

Donovan found himself on the defensive. The quantity and type of arms was a disaster. "It's not too good, I'll agree." No binoculars, he noticed. Which meant that all they had was Gerry Steinberg's personal pair between them all.

"Not too good?" Maxwell knew he had a winning hand. "These are straight from the ark. Not an automatic rifle among them.

"There are Stens and Brens."

Maxwell checked Ossie Jenkins' list. "Two Brens, three Stens, thirty-nine bolt action rifles, parts of a 3 inch mortar, five pistols, non-plastic explosives and, gentlemen, all the way from the Imperial War Museum, a Boys Anti-Tank Rifle." He swung round on Donovan. "I can't believe it."

Sick at heart, Donovan remained calm-faced. They'd been promised *twenty-five* Stens, *five* Brens. More if possible. Thirty automatic weapons excluding pistols. All they had were *five* in total. Even the pistols were less than those ordered. "There're two boxes of grenades," he said defensively.

"Aye, and I bet those bastards are obsolete seven second fuses." Maxwell wandered over to the boxes, picked up a grenade, holding it critically. He tried to unscrew the baseplug but it would not turn. "The bloody thing's so old it's corroded in. I canna shift it."

Thompson tried, then handed it back. Maxwell gazed about him. "No primers, I see. So either the bloody things are already primed, which they shouldna' be, or we've no way of fusing them." He glared at Donovan. "If they're primed the chances are the striker is just as rusted as the plug. It'll stick halfway down the sleeve. The twenty-two cap won't be struck and the Fulminate of Mercury detonator won't explode."

Maxwell had taken the opportunity to air his knowledge in front of the men. Donovan knew it. He knew too, that Maxwell was right. He held his hand out for the grenade but Maxwell drew it back adding, "The only way to find out if it works and whether it's a four or seven second fuse is to try it now." He started to pull the pin.

"Hold it." Donovan grabbed Maxwell's hand. "You can't try it now. There are African troops about somewhere. We were stopped."

"That's all we need." Maxwell contemptuously threw the grenade back in the box.

Thompson wandered over and picked up the anti-tank rifle. He made it look easy. "Well, she might not do much to a tank but she's so darned accurate she'll take the cork from your whisky bottle. *That* should interest you, Maxwell."

Maxwell ignored him, knowing he was on safe ground. "You're in charge," he said to Donovan. "What are you going to do?"

Behind him Frascelli, who had picked up the drift from Thompson, was examining the explosive; he called out, "There's plenty of fuse wire, slow and instantaneous. Plenty of slabs of ammonal and gun cotton plugs, detonators! Excellent, eh!"

Thompson lowered the Boys and picked up a Lee Enfield. With apparent ease he held it over his shoulder by thumb and two fingers behind the foresight, the butt sticking up in the air. "Should be able to dip them in the ink and write with them." He scribbled in mid air.

Even Maxwell was impressed, the soldier in him appreciating the control and strength. "Your old boys' club is loyal, I'll gi' you that. But they've played for enough time for you. Do you expect us to fight terrorists with this rubbish? My men's lives are at stake."

Donovan was not so easily pushed. He studied the arms again. In spite of what Maxwell had said the three inch mortar was there: tripod, baseplate, barrel, even though they looked as if they'd been buried for years. There were canisters of high explosive and smoke bombs, extra tail fin charges for increased range. Could he ever remember how to align the spirit levels and drum sights? Firing the bombs themselves was easy if the fuses were self-priming. The 152 fuse? The ball bearing releasing, arming the fuse by the very jolt of leaving the barrel. It was slowly coming back. No field telephone but there were three old thirty-eight sets with throat microphones. Chianda had joined him.

Two .38 Smith and Wesson pistols, one .45 breakback Webley, two nine-millimetre Birettas. All round ammunition seemed adequate. As Maxwell was about to force his hand again, Donovan waved him down. He had to think it out.

Any attacking force should have superiority of arms and men; they were taking far more risk than entrenched defenders. He could not afford any form of protracted battle and must be in a position to drench Hassan Kilewe with fire power from the outset. In and out. That's what Smithy had wanted but Smithy hadn't supplied the right kind of arms for the job. That was a fact.

For a force of fifty-three men there were fifty-one weapons including the mortar, the anti-tank rifle and the five automatic pistols which were useless unless in close range and even then of limited value. More Stens were desperately needed. Effectively they were nine firearms short and the bulk were the wrong kind.

A sudden muted explosion, like a pencil breaking, startled everyone but when they looked round they saw Pietro Frascelli was calmly timing a length of fuse with a detonator. He left no one in doubt of how he felt about things. Maxwell's attitude was not founded on fear; in the right mood he would go in with bare hands. What was important was to show that he could lead as an officer; that above all, when the British Army had rejected him above the rank of Company Sergeant Major. And now he was surrounded by ex-officers, middle-aged layabouts like that has-been Vale who was scratching around searching for something in the trucks. He resented losing total control to men like these at a time when he had achieved the very ambition he had for so long secretly nurtured.

Donovan took Maxwell aside, sensing a hesitation, but not fully understanding it. "Max, there are totally bewildered girls out there. Princess, lady in waiting. When it comes down to it whatever brave face they put on they are still young girls with a breaking point like everyone else. They'll be suffering right now. They won't know what's going on but they'll know that the odds are heavily against them. They'll remember Peggy McKenzie, too, and they'll assess their chances intelligently, which means they've prepared for the worst. Let's give them a hand."

"I'm more concerned for my men than for a slip of a Princess. These arms are bloody useless."

Donovan groped for an insight, saw a glimpse of one. "Princess is just a handle, Max. Young girls. Defenceless. Living in considerable terror. British. One of them's the granddaughter of a Scot."

"What distance have we to go and what's the strength of the enemy?"

Donovan saw no end to it. There simply wasn't the time. "The distance is about two hundred and seventy-five miles, once we reach the border and the going is a fair bastard. I'm told Hassan Kilewe has twenty to twenty-five men. Don't you believe it. He never operated with so few and they'll be infinitely better equipped. It's not for the faint-hearted, Max. Only for men. Load up or take one of the trucks and clear out."

Steinberg came crashing through the bush at that point. He climbed out of the Rover, stiff-legged and grimy-faced. He bawled at Jimmy King, "I've done the best I can for your brakes. You'll have to play on your gears. You always were a lousy driver, anyway." He strode over to the arms dump, looking down critically, closely watched by Maxwell. To no one in particular he said aloud, "Some of these were smuggled up in my plane. Thought I wouldn't know."

My plane. Maxwell eyed the matter-of-fact South

African. What kind of people were these oldies? Why were they doing it, for Chrissake?

Donovan was bawling out, "Distribute the arms in all vehicles except the second three-tonner and the breakdown truck. Gerry, you won't be armed nor Ossie Jenkins as quartermaster." He wheeled round on Maxwell. "Take the spare three-tonner and those men who don't want to go. Make it quick." He strode away to organise the distribution of the arms. It was important for each vehicle to carry as many weapons and ammunition as were necessary for the men who travelled with it. He saw that the mortar was put in his own Rover together with the bombs. He took no other form of weapon for himself.

Maxwell was standing aside unnoticed in the general activity, a compact, bull-like figure, ready to charge in any direction. His men should be obeying *his* orders. But he hadn't given any. Well, he'd soon bloody well change that. He strode forward belligerently to find a central spot where he could command attention. As he opened his mouth as a first move to resume command, Chianda's voice cut across everything.

"Cars coming. Many."

Chianda hadn't shouted but immediately there was silence, every man freezing. Crates of ammunition half on boards were held there, some guns still poised, one or two held ready, though unloaded.

There was no sound, the silence of the wilderness held in uncanny suspension. All eyes swivelled to Chianda who was completely still facing south-west. One or two men grinned when they could hear nothing. Chianda said, "Seven. Jeeps maybe." As if he could almost see them.

Disbelief showed on some faces. Donovan snapped, "If he says he can hear them then he can hear them. Get the bloody stuff on board and covered over with blankets. Move it."

There was a flurry of activity and from a confused situation came an astounding amount of good order as they fell into an emergency routine of teamwork, working with and for each other. All they needed was leadership. And Maxwell, confronted with danger, dropped his grievance and strove harder than anyone.

Donovan looked at his watch. In half an hour the light would go. Already time was against them. Maxwell, suddenly hearing the sound of engines and the brittle crushing of the brush, ran round starting up the transport in readiness to leave. Those ready first pulled out on Donovan's instructions. Most of them were on the move when the first of the jeeps nosed forward, the bush hats of the askaris mounted at its rear, just visible above the growth before they reached the clearing.

8

COLIN VALE HAD instructed a mercenary to take the wheel of his three-tonner while he supervised the loading at the back. The last man and arms were on board when he saw the jeep. He bawled out to his driver and swung himself onto the tailboard as the truck moved forward. Donovan, in his Rover, would not move until the last vehicle had gone. And Chianda wouldn't move without Donovan.

Helping hands pulled Vale under the canvas canopy as the driver accelerated. Chianda, on the running board of Donovan's Rover saw this and on the periphery of his vision noticed the lead jeep of the Kenya Rifles speed forward to cut off the truck. Instead of jumping into the cab Chianda scrambled into the back of the now moving Rover helped by the few mercenaries already there. By the time he reached the tailboard eight or nine jeeps, their superstructure and askaris visible above the brush line some distance away, were half mooning towards them at reckless speed.

Shots were fired but whether they were deliberately high or merely wild because of the rolling movement of the jeeps was difficult to decide. Chianda, checking the route of Vale's truck, produced a big box of matches, pulled a bunch out and crammed their stems in the lid before closing it tight. They protruded head first from the box. He lit them and threw the box overboard.

The jeeps were already in top flight as Donovan went through his gears but he had to ease off to make allowance for the slower acceleration of Vale's truck, and the lead jeep was forcing the truck driver to veer. Vale had watched Chianda's action before seeing one of the calor stoves still flickering in the clearing. He called for a rifle, a round and physical support.

It was almost impossible to stand upright. The truck was operating on square wheels and as the jeep swung across their front the truck driver found he was heading nearer to the clearing instead of away from it. Four men supported Vale by each clinging to the superstructure with one hand and trying to hold him steady with the other. Vale had crammed a round into the bolt action breech of the Lee Enfield. There was no time for anything more. One of the mercenaries guessing what was in his mind, said, "You'll never do it."

"Just hold me steady, dear boy." The rifle came up. Standing was never the best of aiming positions; in a careering truck over rough terrain at best it was optimistic. Vale timed it to the split second as he steadied, instinctively rode a bump, then squeezed the trigger. Eighty yards away the calor stove shattered, its flame spilling onto dried grass that had seen no rain for six months. The flame caught, gripped, then burst with unbelievable speed and as if following a gunpowder trail either side.

The jeep that had been harassing the truck swung away as the driver saw the danger to the following jeeps, knowing that in only seconds the fire could spread at uncontrollable speed. The truck driver cut inside the jeep and circled north again. On the back of the jeep the askaris were confused, not sure whether to fire at the truck or concentrate on quickly quelling a new danger to their following colleagues. If there is one thing an African understands above all others it's the terrifying dangers of a bush fire. Anyway the truck was heading ultimately to nothing but waterless desert. Instinct dictated that they stopped the blaze. They could not just then, understand why their approaching colleagues were pointing dramatically behind them.

The truck driver found out. As he made his final directional turn he could not fail to see the bush fire ahead of him. The racing line of flame was following Donovan's Rover which had been forced out to the east of it away from the diversionary tactic he had attempted in an effort to relieve the harassment of the truck. Chianda's fire had been no less effective than Vale's, no less dramatic in its incredible speed. Brushwood, grass, stunted dry trees went up as if petrol soaked. The truck was caught between the two lines of blaze that were expanding both laterally and vertically and closing together like a molten clamp. There was no way back. Behind them askaris were already dismounting from jeeps placed at a safe distance. It had to be forward. The driver followed the Rover now accelerating as Chianda bawled the news down to Donovan. The heat was increasing in the truck. The converging lines of fire were devouring the oxygen from the fiery chasm, but the truck was closing with the Rover which turned north when it became clear that the truck would survive once it outsped the fire line. Behind them the second fire was sending rippling heat haze above the flames and the rising smoke pall. Those in the back were pleased at the red black screen that was cutting them off from the askaris. They could endure the immense heat that was sucking them dry in the relief of escape. A life sentence in an African prison, or worse, bearing in mind the arms they carried, had no appeal to any of them.

The Kenya Rifles captain, his men now fighting a difficult battle against the bush fire, suffered the chagrin of losing on both fronts. The fire had got too fast a hold at the near end of the dry season and his quarry was escaping. A field officer with reinforcements was a few minutes behind them and instead of handing over a coup, the captain could only produce failure. In exasperation and in a last attempt to salvage something, he detached a section of men to open fire on the truck, now nearing the end of the northern bush fire line and just discernible from where he stood on the fringe of the southern inferno. The sweat stood out on his glistening black skin like glass beads as he shouted out his orders.

Vale and his men who had been thrown down to the floor of the truck by its speed and rough movement were saved by their very discomfort. The canvas canopy was holed by a volley of shots, some penetrating the metalwork. It was a miracle no one was hit. The driver, on the verge of the eastern extremity of the blaze, outpacing it, almost ready to turn to get north of it, suddenly felt a rush of air in front of his face which left a lingering whine in the cab. When the metal door ruptured above his knee he knew they were being fired at. His decision had to be split second. He was flank on to the askaris. Luck wouldn't sit with him forever. He pulled on the wheel and shot diagonally into the blaze at its thinnest point knowing that the next few seconds governed life and death.

Even one or two seconds can be an eternity during extreme suffering. As soon as he was in he barely had time to reflect that he had made a dreadful mistake. It would have been better that they were shot. The intense heat was unbearable. He had wound up his window as he turned, and had created an incinerator for himself. Flame and smoke engulfed the truck. With what they were carrying it would blow up any minute, but with the incredible agony he suffered, the burning suffocation, that would have been a relief. He shouted in agony, certain that his skin was on fire, his face singeing as he shook his head in pain.

And then he was clear, gulping hot air, winding down the window, half sobbing with relief, still in one piece. His thoughts quickly flew to those in the back. In his wing mirror he saw the canopy was ablaze. He slowed, leaned out, keeping his flesh clear of the metal. In the back Vale called out, "Drive on. We can cope." The rear end of the canopy was on fire, but shaken, singed, sweat and soot covered men beat at the flames with blankets. They had survived two quick intense attempts on their lives and showed their relief in the way they doused the flames. A good quarter of their cover had gone and there was still danger to the petrol and ammunition boxes from sparks but the containers were well sealed. The men endured being thrown around by the lumbering truck as they continued to blanket the last active smoulder. In the greater space on the back they had fared just marginally better than the driver.

They had time to look back now. Black smoke obscured a brilliant sky, arching like a canopy bringing a premature dusk. For a while the flames were lost in the cloud they created. They would spread miles yet at increasing speed, the dry scrubland turning to black powder. It would not stop until either fire breaks were dug by the askaris or the flames reached an unjumpable barrier like a river or total desert. Started by an exploding box of matches and a calor stove.

Donovan had raced back on seeing the truck alight in his mirror. The noise of the raging blaze had drowned the sounds of the shots and he had been startled when the truck had emerged through the tail end of the inferno itself. He got behind it, grinned when the men waved, saw something of what they had suffered from their soot covered figures, then stayed behind them as they raced to catch up with the rest of the convoy.

Donovan drew ahead when they were back in line and raced up the side of the convoy. As he passed Gerry Steinberg in the Maxwell, ginger hair peppered with dust and smoke, grim faced, eyes front. Brown grinned over as he drew away. Pietro Frascelli had grabbed the second three-toner, perhaps because much of his explosive was on the back. He waved cheerfully and so did Jimmy King who leaned across beside him. The lead vehicle was a Rover driven by Tommy Thompson with Digger Williams, Maxwell's 2 i/c next to him. Tommy gave the V sign, looking as if he were enjoying himself.

For a few minutes the two vehicles travelled side by side contentedly, only one safe direction to go. Safe? Donovan turned to Chianda who had climbed from the back with incredible agility and had joined him in the cab. "You wanted it to be like old times? The next lot will be for real."

Chianda looked ahead, then at the sky. "No light left soon. Minutes."

The dust cloud behind them was deepening in the dusk, filling the cab of the truck behind them. The scrub was thinning noticeably, mile upon mile of parched plain. The rich sunset cast blood-red pockets across a changing sky, often reflecting into the shallow hollows of the spreading, heat-filled wilderness.

Donovan glanced at his watch. "We'd better get ahead and set course."

In the rear of the trucks the men were cleaning arms and checking them before loading. They did not want to be caught again and it was almost dark.

The British Foreign Secretary arrived in Nairobi two hours after the Kenya Rifles force, aided by reinforcements, had fought the bush fire. Word was radio'd back and relayed to Nairobi.

By the time the Foreign Secretary was ensconced with the Kenyan Minister for Internal Affairs the brush with the task force was known and the Kenyan Government, as a body, was livid. By the coolness of his reception, which previously had invariably been warm, he guessed that something had already gone wrong.

Behind closed doors the Kenyan Minister did not mince words. "You have violated every international code with this task force. Mr. Kenyatta is personally sending a protest to your Prime Minister and we are making a formal complaint to the United Nations. How dare you do such a thing on our territory without even raising the question with us?"

The Foreign Secretary smiled tolerantly, "Come, now, Joshua, get off your high horse. Why do you think I'm here?"

"To see how they get on. To make paltry excuses. To say that you know nothing about them. You put at risk the tenuous contact we have made with Hassan Kilewe."

"And have you got anywhere with him?"

"At the moment nothing beyond the ransom demand. That does not give you the right to invade our land and to destroy what we've been trying to do to save *your* Princess. If matters go wrong we will make it clear to the world that it was caused by criminal British interference."

The Foreign Secretary offered a cigarette, accepted a rebuff, then lit his own, placing an elbow on the heavy desk as he blew at the ceiling. "You've made your protest. Now switch off the tape and let's get down to it. You know very well that we would never send British troops into Kenya. Not in any circumstances. Not even for Princess Anne. Poor, poor girl."

"You think we don't care about her? What you have done has worsened the situation."

"Why must you insist that we sent these men?"

"You clearly knew about them."

"It was one of the issues I intended to raise with you. We had reports too late to act upon. They had already left the country. They are a bunch of mercenaries, *employed by you and other African states*, if not officially then clandestinely, to set up flying columns in Southern Africa. We don't know who but obviously some misguided patriot, has taken them on loan and has used them for this purpose. There are plenty of wealthy men in Britain who would spend vast sums of money to protect any part of the Royal family."

The African smiled, his dark eyes humorous for a moment. "I would almost believe you if they hadn't so conveniently managed to obtain seats on already heavily booked flights."

"They were booked days ago, Joshua. It will be easy for you to check with British Airways. While you're doing that why not check the onward flights from Nairobi to Lusaka? That's where they were originally going as you know better than any of us."

"We'd never enter into anything like that."

"Of course not. Nor would we. You have your misguided patriots as we do."

"And Peter Hayton-James? He had contact with them. He must have arranged this end."

"Peter Hayton-James?"

"Don't take us too much for fools."

"I believe he was once used by the Foreign Office. Benign intelligence reports. Not for a long time though. He was no damned good. If someone has paid him to organise this end then God help them."

"Your misguided patriot would seem to have convenient contacts wouldn't you say?"

"Rich men do. They can pull strings much faster than we can. Joshua, why are we arguing? For God's sake, the Princess and her friend's lives are at stake but much more than that. The world is waiting to see how we, and you in particular, handle it. Political terrorists around the world are waiting and are laughing up their sleeves. One particular life is not expendable. Centuries of tradition, a national heritage, is centred round it. If there were time for a referendum in Britain today, if the people knew the true facts of the case, they would vote for invasion and to hell with the lot of you.

"We're arguing because we're barren of ideas and you've already found a scapegoat in some draggletail force that you can blame us for. It won't work and in your heart you know it. Why don't we cash in on it? They're here. Keep it quiet and let them go. If they succeed it's to your credit. If they don't then you can place your blame. They've provided you with a safe each way bet."

The Kenyan considered it. "How do you rate their chances?"

The Foreign Secretary side-stepped the trap. "How can I know? I'm not sure of how many or how they are armed and equipped."

The Kenyan studied a note on his desk. "Perhaps fifty or sixty men and, whilst we can't be absolutely certain, some of our men glimpsed the hurried loading of rifles that are well out of date."

The Foreign Secretary stirred uneasily. "So *you* don't rate their chances highly?"

The black hand picked up another note. "Let me put it this way. It would seem that Hassan Kilewe has a small army. This has only just come through. They are fully equipped with modern weapons and Russian Kalaschnikov machine pistols, these days standard Arab guerrilla equipment. How would you rate your raggle-taggle band of poorly armed warriors?"

The Foreign Secretary was quiet. They should never have embarked on it. It was true that he himself hadn't known until he had been needed to clear the way to Swaziland. There had been no time to organise the force properly. To recall them was to acknowledge responsibility for them and that was out of the question. He looked across the desk grimly. "No chance at all?"

Joshua shook his head. "None. The only reason they escaped my men was because an inexperienced officer let his initiative slip. Had the senior officer with the reinforcements been there it would not have happened. That and a compassion that we in Government sometimes foolishly allow. Hassan Kilewe won't show them any."

"Suicide?"

"Undoubtedly. It can only strengthen Kilewe's hand."

"Poor misguided fellows. Whatever possessed them?"

The Kenyan made no comment. He was not misled but was satisfied with the answers he had received. They would do for the moment.

"If they're massacred they'll at least attract world sympathy, turn a lot of feeling against Kilewe?"

"You don't really believe that will worry Kilewe?"

"No. Why don't you send your boys in? They're ideal for that type of warfare?"

"And invite the Russians back? And what of our friendly neighbours? Amin? Kaunda? Nyerere? Micombero? Habyalimana? Don't overlook the treaty signed by Siyad of Somalia and Podgorny of Russia in '74. Nor the fact that the United Liberation Front of Western Somalia have been demanding the transfer of a considerable area of Kenya to Somalia. Are these factors less important to us than your Princess?"

"The least you can do is to protest to the Russians."

"We already have, and I've no doubt so have you. They referred us to the Supreme Revolutionary Council of Somalia. We had already protested there, of course, with all the right noises and no results. Although the Somalis are not Arabs they were admitted to the Arab League as its twentieth member. Their interests are purely Arab and we can expect little help even if Faisal of Saudi Arabia puts on pressure." Joshua raised his hands. "Why am I preaching things you already know?"

"Because we're both chasing our tails. It's not that we object to the £10,000,000. Her Majesty herself has intervened on this score. It's merely that we believe with reason that payment will make no difference. Kilewe will have all the back-door support he needs from the Libyans and Syrians and others the Russians don't want to upset. Whether we like it or not we're back to a misguided patriot who has backed this badly-armed bunch. Let them go, Joshua. Take the pressure off them. They're our only hope."

The Kenyan raised his brows. "Didn't I tell you that I have?"

The Foreign Secretary was satisfied. He hesitated. "Tell

me what positive proof there is that Kilewe is holding the Princess."

"His claims and his demands to some of the survivors radio'd via intermediaries. Captain Mark Phillips was one of those found. Apparently he fought desperately for his Princess. By all the laws of survival he should be very dead. It is clear that Kilewe wanted him neither dead nor captive. He was needed as a reluctant emissary of the terrorists. We have him under close guard in a safe place of secrecy and he well understands the present need for silence. He wants nothing said that might jeopardise the life of his wife. Apart from the Princess, one other woman is missing. Two men were killed outright, two were critically wounded. Of those who fled into the bush one was found this morning, wounded in need of water and hopelessly lost. It's wild, thick growth around the river. Unless signals are made or they reach open ground, survivors will be impossible to locate from the air. Ground searchers are hard at it but it's tough tedious work." After a thoughtful silence he added, "When we've seen Jomo we will take you to him."

The lips were near negroid, the face thin like his Somali mother's used to be. The nose was as straight as a Somali's, splayed only slightly at the nostrils. The skin was faded sepia, cracked here and there like the desert in which he lived. Clear eyes of light brown could be unblinking when he chose, the resulting stare unnatural and chilling because feeling was something he almost inevitably kept within his thin, skeletal frame.

Hassan Kilewe had killed and tortured more men than he could remember. He was not obsessed by the number of his conquests, did not keep records to boast of as some male lovers did of their many women. It was true that he did not kill for the sake of killing. If he tortured it was not for revenge but for information. If he castrated it was because he did not want his enemies to breed and impaling decapitated heads had in the old days been a warning to all watching enemies. None of his violence had been directly based on sadism; he lacked, except in one respect, sufficient emotion to pander to this sort of sick whim. His violence had a purpose. All of it as he saw it. He neither enjoyed it nor disapproved and this frightening fact left his unfortunate enemies with no effective appeal because there was nothing emotionally tangible to appeal to.

The two white girls kept in the windowless mud hut with the heat-conducting corrugated iron roof were kept alive simply because they were of value for the one thing in life he cared about: power. Their station was meaningless to him except as a bargaining factor. They would fetch money but they would bring him far more than that.

As a young man Hassan Kilewe had one burning ambition. Now in his early sixties it was still not too late to nuture it. He had never really learned how his father had been a Kikuyu and his mother pure Somali. The only thing he'd gleaned was that it was an incident near the border. *An incident.* His pregnant mother had borne him back to her village in her motherland and on his birth had been virtually ostracised by her own people. The Somalis were a handsome, proud people, the Bantus something inferior. The very understanding was a simple contradiction. The truth was they were different in looks, in habit, in outlook and in religion which was largely Muslim. The Kenya Bantus on the other hand were largely Christian.

Against a background of an unwanted bastard of mixed blood—he had learned that his mother had frequently tried to abort him—he had grown up under the hostility of those who surrounded him. One or two had shown pity and as soon as he was old enough to recognise it as such he reviled it and he spurned those who had offered it. After his mother's death he assumed the Bantu surname out of defiance. By this time, at the age of fifteen, his contemporaries already held him in awe and not a little fear. As soon as he had been old enough to work things out, Hassan Kilewe had decided he could either sink under the pressure of derision or rise to the top to silence the tongues. It was all important to be completely self-sufficient, to rely on no man.

As a teenager he quickly learned how to get what he wanted, to tolerate nothing in his way, to use people and then to discard them if necessary. Instead of being quietly killed, his position was maintained by the terror of some of his enemies. He never lacked informers and had far less scruples in dealing with those who might harm him than they had in dealing with him. He was adept at passing blame and often killed two birds with one stone. Conversely, too, his very difference from the others often saved him. He developed an aura they simply did not understand and he subtly played on their own superstitions.

He had learned to pay lip service to those who ruled his country whoever they might be. When the Italians annexed Ethiopia in the mid thirties he was well on the way to power but too young to adopt its ultimate mantle. He knew the value of patience; in his formative years he could not have survived without it. When Britain and France joined the war in 1939 he weighed their chances, saw the evidence of the Italian strength around him, of the roads and buildings that they had constructed in their short time of occupation and of the money they had poured in and he made his decision.

In the short term he was right. At that time Somaliland was divided by the British, French and Italians. The British were forced out of their section in 1940. The French sector joined the Vichy Government, and, therefore, the whole of Somalia was effectively Axis controlled: a force on whose back Hassan was confident he could climb.

He had a classic example to learn from. Mohammed Abdullah Hassan of the Ogaden had fought the British between 1900 and 1929. Even then, though finally beaten, he was never captured. Better known to the world as the Mad Mullah he escaped to Ethiopia only to die of influenza the following year.

Hassan Kilewe had studied the Mad Mullah's fortunes and had quite early decided to be infinitely more cunning politically. He wanted nothing less than to be President of all Somalia. It meant waiting until he was of sufficient age and of acceptable maturity but he was already far beyond his years and was grafting at the roots of future success.

When the British invaded from Kenya in 1941 he had already organised very effective Banda under Italian auspices. Some of his treatment of prisoners was frowned upon and stopped, but the Italians could not always be to hand. They had their own problems at the time. Hassan Kilewe ran his own war within a war and made an immense reputation for himself among his people, which was exactly what he wanted. His quick, effective skirmishes and the speed and stealth of his harassment against enemy patrols quickly earned him the name of Twinkletoes, a delightful-sounding misnomer if ever there was one.

Backed by money from the Italians, a people who one day he planned to discard, his fame for fearlessness spread throughout the country. His ideas were proceeding according to plan. By adding his own rumours to reality he enjoyed a reputation far in excess of his actual conquests. Even so, there was no doubt that he was a very formidable warrior and a cunning foe. It was better to be killed than to become his prisoner.

The beginning of his downfall was the very speed of the British advance. South, East and West African troops swept through the country in what, originally, had been planned as a foraging attack on the Port of Kismayu. With the rains so close nothing more had been contemplated at that time. Overrun, Hassan attacked the roots of the columns after they had gone through, and with some success. And then he ran into troops who knew the bush and desert and who could survive it as well as his own men. The King's African Rifles from Kenya, Tanganyika, Uganda. The Northern Rhodesian Regiment, Gold Coast and Nigerian troops could read every blade of grass, every grain of sand, as he could. And they were in the mood for fighting and winning. There was no way to stop them. Hassan suffered severe losses, not only in battle. His men started to desert or break away in groups of their own.

His plans began to fall apart. The country was occupied by the British, his Italian contacts were taken prisoner. Once more he was alone, his only advantage his successful avoidance of capture. Worse was to come. The British spurned his entreaties to help them round up stray groups of Italians. As he couldn't identify himself without putting himself behind wire, his reputation, so carefully built, was useless to him. Not only that, but many of his comrades were being formed into a band of irregulars fighting *for* the British. It was a huge slap in the face for which he never forgave them. It suggested, too, that someone might have informed on him. It was strange that his colleagues were being used and not himself. This possibility provided the supreme insult. The British did not rate him sufficiently high to take him in. His reputation floundered with his confidence. His personal battle for survival had to start all over again and his heart was filled with hate.

His surmise was far from the truth. The British would have been delighted to have bagged him had they known who he was but their reason for not using him would have been equally humiliating to him. They simply considered him physically unsuitable. He was small and wiry to a point of thinness. Most Somalis are lean but he was more so. And they found his eagerness suspicious but no more than that. So his own complexes convinced him of what he wanted to believe. His downfall had to be blamed on someone; and who better than his victors?

He went into French Somaliland to whip up feeling there but Djibouti was blockaded by the British Navy and, in 1943, the French there broke away from the Vichy grip and declared themselves Free French. He was now surrounded by enemies in the whole of Somalia and Ethiopia and belatedly realised that the forces were far too formidable to combat. So he waited again for a long time, his hatred for what he believed had caused his downfall burning all the time.

It was not until years later when the war was over and the Revolutionary Council took control under the auspices of the Russians that he began to grow again. This time his force was illegal but there was plenty of external and internal support while he did for them what they preferred not to do openly. Agitation over French Somaliland, now Afars and Issas, and the Kenya borders and even Ethiopia came within his grasp. His power grew but not as it had been. It seemed that his old reputation was permanently tarnished. Unless he could pull a master stroke, gain the attention he had once enjoyed. More than that. *Gain world attention.* There were many precedents for what he had in mind. But he must do better. In one stroke wipe out his old humility and defeats and place himself on an unassailable pinnacle. A focus for the eyes of the world.

Hassan Kilewe rose, left the building and stood on the jutting rock plateau overlooking the untidy village. It was as if the rock was made for him, a rostrum that placed his small figure above all others. He gazed into a dark sky, pricked by millions of stars whose very coldness appealed to him. Yet they served him better than that. The air was stifling, the heat penetrating the thin soles of his sandals. He wore a waistband to his knees, below which veins stood out on spindly legs. His almost emaciated upper body was bare, ribs casting shadows in the poor light. Beneath the off-white loose turban his grizzled hair was dull red, dyed with clay in the Somali tradition.

As he surveyed the dim outlines around him he saw the faint movement of goats and some of his followers. He accepted with rancour the changes that had taken place in his country. He knew that the Russians tolerated him only because he had the support of other extremist groups who were backed by some Arab States with whom they did not want to lose favour. The Russians played their game as he played his. He understood them. They were far more ruthless than any of the preceding occupying powers. Officially they did not occupy but they had Siyad in their pockets so it was the same thing. They would do to him what he would do to them given favourable opportunity and the right political climate. Right now they would leave him alone. There was a lot of support for what he had done in areas that could embarrass the Russians enormously.

He did not dwell much on the two young girls. They were here, they were well guarded and they were fed and watched like cattle. Soon the water would make them suffer. Their hut, though small enough, had been subdivided by a rush screen the other side of which was a Bantu who had been with the Royal party. A Kenya Government public relations man. It had transpired, under torture, that he was the brother of one of the under secretaries to the Kenyan Minister of Internal Affairs. It was strange how reluctant he had been to reveal this small fact. The radio links to Nairobi had been very busy from that point. The radio operator was approaching now. Kilewe listened to the strange, guttural flow of Somali that made the man sound as if he had no palate to his mouth and he nodded in satisfaction. Calling for a lamp, he descended the rock using a long staff and walked very upright in the way of the Somalis to the hut where his remaining prisoners were. The others had already become vultures' meat.

The lamp in the hand of his follower wavered as it was

held high. Shadows moved and the white of eyes shone from them like phosphorescent balls. The uneven, sand-covered rock was thrown into moving undulations by the swaying lamp. As Hassan Kilewe slowly crossed the ground, feet were pulled back from doorways to make way. Behind stone features Kilewe reflected on the news he had just received and on the ease of the raid.

He considered that his shrewdness had sharpened over the years. In the absence of other advances it had been necessary. Now the long years of waiting, of patience, of carefully controlled self-stimulus to avoid the trap of stagnation, were about to be rewarded.

There was a guard at each corner of the hut and two outside the bamboo door. They were squatting, each with a machine pistol across his loins. When they heard Kilewe approach they scrambled to their feet.

Kilewe swept into the humid murk of the hut, the lampholder just behind. The light threw up the gloom rather than relieving it. To anyone but Kilewe airlessness and the torturous build-up of heat was almost unbearable. Always a practical man, he ignored the two crouching forms in the far corner. In any event they were manacled. His business was with the man behind the screen, whose pitiful whimpers he could already hear. He brushed past the suspended rush matting, the light picking out a sobbing wreck of a man on the floor. Immediately the whimpering increased.

The Kenyan had the remnants of a lightweight Western suit on a once sturdy frame. What had been a rounded black face now sagged and poured moisture through dirt no one had troubled to move. His feet were bare and a mass of burn blisters. His lips were bruised and bloodied where he had bitten them in an attempt to hold his tongue and to stop the screams. A brave man, it wasn't until they'd plucked his eyes out that he had finally given in. The empty red sockets stared up at the lamp as if they could locate its glow. The cringing fear was now as permanent as the pain he bore. He could no longer see his torturer but when he had, for a while at least, it had helped.

Before his collapse he had seen the other men tortured, though they'd had nothing to tell. And his own final betrayal had been minute enough. A huge judder ran through him and he couldn't stop quivering in the presence of the evil he knew to be there. Briefly he thought of the two young women the other side of the screen. Oh God!

Hassan Kilewe was unmoved by the broken wretch at his feet. He had seen too many of them. The Russians could keep their disorientation methods. They took too long and he preferred the old methods. He spoke in Swahili, *"Jambo. Habari yako?"*

The Kenyan groaned. The devil in front of him had no need to ask how he was. *He* could see the living death. A passage through hell but could hell be as bad as this? Yet if he did not answer, and in the humblest of tones, he would suffer more if that was possible. It *could* be worse. Only death would be better.

"Jambo, bwana." If only his voice would steady so that he could retain self-respect.

"I have good news for you. I've received information from Nairobi that a British task force is on its way. Your brother even tried to have it stopped and that is worth some reward. He was, however, misguided; we do not want it stopped. I thought you would like to know. You could have saved yourself much suffering by being frank with us at the beginning."

"Would it have made a difference?" the words were out before he could stop them. Could all this have happened in little more than twenty-four hours? Could a wonderfully enjoyable Royal safari turn into a grotesque nightmare of vivid eternal pain? Could he become a blind, bumbling shell in so short a span of time? On the fringe of learning to suffer the physical agonies, the terrifying sightlessness, his only reality was the knowledge that a day ago he knew the joy of life and now all he craved was the relief of death.

"I promised to help you in return for your help. I am a man of my word. I will relieve your burden." Kilewe turned to the lampbearer. "Release him."

The lampbearer placed the lamp down while camel flies attacked it, and untied the cords that bound the bloodied wrists to a wall staple.

Kilewe said, "You are free to go."

This was a new form of torture, "Where? I cannot see." The hands groped. "I cannot stand on my feet."

"You must try."

The gasp of pain filled the hut as the Kenyan tried then collapsed back on his knees, head bowed in agony.

Kilewe called for some guards. Every whimper, scream, sob and protest of the Kenyan reached the young ears behind the screen. There would come a time when this sort of conditioning would have its use. When the guards came he instructed them to lift the Kenyan to his feet. They slung their machine pistols over their shoulders and struggled with the dead weight, used now to ignoring the despairing cries of protest from the far side of the hut but even those were diminishing.

One of the guards, showing momentary compassion as they urged the Kenyan from the hut, got his shoulder well under the arm to take the weight from the blistered feet. His reward was Kilewe's staff coming down sharply on his instep. As he released his grip in pain the Kenyan fell forward on to hands and knees. Now outside the hut he groped about, glad to be in the open but knowing it would do no good.

Kilewe's staff tapped the ground in front of him. "This is the direction of south. Crawl your way back to Kenya."

"Oh, God help me."

"What is it you want? You have your freedom."

The red sockets strained up to the sky. "You promised to reward me."

"I have. What is it you want?"

"Mercy. Show me mercy."

The Kenyan knew that with luck it was over. He mustered his shattered dignity and still on his knees, straightened. Even now he dare not offend for fear of protracting the cat and mouse game. "Release me," he said simply.

Kilewe nodded, held out a hand into which was placed a pistol. He shot the Kenyan through the back of the head and the body fell forward. He handed the pistol back. "Clean it. And remove this carrion." As he walked away he was aware of the faint crying from the hut and the comforting words of the woman they called a Princess. He would break her too. When he was richer and had humiliated the British, ground their nose in the dirt.

He returned to the small plateau, his mind working ahead. He faced south towards Kenya. So they were coming.

Nothing could be better. He would destroy them bit by bit and he would then parade the bits. What had happened to the Kenyan was nothing compared to what would happen to this arrogant bunch of fools. How dare they invade his country? How dare they insult him by sending a small group of ageing ruffians?

By Mohammed, he would teach them a lesson not only they but the whole world would remember.

9

"Oh, My old man's a dustman,
He wears a dustman's hat,
He wears gorblimey trousers,
And an apron on his back."

AS JIMMY KING sang the cockney song off key Pietro Frascelli, who was more than a passable baritone, winced. He hadn't the heart to remonstrate. The Londoner was doing his best to stay awake behind the wheel, as they all had over the last few hours. The air was cooler now, thank God, and the convoy had spaced out to avoid eating each other's dust.

They were driving on dipped headlights, the experience eerie in the bush, the beams floating, bouncing, picking up the haze of dust that was late to settle and pulling clouds of insect life both on to the lights and the windscreen.

Periodically they had to run the washers and the wipers to clear the crushed, flying nightlife from the glass.

The sheer monotony was already beginning to tell. There was no road to follow, nothing except the distant lights ahead which they dared not lose. The course was set by Donovan and if he was wrong they were all wrong. At first it had been bearable, even exciting, particularly after fleeing from the Kenya Rifles and the fire. Now their backs were wet and aching and there was no room to change position.

Jimmy King, like some of the others, was feeling his age just then. All he wanted was a good night's sleep. As he sang songs most of the words of which he had long since forgotten, he thumped the steering wheel to the beat. When he finally ran out of words he started to whistle in a way that suggested he must be tone deaf. It was so bad that Frascelli was forced to smile when he should have been snatching some sleep. Like King he could find no comfort.

Apart from the unevenness of the terrain what had irritated them most of all was the constant thudding and thumping of the crushed bush hitting their underside. It continued mile after mile after mile until it became the only sound they'd ever known. The second Rover had an exhaust pipe dislodged by the tangled remains of a tree and the whole convoy had been signalled to a stop by the flashing of lights as agreed. They had waited and smoked and talked in the dark, Donovan anxious to get on, while Gerry Steinberg worked his miracles with thick, insulated gloves to avoid being burned.

Donovan had reluctantly used the break to make tea and to open a few cans of food. Every few seconds he glanced at his watch impatiently. Water, petrol and oil were topped up. They had then been travelling for about four hours at an average of about twenty-eight miles an hour which, under the conditions, was better than they could have hoped.

The front of the vehicles had been thrashed and dented by the scrub but they had now entered the fringe of the desert. On occasion their wheels had started to sink or slide. It was a brief opportunity to distribute the arms and ammunition.

Maxwell indicated that he wanted to speak to Donovan alone. The two men moved away. Donovan, desperate to push on, expected difficulty from him but Maxwell surprisingly made no mention of his earlier objections.

"I don't think the Vicar should be a platoon commander. His mind's not always on the job."

"Colin Vale? He helped save all our skins with a brilliant shot."

"The lads are still talking about it. It's not tha'. He gets lost in himself sometimes and this job needs a hundred per cent concentration. The men have nothing against him. It's just a gut feeling I have."

Donovan looked across at Vale who was leaning against a truck, abstractedly fingering the crucifix at his throat. Just then the others didn't exist for the clergyman.

"I can leave him loose like Frascelli. What about Bill Brown?"

"Aye, he'll do fine. A tough bugger."

"You've fought with him before?"

Maxwell grinned in the darkness. "Anyone who's been in S.A.S. 's a tough bugger." He showed a trace of humour. "Some say tougher than the Paras and the Commandos but it's a lousy rumour."

"So we're agreed?"

"Agreed. You still insist on not being armed yerself?"

"I've got the mortar." If he could remember what to do with it.

"You'll have trouble popping that off from the hip."

Donovan took the opportunity, "I don't want to get on your back. We've got to pull together or we're in trouble."

"Och, I've had officers breathing down my neck all my life." Maxwell walked away. Donovan wasn't sure whether he'd made a mistake or not but at least he'd learned something. He heard the faint drone and looked up at the sky. Breathtaking. Nowhere were there so many stars. He located the navigational lights slowly circling. So a spotter was following their own light trail. It confirmed that they hadn't reached the border which he calculated to be about another fifty miles. It also meant that the Kenyans were willing to let them go or they'd have sent in their Air Force. It wasn't difficult to guess why.

They started up again, stiff-legged and stiff-backed, having agreed to ten-minute stops every two hours to stretch and to change drivers. The strumming under the chassis was less now but any semblance of sleep was destroyed by a sudden slewing or spinning of wheels in loose sand. By sheer skill of driving and of keeping their wits about them, they avoided bogging down, using gears and variation of acceleration to keep going. Donovan saw no point in driving on anything but headlamps. Little lived in this wilderness except snakes and the odd herd of game. Beside him Chianda nursed a Sten gun.

During the hours that followed a chill began to creep into the cabs, working up the legs, into the stomach. Conversation had died long since. To break the monotony as many men as possible were given the opportunity to drive with the exception of the Donovan, Chianda team in the lead truck. No one else wanted the responsibility of direction and Donovan didn't want to delegate it. The remaining men dozed as best they could in the back of endlessly shaking vehicles.

The disappearance of the spotter plane at the next stop raised feeble cheers and a sense of expectation as everyone realised they were now over the border. The chips were down.

A breeze had whipped up the hard gritty sand which stuck on the lips and got in mouths and nostrils. There was a bigger danger; the ground was collapsing here and there. They were travelling on a mosaic stretch of baked earth that frequently crumbled under the skin. Any form of rest was out of the question as drivers struggled to extricate wheels. Periodically the convoy stopped while the men jumped off to push a vehicle from a rut. Sometimes it was necessary to call up Gerry Steinberg to examine a spring and the delays began to mount. They avoided the really deep craters and the convoy stood up.

Throughout it all, in spite of acute discomfort and tiredness, the sense of urgency had spread to every man. Every false halt was a personal obstacle and they sweated and worked and heaved to keep the convoy moving, to cover as much ground and to gain as much advantage as they could in darkness.

They reached the Juba River at about four thirty in the morning, well north of Bardera which straddled the river and which Donovan wanted to avoid. It was difficult in the dark for there were Somali villages along the course of the river and they were impossible to pin-point under a thin tree line that hugged the sandy banks. They had switched off all lights and Donovan and Chianda went forward to recce. The breeze caressed the upper fronds of the palms as if sending a warning whisper of their approach. They sensed rather than saw someone behind them and Chianda swung in an arc, dropping on one knee as he raised the Sten.

"It's me. Bill Brown." The lean form joined them. "Sorry, boss, but if there's a village around I want some Somali clothes."

"What's the idea?"

"With the S.A.S. I operated in the Crater district of Aden during the troubles there. I speak Arabic."

"These people speak Somali."

"There must be similarities and there's probably some Arab trading. Boss, I lived with them for a long time behind the lines."

"Chianda?" Donovan turned to the African.

Chianda raised his head, nose dilating, eyes roaming. "Down stream."

"Okay, go with Chianda. No noise. Get what you need and straight back."

After they'd faded Donovan crept nearer to the river bank. Crouching played up his back. They had to cross but it was too risky in darkness in spite of the urgency to move on. At its widest and deepest it couldn't be crossed without a bridge. He waited impatiently, consoled by the fact that Gerry Steinberg was organising, refueling, and servicing two hundred yards back. He felt strange being so near to a tropical river he'd never expected to see again. This was where his eardrum had been punctured searching out a machine gun post. He could smell the area, feel the resting heat of it and its atmosphere wrapped round him like a damp blanket. Suddenly he felt very lonely.

Chianda and Brown were back, two patches from the gloom. Brown carried a bundle under his arm.

Donovan found himself forced to say, "Did you—?"

"No, Guv. Dirty washing. Ready for the rock bashing."

Chianda said, "There's a way across. Wheel tracks by the river."

They followed him down. He pointed to tracks in the sand

which only he could see. They could feel people around and when a camel stirred they knew how near.

Time was against them. "Try it."

Chianda slipped into the water, his white shirt a focus to concentrate on. The moon was lost somewhere behind the ridge of palms but it was light on the river which trickled gently over sand and rocks. They saw him sink to knee level, then lower, before they lost him entirely. The far bank was out of sight but for the uneven skyline and, perhaps with imagination, the pale glow of the sandbank strip.

Brown whispered, "A useful bloke to have around."

"We were supposed to teach them fieldcraft."

The two men grinned in the darkness, straining ears as well as sight. By his relaxed attitude it was clear that Brown was well used to the waiting game. He held his Sten in his left hand, the bundle of dirty clothes, their odour faintly rising, screwed in a ball in front of him. Donovan felt that the three Sten guns were in the right hands and even as he considered it one rose like an arch in front of him, held by Chianda's raised arms to ensure the weapon stayed dry.

"Okay, bwana. It's safe. Keep the men on the back to give weight. *Pangona. Pangona.*"

Donovan remembered. "I'll tell the drivers to keep it slow."

They scrambled back to the convoy. Donovan passed his instruction. There was enough visibility from water reflection to cross without lights. Engines were started. There was no way to make them quieter. The convoy pulled up in close formation to maintain contact and, hopefully, to disguise its size.

Donovan moved forward following a route that Chianda claimed was discernible. They moved over a mixture of loose sand, rock and pockets of shrub. He could hardly see a thing in spite of Chianda's reassurances, so he had to depend on the African's guidance. They were rocking quite a lot. They had traversed Ethiopian escarpments like this. What the hell was he worrying about?

They took the dip towards the river, sandier now, while Chianda, standing on the running board, guided Donovan to the precise point of entry. They had to pass through a jagged gateway of rock outcrop then, as their wheels entered the water Donovan was totally occupied with a Range Rover that had become a camel.

Chianda climbed in, his already wet clothes soaking the leather of the seat. "Keep going. It's okay."

The steering wheel spun, direction governed by underwater obstacles.

He coped with the gulleys and troughs and hidden outcrops wondering how the ballast of men were faring at the back. Before reaching mid river the water had lapped in under the door but he kept going, keeping a tight grip on a wheel that wanted its own way.

The far bank came up like a faint ground mist, changing to an artificial horizon that wouldn't keep straight. The water drained off as the Rover climbed the shallow bank and finally they were on sand, slipping, then gripping and revving thunder into startled ears. Ahead, a hobbled camel reared in fright. Donovan saw it late but Chianda bawled for him to pull his right hand down and somehow truck and animal survived.

They traced a rough gap in the tree line and followed its course. After about three hundred yards they pulled up to take stock. The rest of the convoy crept up behind them and Donovan went back to do a check. The three-tonners which had worried him most had fared best with their extra height and weight. The men were in fair spirits and Gerry Steinberg reported no problems.

The convoy pushed on, travelling away from the river, still without lights until Donovan was satisfied that they were now away from habitation. The beams cut across the desert, lost in the slow moving dust clouds before the trucks gathered speed again and spaced well out, contact being maintained through the lights once more. Donovan glanced at his watch. They had not done badly but he reckoned there was still a hundred and seventy odd miles to go.

In and out in four days. They were already into the third day. They had to find the enemy, rescue the hostages and be back over the border in the next forty-two hours. They made the best of a smoother run knowing it would worsen later on. The real hazards of negotiating the terrain lay ahead. A pastel pink vacillation toyed along the horizon to their right.

They were forced to halt at the foot of a scarp that

appeared impossibly high and totally unscalable except on foot. The rising sun was releasing a spectrum into a clear sky, its range of blues starting from the palest wash in the east, to aquamarine in the middle and Royal blue in the west.

They grouped round the scarp. There was no way round. Steinberg, who had an instinct for coping with problems of this kind, took his breakdown truck a few hundred yards along the base in each direction. The sky was lightening by the minute. He came back and climbed out, a small figure looking as if he'd lived in the desert all his life. It was difficult to find his eyes in the creases of his face as the sun suddenly shed a shaft of blood-red light on the group.

"We may as well do it from here. It's no better anywhere else."

Donovan was about to climb in when Steinberg stopped him.

"Bind the drums to the frame just behind the cab. Do it on all of them. And make bleddy sure the pressure won't break the ropes. That should sort out the centre of gravity. Offload everything that's loose. They'll have to be carried up by hand."

The men knew what was needed and started uncoiling the ropes, circling the oil and water drums, binding them to the metal canopy frames. Meanwhile, Steinberg was doing the same to his breakdown truck with the help of Digger Williams. They worked in teams and they worked well, men versed in the art of survival. Afterwards Steinberg inspected every knot, satisfied himself on every rope.

"Okay, I'll take the fifteen hundredweight up first." When Digger went to get in with him Steinberg stopped him. "Won't take the extra weight, man. I'll have to go it alone."

They all understood. The South African had to prove that it would work and would endanger no one else. The younger men looked on in respect. Maybe some of these oldies had something to offer.

Steinberg eased her forward over loose boulders. He didn't hesitate when the wheels slipped, knowing there was something solid to grip elsewhere, that the slide would be momentary. It wasn't slipping that worried him, although higher up it might be hairy. His fear was for balance. He picked his way like a mountain climber but with a fraction of the time to think. There was no time for hesitation, he had to keep moving. If he slid back it could shift the centre of gravity and the truck would come crashing down.

Gerry Steinberg picked his route as he travelled it. His split-second timing and uncanny perception silenced every man below. To them, there were times when the rock face appeared perpendicular. Even with adequate tyre grip, the surface was so uneven that he might surely have some form of computer mind that told him what the rear wheels were going to pass over while he coped with the front. There were times when they literally held their breath as the truck appeared suspended on its tail and they waited for it to fall back thirty feet on to its spine. Yet always Steinberg would find a depression for his front wheels to drop into, lowering the angle while he twisted and turned and found his way up.

When he arched over the top, without exception the men took off their hats and cheered. Gerry Steinberg had made his mark. He came forward on foot to the edge of the scarp, hat pushed back, his crinkled face one big grin. It was better than banking.

Steinberg had set an example. Donovan took his Rover up next; it was easier than the fifteen hundredweight but no less hair-raising. Steinberg stood at the top signalling the odd direction. It was like the four-minute mile: once someone had paved the way the rest would follow. The remaining two Range Rovers were next with Digger Williams and Stuart Maxwell. The two three-tonners would be difficult.

King took the first and the luck that had helped him through life with everything but his extra-marital affairs held as he took the truck up, almost letting it have its head and, ostensibly at any rate, made the easiest climb of all. He gave them all the soldier's salute when he reached the top.

Disaster came when they least expected it. With one truck to go and with Tommy Thompson driving it, a man whose very rock-like stature suggested that he could *will* the truck to move on its own, success suddenly turned to tragedy.

Thompson had the truck halfway up at a very awkward angle but still moving slowly when, under enormous pressure, one of the ropes slipped round the drums. The drums moved back and changed the balance of the truck which hung suspended. Thompson braked hard, afraid to move one way or the other knowing that he was so poised, the truck already tilted sideways and practically standing on its tail, that if the drums slipped further their weight could topple him backwards.

The men below, so certain that the obstacle course was conquered, had loaded themselves with arms and equipment ready to climb up. There was complete silence as everyone watched and prayed that the ropes would hold.

In the cab Thompson felt another shift of direction as his rear offside wheel slipped down. It was a critical shift of weight, particularly as he could *feel* the drums slipping further back. He could save himself by jumping out but it never occurred to him. It was a measure of the men's subconscious belief in him that it never occurred to them either for no one, as yet, had moved from the line of danger.

Thompson tried to adjust the slip by using both brake and accelerator, but with a changed centre of gravity the wheels weren't responding as they had before. He came halfway over a small boulder then hung there, his position slightly better.

The men at the top of the scarp watched helplessly. For once Steinberg signalled no direction because there was no direction he could give. None of them had control over the movement of the drums or the acute tension on the ropes.

Those down below could see the drums slipping slowly, they could see the way the rear wheels were suspended ready to fall back if they did not grip sufficiently to ride the hump. Thompson had appraised the situation with icy calmness, using his accelerator just right. Sudden movement either way could pressure the ropes into snapping.

Everyone was paralysed as they watched. The truck wouldn't move. Gradual acceleration was countered by a gradual shift from the drums as if the vibration from the engine was attuned to the tension of the ropes.

No one moved as if the very act could endanger Thompson. They watched as he hung there and the rear wheels began to spin slowly on the outcrop, blue tyre smoke puffing out from the friction. It broke the spell. With a flurry of movement the men at the foot of the scarp threw down their arms and surged over the rocks towards the truck. Half climbing, half running, they moved up as one man. The few at the top of the scarp, unable to see the wheel spin, guessed what had happened and clambered down to meet them, sliding on their behinds and hands, digging in heels, keeping well to the side of the truck so that dislodged stones wouldn't worsen matters

The first two men had reached the tail when the rope gave way and the drums burst out towards them.

10

As THE HUGE drums jumped the truck the nearest man took the full weight of one. His scream was stifled as the drum crushed his chest before bouncing towards the others. The second man had been slightly luckier. A drum had crashed straight on to his head and he was already unconscious before the next two smashed him to follow the contours of the rocks. The remaining men were scattering wildly. Donovan's group had reached the truck, grabbed, pulled and plucked at it until the wheels gripped and Thompson did the only thing left open to him, to continue to the top now he was relieved of the crippling weight.

As Thompson went up, Donovan and company continued down, appalled by the sight of drums crashing over rocks, flying high, shedding oil, petrol and water over men racing for their lives. Men who were smoking saw the danger.

They hand cupped cigarettes and scrambled to get clear. To be burned alive was no more attractive than being crushed. One man, petrol soaked, was self ignited as he ran. He had the presence of mind to throw himself flat and to roll down the rough slope, hands and arms protecting his head. When he reached the bottom nearby colleagues smothered the flames.

The screech of tearing metal, the clang as drums dented, cracked and ruptured, their spilled contents flowing down the scarp, gradually subsided until the last drum rolled slowly across the desert to be halted by a stone little bigger than a pebble. The last bitter irony was complete as it rocked to a creaking standstill.

Cigarettes were carefully stubbed out, the last spark killed. Weary men took stock as a white-faced Thompson came scudding down to join them. Before Thompson could open his mouth Steinberg said grimly, "Not a word from you. No recrimination. I was the one who checked the ropes." It was left at that but it was clear from Thompson's face that he accepted blame.

Maxwell and Donovan followed by King, Brown, Williams, Vale and Chianda had reached the bottom of the scarp to check on the human misery and loss of life. Most of the men had escaped with nothing more than the scratches and bruises. A few were oil and petrol soaked and were at present stripping, others had been luckier in being drenched by water. Some were covered by both.

Steinberg had gone back up the scarp with Thompson to get the first-aid box from the fifteen-hundredweight. Weapons lay scattered amongst the rocks, some oil covered. Precious water filtered through crevices into earth baked hard by need of it. Gallons of it disappeared with magical speed leaving faint, damp traces that vanished in seconds until it was impossible to see where it had gone.

The man who had caught fire had been saved by his own presence of mind and by the speed of his comrades. His burns were largely superficial and Vale made himself useful when Steinberg and Thompson arrived back with the medical kit. Shock was quickly wearing off as the men took stock, searched for their arms.

Some clothing was simply discarded, thrown into blackened balls among the rocks. A few men, naked but for socks and boots, rubbed oil off with the help of colleagues, using sand. Water wouldn't do it and no one needed telling that water was now short. Those soaked by petrol had laid their clothes out on the ground. The rising sun was already warm, evaporation should be quick. The smell of the fuel was stifling on the still air. It overrode everything else, a constant reminder of danger. Black streaks marked the scarp like a petrified waterfall where oil had flowed. Six drums lay scattered away from the scarp, five of them torn shells, gaping holes letting out the last trickles.

From chaos came calm appraisal. Donovan and Maxwell climbed the scarp to the point where the two men were so brutally killed. Thompson and some others followed behind. The crushed remains were not pleasant to look at. Thompson went close. Two men he did not know, yet who had tried to help him, lay in a bloody mess of bone and blood. He felt ready to burst. Donovan said, "It wasn't your fault. It wasn't anyone's. These things happen." It was reality.

Maxwell seemed unmoved. He'd seen worse when a comrade's parachute had failed to open. He looked at Donovan. "We'd better get 'em buried. Poor buggers."

"There's no time." It was a long time since Donovan had gazed at young death. He had hidden his feelings behind granite. These men had tried to help a friend of his.

"We'll make bloody time. We're not leaving 'em like tha'."

Donovan said wearily, "I've buried people in this stuff. Under the skin of sand it's rock hard. We must push on."

Maxwell glared at Donovan who was still looking at the mangled remains. "I'll get the men and the spades." He turned to go when Thompson put a hand out to stop him. "How d'you think I feel about it? But it would take too long. They're dead. We've got the living to think about."

Maxwell brushed his hand away. "Outa my way."

"We'll heap stones over them," Donovan called to some others. "It's all there's time for."

"They deserve better than that." Maxwell started to walk round Thompson.

"Infinitely better. Maybe on the way back . . ."

"I'm doing it now."

Thompson said, "You awkward bastard. If it was one of us you wouldn't give a shit."

Maxwell gripped his Sten with his left hand and hit Thompson on the jaw with his right. Thompson, legs splayed on the slope, lost balance and went rolling down the scarp the way the drums had done. Donovan, pent up by the tragedy, his own necessary callousness and Maxwell's obstinacy was grateful then for not having a gun, or he might well have shot Maxwell. The knots of tension were tightening inside him. He saw Thompson bouncing from rock to rock as Maxwell stood watching. He moved towards Maxwell as Bill Brown caught his arm.

"Don't worry about it, Guv. I'll get them covered up while you see to your mate."

Donovan eased down and nodded his gratitude to Brown. Thompson was inert at the foot of the scarp being approached by some of the men. Brown, helped by the others, started collecting small rocks to cover the bodies. Hearing them, Maxwell swung round. "I want them properly buried."

Brown stood up, moved a rock closer with his foot. "You scrape the remains off and we'll do it your way."

Maxwell strode over towards Brown. He was not going to be undermined.

Vale came up then, Bible in hand, to gaze with strained face at the mess that had once been two men. He gave Brown a sombre nod, then started to bless the dead in a clear voice that silenced the rage in Maxwell, who was torn between dealing with Brown and worry over Thompson. He was reluctant to cut across Vale's intonations. He looked down at the group that had gathered at the foot of the scarp. He glanced back at Brown, at the remains. He kept his voice low. "Don't ever talk to me like tha' again." He nodded briefly. "All right. Make sure the buzzards don't get at them."

Brown and his friends were satisfied. Command was never too easy with Mercenaries. They knew it and accepted that at times it became more a matter of understanding. They had just reached one. Maxwell scrabbled down the scarp while they continued covering the remains and Vale finished his blessing, sprinkling the gritty sand over the dead.

At the foot of the scarp Thompson's pulse rate was sound. There was a little blood on the back of his head which had cracked against a rock and he was barely conscious. Maxwell approached. "He all right?"

It was Maxwell's gruff enquiry that brought Thompson round more than anything else. He stared up at the sea of faces, at Pat Donovan kneeling beside him, strained and worried. He rubbed the back of his head and sat up with Donovan's help. "Just about. I hit several rocks on the way down. After losing my balance."

The men grinned. It was going to blow over. Donovan looked relieved. Thompson climbed to his feet, insisting on doing so without help. Donovan turned to the rest. "Okay. Let's see what we've lost and then get moving."

When the men fanned out to make a last search of the scarp for missing weapons, Thompson smiled ruefully.

"My reflexes have slowed. That awkward bastard should never have caught me with a wild swing like that." Thompson looked up the hill, saw Brown and his men and his smile died. "I'll go up and help them."

They counted the cost. Eighty-eight gallons of petrol, the same in water, forty-four gallons of oil. They roped the remaining drum of water and manhandled it to the top. It was dented in several places but had somehow survived. The men who had lost their clothing went to their respective trucks to change. The losses were severe. Immediately Donovan rationed water to one bottle per man per day to conserve what was left.

It was eight thirty a.m. before they were moving again. They had lost valuable time. They left behind a trail of broken metal, oil, clothing, the smell of vapourised petrol, one smashed rifle and two neat mounds of stones. It was already sticky by the time Donovan led off. He sat beside Chianda, depressed and moody, driving recklessly at times. Two men dead, loss of fuel and water and a weapon. Friction at a time when he thought Maxwell might have lost his chip but he supposed now that he never would. Behind him, in his and other vehicles men were trying to rid their equipment of oil before they would be fit to use.

The tragedy had thrown up one other factor. The men themselves were pulling well together. Gradually, as he drove across an increasingly heat-filled desert, Donovan grasped at the straws that reduced his depression to sufferable proportions. He paid more heed to his driving and the silent Chianda saw the mood working off. During the five years service he had spent with Donovan, Chianda recalled that whatever struck him Donovan never lost sight of the objective.

With the rising heat came the camel flies. They hovered like brown beetles, deceptively slow, settling on flesh, avoiding all attempts to catch them. There was, about their touch an obscure softness that drove men to shift them. The lazy, insolent way they removed themselves from a descending hand, then hovered just above it before alighting again, could drive a man crazy. They are virtually indestructible, some say even to hammer blows. The only certain way to kill them is to pull off their heads. But they are uncatchable.

They didn't worry Chianda. They never had. Donovan and his friends remembered and knew how to cope. Those mercenaries not used to these conditions annoyed their more tropically-experienced comrades in their mad endeavours to get rid of the flies. The driving cabs were a haven for them.

The heat became unbearable; it was impossible to touch any metal part of a vehicle. The cabs were like ovens. Sweat started to roll, shirts turned black, the backs of knees stuck uncomfortably to seats, the camel flies found ample drinking water in the sweat on arms, face and chest. In the back of the trucks, under the thick canvas canopies, the men suffered the heat in a different way, unable to get settled with the jarring motion. They clung to the frames and endured the stifling airlessness the canopy trapped. Yet if they removed it the scorching sun would bake them.

It was even worse in the three-tonner whose canopy had part burned away. The men crowded under what was left which sometimes meant body contact and the discomfort of another man's sweat. Yet they somehow cleaned up the arms that had been spoiled at the scarp.

Donovan called a halt late morning, and the convoy grouped in a rough circle. There was no shade once they stepped from the trucks. Steinberg came hustling up, the only one who appeared not to be sweating. He supervised the usual oil, petrol and tyre check and tanks and sumps were filled. Radiators were topped up with precious water. They were using more fuel than Steinberg had hoped and he was concerned.

Donovan spread the map out on the superficial covering of coarse sand and called his platoon commanders. The map lay flat. It needed no anchorage for there was no breeze, no relief from the fireball almost directly overhead. Wherever they looked there was nothing but an immense hard ochre blanket ruckled at times by outcrops of dun-coloured rock, buckled and barren and gradually powdering under the eternal process of relentlessly excessive heat. Here and there the sanded waste had collapsed under the struggle to form gulleys and depressions and pot holes for the unwary. There was nothing to break the remorseless monotony, no growth of any kind in sight. They sank on to the hot surface watching Donovan's prodding finger.

"There's a well about twenty-five miles ahead northwestwards of our route. Kilewe, if our information is right, holds Ober Uen about thirty-five miles ahead. The question is, do we deviate to get some water we badly need to make up our loss?"

Donovan looked round. They understood the problem. They looked at him, they looked at the map. Men he knew, some he was getting to know, one he used to know better. Vale's Bible was stuck in his pocket, its cover torn, the pages thumbed and damp. The heat was taking more out of him than any of them. He looked pale in spite of the sun.

"Just 'ow badly are we off cocker?"

"We could just about do it if everything goes right for us."

"Nothing ever does, man. But that bleddy well water will hang out our guts."

"Not for a couple of days." Donovan rubbed a lip that was already cracking, a fly trying to explore the crevice. He wiped the sweat from his face. "I think we may regret it if we don't try to replenish. But Kilewe may have spies there as it's so near to his base."

Digger Williams shrugged. "On this frying pancake there's no way to surprise him anyway."

Maxwell said nothing. He wanted action; that's what he was here for. Donovan looked across at him but Maxwell was drawn only to say, "You make the decisions."

Donovan nodded. "We've lost almost two gallons a man. I'd be happier if we could get some of it back." To Maxwell he said, "Get Ossie Jenkins to syphon off one half empty drum into another. We'll do another twenty miles, then a Range Rover pushes off to the well with the drum."

Jimmy King called out, "Gerry, lend me your goggles."

Steinberg handed over his binoculars. King looked at a small lonely figure slowly coming towards them. "A hunter." Brown borrowed the glasses then raced for the nearest Rover. He was away before anyone realised what had happened. The only one showing no surprise was Donovan who was attuned to Brown's thinking.

Brown homed in warily on the lone figure. The hunter was shorter than the average Somali. A small bow was over one shoulder and a quiver of arrows hung on his back. A man alone, seemingly from nowhere and going nowhere, for there was no other sign of life apart from themselves. What was there to hunt in a scorched wilderness? Yet he survived. The Somali was nervous of the approaching Rover and his bow came down from his shoulder. Before he could pluck an arrow Brown skidded in an arc sending a sand cloud over the sinewy figure. Braking hard, Brown jumped out, Sten levelled, "Get in." If the Arabic was not understood the movement of the gun was clear.

The Somali was frightened. He'd seen guns before. His hand was still over his shoulder, fingers grasping an arrow. He pulled sharply with surprising speed and the feathered end was stretching the bow. Brown moved and fired a short burst at the side of the Somali who jumped with fright as his arrow passed straight through the open cab window while a spray of bullets raised a dust storm beside his feet.

"The next burst goes straight through you." Brown felt he was going soft. Maybe it was Donovan's unspoken influence. There was something about the man. All he knew was that at any other time in a situation as tight as this he'd have shot the Somali and saved time.

The Somali held his bow out in surrender and Brown took it, then the quiver from the lean shoulder. He knotted the narrow wrists behind the man's back with the loose turban he removed from the bush of hair then prodded him towards the Rover. He drove back to the convoy.

He pulled the Somali from the cab. The man was really scared now, seeing so many armed men. Brown jerked him in front of Donovan. "We can kill him or keep him. It's up to you, Guv."

"Which part of him do you want?"

"His bow and arrow." Brown removed an arrow. It was short, not more than eighteen inches from feathered end to the very sharp beautifully-fashioned metal head. The bamboo shaft was thin but strong. Behind the head was tied a blob of brown poison that would dissolve in an animal's bloodstream. The veterans had seen them before.

"You can use the thing?"

"Part of our training. Known ways to kill a man."

Colin Vale stepped between them. "This man has done us no harm."

"He might do if we let him go."

Vale swung an arm to indicate the empty desert.

"Where can he go? Who can he tell?"

Donovan put a hand on Vale's shoulder. "You know better, Colin. Where's he going, anyway? Where'd the bamboo, the metal, the grass come from? He knows and it can't be too far to walk. You release him without his weapons and you might be killing him the hard way."

"Then give them back."

Brown shook his head at Donovan who broke it up. "He can come in the back of our Rover. Let's move."

Before they set off, Brown changed into the dirty Somali wraps he had stolen on the Juba. He tied the turban loosely with surprising deftness and his bare legs were dark beneath the dirty white, his feet slipping into sandals a little too big for him. Dark hair, what could be seen of it, darkish skin and clothes that smelled of use, but that was an inconvenience he had long learned to live with. More than anything it was his poise, and the way he had mentally attuned to the part, that so drastically changed him. From an almost lazy way of holding himself he had instinctively straightened into an easy grace. The bow and quiver of arrows completed the image well. When he spoke to them in Arabic his colleagues grinned approval. He would pass on short encounters.

Donovan had the Somali securely roped to one of the staves at the back of his Rover. They set off to do a precise twenty miles before the final run in on Kilewe. The sun was almost at its culminating point and there was no escape from its scorching fury. As Tommy Thompson drove his three-tonner he mentally rehearsed every scrap of weapon drill he could remember.

Pietro Frascelli had left Jimmy King to do the driving while he rode with the men on the back of the three-tonner and did a more exact count and check of the explosive, fuses and fuse wire. In one tightly wound coil of instantaneous fuse wire, he found a box of fuse matches. There was a pathetic irony about it; ordinary matches would have done as well for there was no movement of air to blow them out.

The distance was covered in well under an hour. The convoy drew up in line as if it were about to charge. The terrain had not changed. Loose gritty sand covering rock or hard-baked earth. The only relief were outcrops of rock, sometimes with pathetic traces of almost colourless grass in the crevices.

Steinberg's binoculars revealed nothing but a heat haze that shimmered like reeded glass. It was impossible to penetrate it except to see the wavering suggestion of a mirage of dwellings that they were too experienced to heed. Brown took the two mercenaries to ride in the front of the Rover while he travelled in the back. They hoisted the empty drum on board, removed all arms from the rear. All three men were given automatic pistols because any other weapon would be too conspicuous to carry.

They checked direction with map and compass while Chianda sensed out the position of the well in his own way. He used Steinberg's glasses, his nose, his considerable instinct and gave the men direction. They set off, the empty drum clanging in the back, while Brown tried to wedge it. They should be back inside the hour for they had little more than five miles to cover in each direction although the filling of the drum would take time. They had rope and cord and a few of the largest spare water bottles.

Bill Brown stood in the back, leaning forward to gaze between canopy and cab roof to get some sight of the well.

Suddenly he banged on the cab roof and the Rover slowed to a crawl. Brown dropped off and thumped the side of the vehicle as his feet touched the ground. He ran a few paces, the grit getting between his feet and sandals as the Rover drew away. He didn't object to the sand he swallowed for the cloud gave him cover. He slowed to a fast walk calculating that he had less than a mile to go. Say twenty minutes in this heat. He did not see it as wasted time but as a safety measure.

He fell into the easy style of walking from the hips as the Somalis did, the bow and quiver over his shoulder, his own knife and the gun in the folds of his draped waistband. When he located the well he slowed instinctively. As he drew closer he saw a solitary palm like a worn sentinel, the sparse fronds almost dead as they hung limply as if in mourning. It was the only growth that he could see. The well itself emerged as a big flat square mound with steps built up around it. Somalis moved slowly around it with camels, sheep and goats. God knew where they had come from, for there was no grazing that he could see in any direction.

Water was life out here and almost the whole concentration of natives was by the well itself. The tableau drew nearer. The animals were being fed from goatskin troughs, a few at a time. The water was being drawn up by the simple process of lowering a skin scoop on the end of a rope. It was clear that the well was deep, thirty or forty feet. There were some small stone buildings sprinkled haphazardly, some with blank gaps for windows.

As Brown drew near he saw no sign of the Rover. No sign of the water drum or of his two colleagues. Christ, he could see the whole bloody place unobstructed and beyond to the open desert. There was nothing that could be missed. The Somalis, maybe forty of them in total, were loose packed, there was nothing they could hide. So what in God's name had happened?

Brown had a gut feeling that he couldn't ignore. He did not go directly to the well; he had no water carrier; one of the issue bottles would have been a giveaway. He went past, attracting no specific attention and conveniently placed apart from the others by his apparent calling. The domestic Somali had respect for the hunter.

He took a central course past the few scattered buildings,

one long and low. He had traced the tyre tracks by the very faint indentations in the loose surface sand. He'd had to strain to pick them out. They had completely disappeared at the point where the animals were being herded. If it was a coincidence it was a convenient one. He needed Chianda. He dare not voice interest in a missing vehicle.

Some Somalis were squatting round the well, others against the stone walls of the buildings. Most were standing, almost all had the long staffs they used. Brown chose a shaded wall within earshot of a small group and sank on his haunches. He hung on hoping to glean something but apart from the language differences he did not think that anything of importance was said. The Rover had come and gone as if nobody had seen it. In a place like this it would create a talking point for a week or more.

At what point he felt himself to be in danger he wasn't sure and it did not matter. The feeling was slow to come but suddenly he realised he dared not stay longer. None of the Somalis were armed but that did not mean that spies for Kilewe were not among them. Rising slowly he walked north, away from the well and the direction from where he had come. Instinct told him it would be a mistake to go back directly. He did not hurry nor did he look back but he was satisfied that he was being watched and would be until he was out of sight. That meant walking the best part of a mile, under desert-trained eyes, before he could circle round. It was going to put three miles onto his journey back; a journey he had expected to complete in the returning Rover. He could not expect the convoy to wait for him. Already he was thirsty, the heat dehydrating him at every step, but he could cope with that. What was worrying was that he'd create no dust cloud for the main party to trace. He had no compass, was caught unaware by what had happened and he was annoyed with himself.

There was a more worrying aspect than his own plight. He was expendable. In his job he'd always accepted it. Donovan would not know what had happened. And Donovan wasn't a man to sit about wondering. He would act. In so doing he could easily fall into the same trap. Hassan Kilewe had made his first move. *Which meant he was expecting them.*

11

DONOVAN WAS INCREASINGLY restless, glancing at his watch every few seconds. Two forty-five. More than an hour, and no sign. Time was running out. When he wasn't looking at his watch he was scanning the desert through Steinberg's glasses until the sweat poured into his eyes misting the lens. He would wipe both and start again.

The men had cleaned their weapons for the last time, had distributed grenades and ammunition, cramming them into pockets until they were uncomfortably weighted down. There was no shade except the thinnest of strips beside each vehicle, which was too hot to touch. Only Steinberg appeared reasonably relaxed. He watched Donovan pacing restlessly in the heat when he should have been conserving his energy. Jimmy King was getting pent up merely watching Donovan. Frascelli was also watching Donovan, feeling for him and for the others somewhere out in the desert. Thompson was lying face down, unmoved by the heat as he sighted behind a Bren gun, moving it again and again, anxious to use it. Chianda, better at waiting than any of them, squatted on his haunches, plucking at the sand with one long black finger. Stuart Maxwell was as restless as Donovan, wanting only to push on, to face the enemy. Colin Vale stared thoughtfully into space.

"Get the canvas off the frame of my Rover and tie that Somali to something else."

Donovan had made up his mind. He gave them a hand to strip the back. "Mount the two Brens, manned by Jimmy and Tommy. Max, take your Sten in front and Pietro, you drive. Take a rifle with you." Donovan turned to Steinberg. "Gerry, you're in charge while we're away. Digger's your 2 i/c. If we're not back within the hour do what you think fit. My advice will be to pull out but it's up to you."

"You realise you're taking most of the leaders with you?" Steinberg pointed it out as he might an apparent mismanagement on a business deal.

"I know what I'm doing. We must know what's happened to them."

Steinberg flipped a hand. "Good luck."

The Brens were mounted with Thompson and King behind them. Donovan took a rifle. When Frascelli started up Donovan told him, "One thump on the right, half right turn; two thumps, right angles; three thumps, go like the clappers. Same for the other side. Quick series of thumps, stop. Chianda, you come with me."

Chianda clutched his Sten and climbed in the back with Donovan, who had slung the binoculars round his neck. He thumped the cab roof three times and Frascelli drew away, going through the gear changes as if he were in a sports car. Donovan cleaned the glasses again, propped himself against one of the stanchions and swept the area ahead of them.

For the first three miles they followed the course of the missing Rover, Frascelli picking out the tyre tracks but comforted by Chianda's presence in the back. At the three mile point Donovan thumped twice on the right hand side and Frascelli changed direction. Donovan now scanned obliquely to his left. When he picked out the distant smudge of the well he signalled a stop.

Frascelli poked his head out as Donovan leaned down towards him. "It's in sight, Pietro. Ninety degrees left. I want to circle it but far enough away for safety." As the Rover moved off Donovan turned to the three with him on the back. "The slightest suspicion from anyone we meet, fire. Don't take chances."

Thompson immediately released the safety catch of his Bren. He and King were back to back flanking the Rover. Chianda was covering front and rear with Donovan. They moved at reduced speed, coming closer to the well for Donovan to pick it out clearly with the glasses. He pulled back, wiping his eyes. "There's not a bloody sign. I can't understand it. There's no sign of the Rover. Not anywhere."

"You mean they never got there?"

"I don't know."

"Bwana, the trail was leading there before we left it. If we circle I can pick it up again."

Donovan signalled stop, told Frascelli what he wanted and they moved off again at speed. It was difficult for those on the back as they struggled to keep the Brens upright. They had closed in to within half a mile of the well. There was little doubt that they would be seen, their sand plume alone a giveaway, but they were ready for trouble. All the time Donovan scanned with the glasses, searching around the buildings, groups of camels. Chianda called out that he had seen the tracks as they passed over them and they were still heading straight for the well. They *must* have completed the other half mile.

Donovan was just thinking as Brown had done, that Hassan Kilewe had made his first move when he picked out a sand cloud to the east of the well. He thumped instructions for Frascelli to change direction and they moved towards the other vehicle while Donovan searched behind it. When he finally picked out the detail of it he yelled, "It's ours." He was relieved and puzzled at the same time. An arm came out of the driver's side of the approaching Rover and waved. Where the hell had they been?

Chianda stood next to Donovan, holding onto a stanchion as they struck shallow rock. He was squinting ahead, the sun hitting the windscreen of the racing vehicle that was closing in. They were head on. Frascelli slowed but the other one was still travelling fast. The arm was still waving. Chianda shouted, "The glasses, bwana." Donovan passed them over. Chianda yelled, "They're not our men." And then at the top of his voice, *"Maliwongo."*

Donovan thumped frantically on the cab hoping Frascelli would understand. At the same time he leaned down and bawled, "It's the enemy." Frascelli accelerated and swerved, almost throwing his passengers out. They clung on as machine gun fire burst at the side of them. Chianda let off a burst at the windscreen of the other Rover but his aim was spoiled by the frantic swerve.

In this most unlikely conflict across the desert sands Donovan was putting his trust in the brilliance of Frascelli's driving. A sudden burst of fire from the other Rover left no doubt of the fire power that was there. Several machine pistols had opened up at once but Frascelli operated a series of hard braking, skidding and quick acceleration movements which had those on the back tumbling around, clinging to anything they could find. And he opened up a cunning range to give the more powerful Brens a chance. With sudden swerves at changing speeds he destroyed the aim of the enemy and saved the lives of his friends as several bursts thudded short. Behind him the men were bruised and battered and unable to fire back.

Frascelli manoeuvred into an oblique approach to restrict the firepower of the others and give Donovan's men a chance to finish it. He prayed that they would understand what he was doing, and that he was exposing Maxwell and himself. Even so he drove an evasion course, zigzagging in a series of uneven swerves that must have been difficult to aim at with accuracy. Shots came. He could hear and feel them thudding into the metal. If it created a firing opportunity for those on the back, it prevented Maxwell from using his Sten through the window. The Rover, closing in again, had swerved to reveal its flank, the driver possibly reading Frascelli's tactics, so as to give his own gunpower better chance.

Maxwell bawled above the engine roar, "Brake hard, and swing left to shield me." He had the door open. Frascelli picked up the meaning, braked without warning and pulled his left hand down frantically. Maxwell disappeared from sight as the Rover accelerated again in the face of sustained fire. The windshield was shattered and Frascelli felt blood oozing down his face and chest. Where Maxwell had been the back of the seat was a mass of holes, padding popping out like bubble gum. Frascelli punched a hole through the windscreen so that he could see and withdrew a badly bleeding hand.

As Maxwell landed, he rolled. He was on his feet while the Rover as still accelerating beside him. He crouched in the engulfing dust eyes screwed against the grit, waiting for the shadow that would pass him. It was braking as it came clear. The driver was turning to get Frascelli back in sight. Somalis were firing machine pistols from the hip at Frascelli's dust cloud but their own movement did not help them, and they were falling about. Maxwell dropped to one knee, took aim and fired a continuing burst. He changed aim while still firing and put a burst into the front offside tyre before bringing it up again to a startled driver who never had an opportunity to correct the skid. The Rover wheeled in an arc while Maxwell emptied his magazine into it.

He had hit some. As he whipped out the empty magazine and grabbed a fistful of bullets from his pockets he could see three or four men yelling, trying to regain balance. As he looked he was thumbing rounds into the magazine, one ear cocked for sound of the returning Frascelli. And then the surviving Somalis saw him. He had no time to finish reloading. His magazine was about a quarter full when he whipped it into the Sten and cocked.

The Somalis' Rover had slowed to a stop. Maxwell's Sten came up and the Somalis jumped in all directions making it impossible for him to cover them all. Maxwell accepted then that he was finished. He stood up; it was more comfortable. He gave a short burst at one retreating brown form as two of the others found a measure of cover behind the vehicle. The Somali fell. Maxwell gave a quick look round to see what had happened to Frascelli. The bloody truck had stuck. And then he heard the sweet sound of automatic fire from its direction and he threw himself flat as the Somalis opened up in return.

Frascelli, responding to the yells and thumps at his back, had turned round, seen the back end of Maxwell's action, then stopped as he saw the after development. Thompson and King grabbed their Brens, rammed the bipods on the roof of the cab and started to get Maxwell off the hook. Now steady, they were firing with deadly effect, the return fire desperately wild. Donovan was aligned beside them with the rifle, and Chianda had jumped from the back to cope with a man too well hidden behind the crippled Rover.

It was difficult to know for certain how many men they hit but the accuracy of the Brens was clearly telling as the opposing fire rate diminished, then stopped. Donovan jumped off with Thompson. Jimmy King stayed with his Bren on the cab roof and Frascelli nosed the Rover cautiously forward. The others fanned out. Donovan waved at Maxwell and was relieved when he received a return wave. Maxwell was at last doing what he did best.

An off-white, unwound turban tied to the end of a machine pistol appeared from behind the stationary Rover. Thompson hurried forward. There was a sudden burst of fire, Thompson spun round and fell and King opened up from the cab roof as he located the source. Donovan went to Thompson who was already rising, his face red with rage. "The bastard nearly got me." His left shoulder was bleeding. He brushed Donovan aside. "I'm okay. Let's finish these bastards." He was holding the Bren under his right arm without apparent effort, finger still on the trigger.

Donovan didn't argue. They closed in on the Rover, well spread out, with Maxwell taking the other side and Frascelli and King coming head on. It was a bloody scene. One Somali was alive with a hole through his arm. Another was lying awkwardly, his stomach a red mess. Five others including the driver were dead.

Donovan's men had instinctively fallen into a back to back routine searching for others on any approach from the well. No one came near and yet the battle must have been heard. Maxwell pulled the dead driver from his seat, callously letting the corpse fall to the ground; he was wearing some of the missing men's clothes and so was his dead co-driver. They searched the back and found the two missing mercenaries. Naked, the sun had already played cruelly on their mutilated bodies. Donovan climbed down and thought he was going to be sick. Chianda showed no sign of being moved but Frascelli swung away quickly. Even Maxwell tightened his jawline. King, still with his Bren on the back of the other Rover, was too far away to see. Thompson was to one side trying to stem his blood flow.

To cover his nausea Frascelli said, "Brown's not there."

"He'd have dropped off before they reached the well. It was his scene to follow up an operation."

"Wha' about these bastards?"

"Leave them."

Maxwell released the bonnet catch of the stranded Rover. A mass of bullet holes showed above the burst tyre.

"We've had tha'. Even Steinberg couldna fix that mess. We've lost a truck but we've gained ourselves some Kalaschnikov machine pistols with bugger all ammunition, I would'na be surprised." Maxwell's accent, rekindled by action, was noticeably thicker.

There were six machine pistols. The driver had been unarmed but for a long knife. One weapon had been smashed by their own gunfire. The other five were in good order but Maxwell was right about the ammunition; most of the magazines were empty or near empty and there was little to spare. They collected what there was and threw them in the back of their own Rover.

Frascelli was wiping some of the blood from his face. They had been so preoccupied that no one had remarked on it, although it was clear from the smashed windscreen what had happened. Chianda helped him pluck out slivers of glass while Donovan helped Thompson with his shoulder; a bullet had torn straight through. Maxwell watched the surviving Somalis. The less injured Somali understood his mood and cowered against the cab.

The empty water drum was missing, the truck emptied of all but the two gruesome corpses. They had to get back to base or a crisis would erupt there.

"We'll have to leave them, Max."

For once Maxwell did not argue. No one wanted to touch them. The only sign he showed of the paternal protection he gave to his men was brutally to pull the clothes from two of the dead Somalis and to drape them over the bodies of his own men.

"What about him?" Thompson indicated the cowering

prisoner. "We might get info from him with a little persuasion."

Donovan shook his head. "Apart from language problems he won't know anything worth knowing. This is typical Kilewe style. These are some of his expendables."

Chianda tried Swahili on him but if he understood there was no response, the whites of the eyes rolling as time ran out for him.

"We canna leave him. And we canna take him. We've barely enough water for ourselves and no one to spare to look after the bastard."

Donovan knew what had to be done. He couldn't ask anyone else to do it although Thompson, Maxwell or Chianda would have had no qualms. Faced with brutal reality, the lives of his own men, the danger if he didn't face up to it, he held out his hand for Chianda's Sten. Before firing he set his mind to the two mutilated bodies and it made it easier to wipe out the terrified wretch in front of him. He felt little remorse as the Somali fell forward, only a deep sadness at his own weakness and a revulsion over the need of what he'd done. When he checked the Somali with the stomach wounds, he was dead. Thank God.

As they turned towards their Rover Donovan felt Frascelli's hand on his shoulder. The understanding made it no easier nor the fact that none of them said anything, no one blamed him. It made it worse. They took up positions as before. The Rover drew away leaving behind it nine dead who, before the day was out, would be mummified and cracked by the fierce, dry heat. Within minutes of their departure the mechanical wreck that lay canted like a dead mammal would be stripped of every piece of metal, of fabric, of rubber. It would disappear in its entirety before the sun went down. Yet, as Donovan searched the well area with the glasses, there was no sign at all that anything untoward had happened. They were ordinary Somalis but there was little doubt that they were intimidated by the proximity of Kilewe.

Chianda gave a shout when they had gone only a few hundred yards. He had spotted a lone figure to the east of the well. It was heading in the same direction as themselves. Donovan swung the glasses. "A hunter. It could be Brown, though he's strangely positioned."

Thompson and King were non-committal. Nothing was certain from now on. There was no response from the figure who must have seen them. Donovan searched behind the man. He thumped the cab for Frascelli to turn sharp left. The two reloaded Brens were hoisted back to the cab roof and, with a steadier course, it was easier to hold them there. Donovan kept sight through the glasses and saw the figure hesitate. Surely Brown would acknowledge them. The hunter then continued at an easy pace as if nothing was happening. Donovan handed the glasses to Chianda. "What do you think?"

They were drawing closer but a flap of the hunter's turban had uncoiled and was covering the side of his face.

Chianda suddenly showed all his teeth. "It's Brown."

"You sure?"

"I'm sure."

Donovan thumped the roof and bawled down to Frascelli who sounded the horn. Those on the back waved their hats. Only then did Brown acknowledge. They helped him onto the back with much back slapping and King gave him his water bottle.

"What happened?"

He told them.

"Why didn't you signal? We might have put a burst into you."

"On the way back the other Rover passed me. It was not too far away that they could have missed me. I didn't trust the direction it was coming from and it ignored me. Our blokes wouldn't have done that. I guessed they had been nobbled when they weren't at the well. And I wasn't sure if you weren't the same mob. If I'd signalled to the wrong crowd I'd have finished up like them."

"You know?"

"I don't have to see to know. These boys aren't messing around. I had to make a detour or be suspected as one of you."

They arrived back at base to find all trucks ready to move north. It was three thirty. Steinberg had talked to the men and Digger Williams had backed him. There was tremendous relief on seeing the Range Rover return. No comment was made about their dead colleagues. It was a safety valve. For the mercenaries it was the only way life could operate.

While Steinberg sand-scrubbed his hands to attend to Thompson and Frascelli with the help of Vale, Donovan addressed the men. He looked at his watch, time the constant problem, feeling the pressure of impatience. Three thirty-five. He dangled one of the captured machine pistols as a psychological sop to show that the enemy were destructible and to illustrate a victory. "You can thank Stuart Maxwell for pulling us through this one. In any other army he'd have got a gallantry medal for what he did." He quickly viewed the men he had first seen as a drunken rabble. Now they were faces he was getting to know, some he was beginning to respect. Others, like a constant niggler called Croft, needed an eye kept on them but that was Maxwell's job.

"We've killed nine of Hassan Kilewe's men against two of ours. But don't kid yourselves. I'm convinced that Kilewe has more men than has been reported. It's his style to knock off ones and twos. He likes to nibble away at his enemies. We still don't know how he lured our men so bear it in mind. If that skirmish had gone the other way you'd have found the remains of our two lads somewhere along the route as a warning. That's Kilewe's sadistic style, too. He wants us to know that he knows."

Digger Williams called out, "You trying to talk us out'vé it, sport?"

Donovan smiled. "I couldn't talk you savage lot of bastards out of anything. But there's no profit in living in a fool's paradise. He's shown he knows we're coming. And he's sent out a warning. And don't forget the two girls in Kilewe's hands just fifteen miles ahead at Ober Uen. Five of us here remember it well, not that there's much to remember." It felt strange talking like that, as if he'd never left Somaliland, a continuation of yesterday and the day before.

"We'll take up positions in daylight which I'll give you as we reach them. Weigh up the enemy. Keep in radio contact. And then we'll decide the final concerted move." He would have said more, somehow reassured them, but he felt they were too experienced to delude. There was nothing he could decide without proper reconnaissance.

Before climbing into the shot-up Rover, Donovan noticed Steinberg standing alone, not moving, just gazing north out of narrowed eyes. He went up to him, slapped him on the shoulder. "You're thinking of Bob."

Steinberg came out of reverie. "That obvious?"

"It's the time and place to rekindle that kind of memory. Would you feel better with a gun of some sort? You can have this." Donovan held out the machine pistol.

Steinberg shook his head. "No. Not now, man. I'll tell you when I want a gun." He walked off, head down, a small grim figure with thoughts well shielded, his inherent humour for once totally missing.

They moved off in close formation. It meant swallowing sand continually but it gave them greater safety. Kilewe was adept at picking off stragglers. Fifteen miles to go. Donovan took a north-westerly route, wanting to approach from the flank for first sight of the stronghold. Brown, who had a predilection for spotting aircraft, leaned out of his cab to see a Russian MIG flying at low altitude from east to west above them. As he was not driving at the time, he watched, guessing that eventually the plane would have to turn if for no other reason than that of reaching the Ethiopian border. Some time later it came back as he had expected. It was at a similar altitude, travelling slowly for a very fast plane, but on a straight course, probably returning to Mogadishu.

The big van rolled drunkenly over the jagged surface. Surprisingly, it had a right-hand drive and its lines were old fashioned. Its blank sides had been painted many times, its present colour that of the sand around it. Even now, at certain angles, a cross could just be discerned on each side. It was, in fact, an old South African Army ambulance that had arrived via Kenya just after the war. It had been carefully nurtured ever since and used sparingly. If its mobility was restricted its sophisticated contents were not.

A bank of up-to-date radio equipment took up most of the interior. The massive aerial was the one possible let-down in an otherwise modern array but only in its erection. To save the batteries, it was hand cranked to its full, disproportionate height above the vehicle. Inside, it was unbearably hot even for a Somali, for the black glassed windows had long since been removed and blocked up. Transmissions flowed with the double doors wide open, usually facing the benefit of any breeze that might bring the slightest relief to the sweat-drenched operator.

The original operator had now been dead for two months. Half Indian, half Arab, he had died painfully before releasing his codes to Kilewe's men. At that time the radio had been slightly smaller and much of the interior was covered by the wares of a mobile 'dukha wallah'. Silks, rushmats, hats, sticks and so on had been fair subterfuge for a long, successful operation. It had been ironic that the Kenyans, who had expelled their Asiatics, had selected one to be an agent for them during the border disputes with Somaliland. Perhaps because there was internal conflict of the two races within Kenya Ramah Singh had made such an unsuspecting and successful operative. So far as the Kenyans were concerned he was still passing useful information. Exactly how useful was, these days, decided by Hassan Kilewe in his state within a state. Siyad might rule from Mogadishu but out here Kilewe was King of the desert Somali. The ploy was useful for another two months when Singh, moments before his death, had revealed that he was due to return over the border.

The radio van had been used to mislead the two mercenaries who had since followed Singh to eternity. The driver, having erected the mast at its highest, so that the purpose of the van could not be missed, had approached them just outside the precincts of the well and had introduced himself in broken English as Kenya's man in Somalia. As information had been reaching Nairobi from somewhere on the Somali Plateau, and as the operator had up-to-date information for them, it was not surprising that they had been misled.

The van now hobbled up the stretch between the widely-spaced buildings of Ober Uen and stopped outside the guarded open entrance set in the stone wall which had deteriorated ever since the Italians had left. A darkened circle over the arch of the entrance showed where once the Italian coat of arms had been suspended, and, even earlier than that, on the top of the arch was that stub that had been the Fascist faggots from whose centre a short flagmast had risen. Once the home of an Italian administrator, it now housed Hassan Kilewe who governed a thousand square miles of sparsely populated wilderness whether the Russians liked it or not.

This land, climatically the antithesis of Siberia, was his.

The courtyard still had a well-watered tree, the only one visible in any direction. And it still sported the original flagmast, one day to take the emblem Kilewe had designed himself on the pattern of the multi-beaded, many coloured and intricately-worked Somali mats. It would be wrong just now to reveal it, but it was ready.

In the brilliant sunshine the stronghold was as revealing as it was misleading. There was Kilewe's several-roomed dwelling and parades were frequently held in the huge courtyard. Across the way and a little further south was a long stone building with a corrugated roof. The walls had more than thirty square-gridded windows, well out of reach, right round its perimeter. There was only one entrance with a small iron canopy to give doubtful shade to the seated guard. It had once been a barracks, then a prison filled mainly with camel thieves. It had now returned to its former use.

Almost opposite Kilewe's near-palatial villa was, incredibly, a Roman Catholic church. It was a square building with octagonal turrets each side of its facia. On the flat roof a much weathered cross still rose and on each of the double doors were, barely visible, the faint traces of white crosses. The only reason it had survived in its present form was its utter remoteness from any form of civilisation. It owed its existence originally to a small Italian desert garrison. It now survived because of its comparative coolness and was used as a general storeroom and armoury.

There were other buildings, all of stone, but the one that housed the prisoners was set strangely at the end of the untidy group and in the middle of the desert stretch that could loosely be termed a square. To emphasize the oddity of its position, nothing had been built beyond it. So it took up the north extremity of the outpost with guards still positioned all round it. Machine-gun posts were hidden elsewhere and motor transport occupied a deep depression sheltered by rush canopies on bamboo supports some distance away. To the south, opposite the barracks, was a huge stone-built well.

The radio operator reported to Kilewe that his men were dead and that the mission had part failed. Kilewe took it philosophically. He didn't mind so much about the men but resented strongly the loss of arms. However, the ridiculous task force had lost two men and a jeep and he now had the vitally important information that they were short of water. The game had so far gone more or less as he had predicted. He already had mobile units of his own in well-chosen wadis which could move in quickly. If the pathetic little British task force could know what arms and men he had waiting for them here, it would surely flee at once.

When the radio operator had gone, Hassan Kilewe joined his second in command on the roof of the villa. Aref Ghalib was shaded by the overhang of the solitary tree, scanning west with binoculars. Ghalib was tall and willowy with high cheekbones and a proud carriage. As the two men stood side by side, their many differences were obvious. Physically polarised they were, nevertheless, on a similar mental wavelength.

Kilewe said, "I want the prisoners transferred to the south section of the barracks. There is a suitable room there."

Ghalib lowered his glasses, inclined his head graciously.

"When the prisoners have been moved double the guards where they are at present."

Ghalib immediately understood. The hut would be empty.

"I then want four machine guns trained on it."

Ghalib showed his first surprise, an eyebrow raising fractionally.

"On our own men?"

"Just four. It will be worth it."

Ghalib was not sure. He kept his counsel and went off to execute the order.

12

CHIANDA, NOW DRESSED as a Somali in clothes he had taken after the action at the well, sat beside Donovan, focusing through the binoculars every few seconds. The squat shape of Ober Uen shimmered through desert in disseminated patches like a disturbing vision to a drugged mind. He told Donovan, who headed north-west of it and, as yet, could see nothing but barren terrain, yellow or fawn depending on the sand depth which mostly was a shallow covering for the hard rock of the plateau. He had approached by using a succession of gulleys and depressions but did not delude himself that they had not been seen. Chianda steadied the wheel for him while he took the glasses.

He detached Thompson and King with their platoons at a gulley about three quarters of a mile south-west of Kilewe's outpost. At the moment he saw it as the strongest position for attack but it was much too soon to be final. He continued north-west, away from Ober Uen. By use of the glasses, Chianda located a depression to the east of the Rover but about a mile due west of the stronghold. Here Donovan detached Maxwell, one platoon and Frascelli. He now changed direction to north-east, circling slightly above Ober Uen until they found a deep wadi which safely sheltered them from view at the acute price of a rise of several degrees of heat. When they had occupied the outpost during the war the average shade temperature had been 124°. It was now worse than that. Some of the men were already suffering the agonies of 'prickly heat'.

The three sections covered a boomerang line west of their objective. Having delivered his men, a three-tonner and Steinberg with his fifteen-hundredweight, Donovan now pulled out in his Rover with Chianda and Brown out of sight in the back. During the last fifteen miles all guns had been loaded, safety catches off, a round in each spout. The Brens had been mounted by King and Thompson and the Stens, in the hands of Maxwell, Chianda and Brown, had been constantly ready. Now, however, Donovan carried a Sten on the passenger seat beside him while Chianda and Brown had nothing but a pistol each plus panga and knife hidden under their drapes, and the bow and the quiver of arrows.

Vale was left in charge in Donovan's absence, the detachment being roughly two miles north-west of Ober Uen, further away from the others due to the fact that Donovan had kept the only pair of binoculars and could bring Kilewe's outpost visually closer.

Donovan headed due west. It was important to drop Chianda and Brown unseen, out of sight of Kilewe, so that at least they had a natural start. When the stronghold was well out of sight he hairpinned, now travelling north-east-east, finally halting about two miles north of his own detachment position. They would have four or five miles to walk back in a heat that would slay lesser men. But Chianda had insisted that he recalled a dry river bed passing north of Ober Uen that could be useful to them. Donovan vaguely remembered but in any event some form of recce was essential and the combination of Brown and Chianda was ideal for it. He used the glasses in the direction of the stronghold. The drop off was safe. He called out and the two men climbed down. Donovan wished them luck and took the same circuitous route back. It was important to cram in as much observation as possible before sundown.

Thompson wiped his eyes, searching through the haze. "What do you think?"

King ground his elbows into the shallow sand. Both he and Thompson were prone, the remainder of their men resting at the foot of the narrow gulley. He took careful stock. "Too good to be true, mate. The place hasn't changed."

The two men stared at each other thoughtfully. "I wonder if that conniving bastard Kilewe has changed?"

"Have we?" Thompson looked out again. "No transport in sight. Not even a camel."

"We need field glasses."

"Yeah, but we've one advantage. About the only one."

King pushed his hat back further to protect his neck. "You're dying for me to ask, cocker."

Thompson grinned. "Hassan bloody Kilewe doesn't know we've been up against him before."

"That helps? That geezer thinks and double thinks." And then quickly as he shielded his eyes to scan the stronghold again, "Come in with me when this caper is over, Tommy."

Thompson was touched. "You know me, Jim. Can't work for anyone."

"I said with, not for. Don't be so bleeding independent."

"Let's see how we both feel if we get out've this." Thompson rolled carefully on to his back to gaze at the men a few feet from them. On the far rise of the gulley a sentry was posted to watch their rear and another at each end. A narrow depression wound from one end of the gulley through which the transport had advanced.

"It's living under a spotlight. I don't like it, Tommy."

"No. I wonder if the girls are still alive?"

"I've been wondering the same. You never know how that bugger's mind will work. Only one thing's for sure; in a few hours time *some of us won't be*."

Thompson nodded calmly. He winced, hand going to bandaged shoulder as he slid down the slope. "It's time for a radio check."

The wadi was deep. Steinberg, clothes black with sweat, was working under a jacked-up three-tonner which had a cracked spring. Two of the men were helping him. Others were lining the ridge watching the distance smudge, like a faded outcrop, that was Ober Uen. Three men were spaced out to guard the rear and the flanks.

It was ten minutes to five. As Donovan scanned he thought it typical of Kilewe to select a spot that could offer only limited protection to his enemies and thereby pinpoint them at the same time. The place hadn't changed except to grow shabbier. He needed more information than the glasses would reveal and wondered about Chianda and Brown. He noted the sentries round the hut. Was that where two very frightened girls were? To take his mind off it he said, "The cross is still on the church."

Colin Vale lying alongside said, "Whatever happens we must protect *that*."

Donovan rested his chin on the backs of his hands and wondered what to do about Vale. "Hassan Kilewe has probably desecrated it. Are you forgetting what we used it for with African troops?" He wanted to move; the sun was scorching him behind his knees.

"I've never forgiven myself for agreeing to that."

"No? Is that the only thing you can't forgive yourself for?" Donovan kept his voice low. As he saw Vale's face stiffen he wondered if he'd gone too far.

"That's not your concern, dear boy."

"It's very much my concern. What's bugging you?"

"It's nothing I can tell you."

"Not tell a friend?"

"It's between God and me."

"Fine. As long as you keep it between God and you. But the moment your personal problems affect the safety of these men it's then between you, God and *me*. Since the bush fire you've become broody. Have you found that you can't run from yourself? That new problems don't solve old ones?

There are times when you're not here at all, when you're corked up, fit to burst."

Vale's face was tight. "I'll do my job. I'm not afraid to die and you know it."

"I'm beginning to think you're banking on it. But suicide is a mortal sin. Do you expect some other poor sod to pull the trigger for you? What sort of man have you become to want to atone for your own sins by creating another sinner? Keep your mind on the job, Colin. There are terrified young girls there who desperately need your help. Wouldn't you be helping yourself at the same time?"

"There's bugger all there tha' we couldna' take care of."

In the middle depression Maxwell lay with Digger Williams and Pietro Frascelli by his side.

"Hassan Kilewe is devious. It would not be so easy."

Maxwell turned to the Italian. "Don't tell me you fought against him too?"

"*With him.* He was on our side then."

"And you think he's got something up his sleeve?"

"He is a man with more than one sleeve. He is waiting for us to try something stupid."

"I reckon you're right, mate." Williams, like the others, kept his gaze on the distant, untidy group of buildings that constantly moved and lost shape behind the heat haze. At times they almost lost sight of the place, the lowering sun playing obliquely behind them like a massive blood drop, bleaching out the sky around it into a pale, sight-robbing glare. "It's too quiet by half. I suppose the Sheilas are in that hut that seems to be guarded. If only we had some bloody glasses."

"I wonder if the lasses are still alive?"

Frascelli was surprised at the concern behind Maxwell's question. He tried to focus on the moving shapes again, for some reason feeling uneasy. Something was happening up there where ostensibly nothing was happening. It was strange that there were no visible signs of any form of animal, unless they were disguised by distance. They were essential to any desert encampment. During the war both British and Italian detachments had often survived by taking their own herds of goats to provide milk and meat. They had to be somewhere, so where were they?"

With his Bren gun slung over his good shoulder Thompson topped the rise to see the figure of the rear sentry squatting behind a shallow rock outcrop. To left and right, well separated were the flank sentries. It was time to change them. The period of concentration they could endure after sleepless nights and in extreme heat was severely limited.

Thompson scanned the desert. Some distance away was a small camel train looking as if it was heading for the well they had left earlier. It was moving away from the stronghold and themselves. A solitary Somali with a few goats brought up the rear and he used his staff as a goat wandered. Approaching the sentry Thompson noticed his head was down and anger boiled quickly in him. Okay, so they were all dead tired having travelled solidly for two nights, but where lives were at stake it was unforgivable. As he neared he unslung his Bren and was later to wonder why.

The sentry heeled over as Thompson reached him, as if the vibration of the footsteps had disturbed his balance. The anger in Thompson changed quickly to the kind of unease Frascelli had felt. When he knelt down the man was dead. There were three widely spaced bullet holes in his chest. He shouted loudly, half expecting the other two sentries to fall over as this one had done. When they raced towards him his relief was immense.

"Someone got him through the chest. Either of you hear a shot?"

No one had, including himself. "Either of you see anything?"

They hadn't. "What about that bloody camel train you stupid buggers. Didn't you see that?" Thompson was furious again. He had warned them before taking up their posts but clearly he hadn't warned them enough. They had seen the train, had kept their arms ready and they had been wary of it. But it had been moving obliquely away, not towards them. The goat herder had been having trouble with strays but he hadn't stopped, knelt or lay down. No. He had been the distractor.

Thompson was filled with self-disgust. His only justification for being here was past experience of the country, its people and in particular one half-breed Somali. Maybe it had been all too long ago.

"Get him down there with the others." As Thompson hurried down the slope he felt he was running in an oven; the gulley was holding the heat, building it up so that even to breathe was to shed body moisture. As he ran he detailed new sentries, instructing them to bawl out a warning however innocuous the distraction. He took the thirty-eight set from the man who was switching to receive for a minute every ten and fifteen minutes starting from the hour, his own sending time being every five minutes from the hour and the third set with Maxwell every ten minutes. He placed the throat mike round his neck, checked the time and channel and realised he would be cutting into Pat Donovan's sending time. He was about to switch to send when a grim-sounding Donovan came over the air:

"All channels. A silenced rifle is loose with a camel train. One man lost. Over."

"*Two* men, Pat. Over."

Maxwell cut in, "Hold it while I check." Fifty long seconds passed. "He musta' missed. But mebbe we're out've the way here."

"No one's out of the way, Max."

"Pat, let Jimmy and me go after them."

"You know better. That's what he wants. Channel four, are you in yet? Channel four, reply. Over."

The channel stayed open and then Donovan's voice almost to himself: "A hundred bloody men and either their set's broken down or they're lost."

"Sammy wouldn't get lost, Pat."

"I hope you're right. Watch your backs and check in as arranged."

By the time Thompson had finished and handed the set back, Jimmy King had been filled in on the loss. Two more men dead. They were now down to forty-five. Thompson joined King on the other ridge. He scanned the whole area again, slowly, carefully, particularly around the building with a tree showing above the outer wall. "Got it. That's why Pat played the Australian Division trick. The bastards are listening in."

"Australian—. The division that didn't exist? The Italians thought the Aussies were up their arse."

Thompson was still scanning. "Pat must've spotted that aerial. A whopper. The sun has turned it to silver." He pulled back from the ridge, wiping his face. "Pat sent out a call to a hundred men. God, if only we had them I'd go in now. Kilewe's chipping away at us, the bastard."

"That's how he pushes his enemies into mistakes."

Brown and Chianda loped easily across the desert, eyes screwed against the glare. Because, under scrutiny, Chianda appeared less Somali than Brown, he had taken the bow and quiver to compensate. They travelled faster than was wise in the excessive heat but they had to make up time. Their course, under Chianda's guidance, would take them obliquely across the north-eastern corner of Ober Uen so they could get a better view and a different angle of the whole compound, and with luck, locate the old river bed. They were silent. Talk meant use of energy.

When Chianda said the stronghold was in sight Brown took his word for it. It was strange territory, flat for the most part as it had been during almost all of their advance, yet hereabouts pockmarked with craters and depressions that gave no warning of being there. At night it would be disastrous with transport.

Without changing step Chianda said, "Hear that?"

"Yeah. Like Errol Garner playing the piano."

Chianda did not understand. "Camel grunts. Don't turn your head. To our left there's a big depression. *Listen*. Goats. Maybe sheep too. That's where they're hidden. Lots of them."

Brown resisted the temptation to look. They themselves were being observed, Chianda on the outside, further from Kilewe's stronghold, which had now shakily risen from the heat mist for Brown to see. Brown's neck prickled. From now on they were on view.

Hassan Kilewe lowered his glasses. He was puzzled. Aref Ghalib still had field glasses trained on the two figures.

"What do you think?"

Aref Ghalib continued to inspect before replying.

"I cannot get proper sight of the hunter. Only occasionally do I see his bow or his quiver. He is dark and thickset. *Very* dark for a Somali."

Kilewe was searching again, the veins like swollen rivers ready to burst over the shrunken skin of his bony hands. "Wait until they're nearer. Have someone watch them constantly." He lowered the glasses again. "Any news from our scouts of the hundred men on our east flank?"

"No, effendi. There is no sign."

"Perhaps they don't exist."

Aref Ghalib broke off his search in surprise. "They can't know we have radio interception."

Kilewe smiled thinly. "The British deceived the Italians with such a trick at Gelib on the Juba River."

The tall figure of Ghalib was ramrod straight at the window. Even movement of his head had enormous grace. "Does that tell us anything?"

"It tells us that I may have encountered some of these men before. That would explain some of their ages."

Ghalib, in his early forties, was curious. He saw the satisfaction in Kilewe's brittle eyes. "That pleases you?"

"It is a double bonus, Aref. To crush some of those who were *actively* engaged in fighting me. Yes, it pleases me very much." He raised his glasses once more, his thin lips tight beneath them. Without moving, he said, "Send armed men to intercept those two. Let them continue if they're harmless. Kill them if they're as odd as I think they are. When you've done that go to the two Englishwomen and tell them that their rescue force has arrived. Tell them that they are divided into three small pockets from north to south on our west side. Tell them that a few might be old protagonists who have long lost sight of the subtleties of battle and are using old tricks because they know no new ones. Tell them that I shall kill them all, a few at a time. And tell them that they will be permitted to attend the mass funeral of their departed compatriots. Don't give them water if they ask."

Brown saw the wavering shapes of two camels approaching.

"Don't look now but a couple of pig-sticking terrorists are on their way." They had appeared suddenly as if from a hole in the ground which was almost right.

Chianda said, "The dry river bed I told you about is ahead." His pursed lips gave direction.

"It's not gonna help us. They'll reach us anyway," and then, "They're armed. Machine pistols across their laps like pussy cats."

To pretend that they hadn't seen the camels approaching would have been as suicidal as making a run for it. Yet they had to cover ground. They compromised by looking round at the advancing terrorists while continuing to walk. When they were signalled to stop Brown touched Chianda's arm and they slowed to a halt. The camels approached, heads high in hauteur, the rolling bodies ungainly.

Brown and Chianda separated to approach the gunmen. They came close, knowing they would not survive examination. The spate of Somali thrown at Brown was answered by him in Arabic. It was sufficient to surprise the rider. Similarly, Chianda answered his man in Swahili, a language not entirely unknown in Somalia. They gained themselves a few seconds. Before any follow-up Brown ducked under the camel's belly and stuck an inch of knife into its ribs. He dived into a frantic roll as the bellowing camel reared huge, splayed hoofs pawing the air.

The rider yelled gutturally, as he was thrown but Brown had risen before diving again as the Somali, on his back, tried to bring his machine pistol into play. Brown reacted as he'd been trained to do. The Somali died with a gurgle in his throat and knife under his ribs. The whites around the sepia eyes were frozen wide as the final pain died with him. In the same movement Brown rolled to bring the Somali on top of him to act as a shield while he weighed his next move.

Chianda had a greater problem. His quick flow of broken Swahili had not saved him. The Somali had already recognised him as a Bantu and that meant he'd come from over the border. It was enough; he fired a burst. His camel, distressed at the cry of his fellow, stirred awkwardly, lunged towards Chianda who kicked hard at the animal's leg and the two simultaneous acts spoiled the aim, the shots spurting sand some distance away. The rider was still trying to control the beast, giving Chianda sufficient time to draw his pistol and to fire. The man fell at his feet, hit in the body but still alive when his own camel, still in pain, stamped on him. To erase the dreadful scream of agony and on seeing the crushed chest, Chianda shot him again and grabbed the camel's halter swinging the hobbling beast round between himself and Kilewe's stronghold. He stooped quickly to pick up the machine pistol then shouted at Brown,

"The river bed, *Msanga*."

Brown needed no interpreter. He rolled from under his victim, grabbed the Kalaschnikov and raced to join Chianda who was running alongside the camel, partly shielded by it. Shots were pumping at them before they'd covered ten yards. As best they could Chianda kept behind the plodding forelegs, while Brown stayed at the rear. So far the firing was wild.

In spite of Chianda's efforts with the halter, the camel was beginning to outstrip the two men, frightened by the gunfire. Finally it broke away, veered towards the encampment and crashed into the second camel which had instinctively followed it. They reared as Brown and Chianda crouched low, running fast for the protection of the river bed. There was a tremendous burst of firing as a machine gun opened up and the camels squealed in agony and terror before keeling over, legs kicking spasmodically. Their action had been a fortuitous break for the two running men, a distraction that gave them just sufficient time to hurl themselves over the ridge to tumble down the crumbling river bank. They lay on the slope, soaked with sweat, while bullets whined above them. With mouths open wide, they gasped at torrid air as if trying to breathe in a vacuum. Chianda managed to move a leg and ease the pressure of the quiver from his back; with the bow still draped over him and the machine pistol clutched in his other hand Brown saw the incongruity of it.

"I'm too old for this." Having said that Chianda, with Brown, started to crawl breathlessly to the ridge. Bursts of fire still came over and they kept low. There was nothing beyond the untidy mounds of the dead camels and the two dead Somalis. Brown gulped for air. "We'd better follow this bed. It might get us near to base."

Chianda nodded, rubbing his chest with the flat of his hand as if suffering from indigestion. Both he and Brown were puzzled by the lack of pursuit.

They eased further down the slope to the bed, the base a

mixture of soft sand, where water had once flowed from the Ethiopian hills, and scattered stone and rock. Unless they were followed there was ample cover down here. Brown, slightly ahead of Chianda was about to straighten when Chianda screamed at him.

"Don't move. Don't move one inch or we're dead."

13

Brown froze. His sweat ran cold.

"*Don't move.*" Chianda advanced cautiously, gaze riveted at Brown's feet. The Zambian came round the rear of Brown, knelt almost behind him. "Don't move your feet." Long black fingers curled round Brown's sand-caked sandals. The fingers gently explored around the feet brushing the toenails as if giving the gentlest of manicures. Awkwardly poised Brown felt a compulsion to move but had too much trust in Chianda. Balance was difficult.

The fingers eased away the sand in delicate movements until Brown, beginning to sway a little, saw part reason why they had not been pursued. The rim of a land mine gradually came into view. The Zambian leaned back on his haunches, critically studied the ground behind them then said softly, "Okay to step back now."

Brown stepped back, sank down beside Chianda to ease the strain from his legs. "We're bitched. Can't go forward and we can't go back."

Chianda didn't reply. He was carefully panning along the river line, taking in every sand stretch, every sigh. "They've mined right along the bed. I can't tell how far from here."

"I'm listening."

Chianda moved slowly along the middle slope, above the old waterway. "It looks safe here. They've just done the bed, I think. Follow me."

"You sure it's all right along here?"

"Sure."

"Sure enough to run like the clappers?" Brown had withdrawn a grenade, had his finger through the loop of the pin.

Chianda understood, approved. He rose as far as he dared and studied the middle bank once more. "Worth a chance, bwana."

Brown withdrew the pin, held down the lever. "You bugger off. I'll follow."

"I'll go with you."

"Piss off, Chianda. I don't know whether this is a seven second or four second fuse. You take your chance with the mines, I'll take mine with the grenade. Okay?"

Chianda set off, scuttling through the loose rubble, rounding the outcrops, displacing stones that bounced down dangerously on the mine strewn river bed. When Brown judged him to be at a safe distance he placed the grenade on the mine, released the lever then ran for his life. As he ran he counted. At four seconds nothing happened to his immense relief, at six he threw himself flat. The double explosion followed as he hit the ground. The river banks created a strange echo chamber that spilit the roar into a multi-directional, multi-volume, mass of sound. Brown, and ahead of him, Chianda, covered their heads with arms and hands as stones, sand and lethal flying metal rained down, setting off a second mine. It took them by surprise and was fortunately further from them than the first. They kept down, safe apart from minor cuts.

As the falling rubble eased off the two continued their run along the bank, sometimes stumbling, slipping but always moving. Both were parched. They had lost far too much body moisture. The low sun was still intense, strength sapping. "Well at least," gasped Brown as they kept moving. "Kilewe will think we've blown ourselves to bits."

"There's a small tributary here. Heads north-west. We'll use it to get out."

"Get that mortar on the Rover." Donovan was hustling. With Chianda and Brown back he now knew exactly what to do. During their absence he had been withstanding pressure from some of the men who resented the captured Somali sharing the meagre tepid water ration. The hunter was now roped under the canopy of a three-tonner.

Baseplate, barrel tripod, bombs were quickly loaded. "Are there any mortar men here?" Donovan glared round impatiently. There were never any mortar men. Never had been. Nobody had wanted to know and commanding officers had not had the remotest idea of how to use them properly, had even been known to refer to them as bloody drainpipes. The oddest memories stirred as Donovan heaved up bomb containers. "Looks like you and me, Chianda."

Before climbing in Donovan took a hasty look round. The men hadn't complained but they had nothing to enthuse about. Sores were breaking out around Vale's lips. "Colin, take over while we're away." He looked to Brown as he spoke, an unvoiced understanding communicated between them. Brown inclined his head almost imperceptibly. Donovan drove off with the knowledge that Brown would cope if Vale cracked.

There was less than an hour of light left but it was essential to get nearer to their target which meant first driving well west of it before circling. Kilewe would see them go and might even pick them off but Donovan was gambling on old knowledge of the terrorist, believing that his main positions would be taken up after dusk. And he possessed mobility in the Rover.

The journey did not take long. Most of it was on the flat but Chianda guided him to a low ridged depression. They offloaded quickly. The oppression here was worse than anything they had yet suffered, as if God had put a lid on the place. But it was the right place for range and observation and the low sun was behind them.

They had difficulty setting the baseplate. The ground was

hard and ungiving. They slid the barrel through the tripod ring and locked it in the baseplate. It was difficult and he wondered if he was doing it the wrong way round. But it was mounted facing the way Chianda had directed. Donovan turned the lateral screw to get the spirit bubble centre and adjusted the elevation screw. All they wanted now was accurate range. Donovan bent for a bomb, his back already aching; if backache was his only problem then he was home and dry. He took the cap off the first bomb while Chianda prepared the others. Donovan held the first bomb over the barrel as Chianda ran to the ridge with the glasses. As the Zambian signalled Donovan released the bomb.

He remembered to sway from the hips as the bomb flew out. The thirty seconds of flight seemed an eternity before the muffled explosion reached them. "About four hundred yards short, bwana."

Four hundred yards. Jesus. Donovan fastened three extra charges to the next bomb fin and adjusted the range drum. The firing pin in the barrel gave the charge instant detonation.

Chianda turned, a grin splitting his grimy, sweat stained face. "Direction, okay. Down a hundred yards."

Donovan raised elevation a fraction. He fired again. It was galling being unable to see where they landed but he trusted Chianda implicity. In spite of the gap of years he could feel an affinity for the weapon returning. It would respond because his use of mortars had not always been by the book but from experience and understanding of them.

Chianda held up a hand, pulled it down. "On target."

Donovan could not believe it. Two bracketing shots and the third on target was better than anyone could expect. His guesswork had been lucky but maybe a dormant instinct had played its part too. He set off five bombs in quick succession. The bursts came back: five, six, seven. They cheered.

"Try thirty seconds right, then left, bwana."

Chianda came back to help with the bombs. Donovan worked quickly now. His mouth was so dry he had to probe with his tongue to create a meagre saliva. Five bombs right, five bombs left. Fourteen explosions. It was unbelievable. He had used eighteen bombs. The last two had fallen short according to Chianda. When he checked the baseplate, it had sunken slightly even in this hard ground. The force of the ejections had put tremendous pressure on it. Donovan checked range and balance, the bubbles dead centre. He fired another twelve bombs in quick succession. The unrifled barrel would assure a carpeting effect and as he fired his final bomb he raced to the ridge in time to see the last four land.

There was more than that to see. The whole area of the river bed had erupted where it bulged north of Ober Uen, explosion following explosion, as the bombs landed in the congested area of the land mines, setting them off with the pressure of near misses, even of the odd direct hit, by the tremendous vibration reverberating and shaking the whole area. Land mines were also set off by blown up rock and debris.

Rays from the waning sun played on the smoke and sand palls like a string of misted camp fires, joining in a single canopy which spread over the whole river bed as if supported by the heat haze. Donovan and Chianda scrambled down to dismantle and load, speeding back to base by the shortest possible route, leaving behind empty bomb canisters to twist and blacken in tomorrow's sun.

Hassan Kilewe paled with rage. With Aref Ghalib he stood on the flat roof of his villa, shaded by the solitary tree, watching the smoke palls rising from the river bed. Apart from the obvious clearance of most of his mines, it told him much. It suggested that the two men who had killed his own men and, more importantly, been responsible for the death of two camels had escaped. That upset him more than the mortar bombing. It suggested a special kind of person out there and for the first time he had qualms. He was not afraid of the outcome; he had too much firepower, too many men to let that worry him, but he had allowed his contempt for the small task force to be aggravated by his hatred of the British and thus he had underestimated them. That was an unforgivable thing to do of any enemy. For an old campaigner like himself it was unbelievable.

The way his men had been killed had both impressed and troubled him. Now they had virtually blown up his minefield but at least it warned him of what was in their minds. The river bed was the only reasonable approach to his stronghold. So far he had only played with them: lopping off a finger here and there as he had intended to humiliate them. It was time to show more teeth. He instructed Aref to have the river bed doubly manned as soon as it was dark. And he instructed mobile units to go into immediate action before the light finally deserted them. Having done that he sent for his radio operator.

Kilewe paced the roof in the shadows of the rampart cast by the dying sun. Aref Ghalib was still watching the smoke pall now almost stationary with no breeze to stir it. When the operator arrived Kilewe spoke thoughtfully. "Send this message back to Nairobi: 'British task force has engaged units of the Somali Independence Army and has suffered heavy losses. At least twenty men killed, unknown number injured. Task force critically short of water and fuel and their position is considered desperate. There is no news of Princess Anne and her companion but they are believed still to be alive. All other prisoners are considered dead.'"

After the operator had gone Kilewe turned to Ghalib who had joined him. He felt better for the dispatch. "It's now time for events to catch up with the news."

Ghalib said nothing, warned by Kilewe's intensity. Yet he was concerned. Like his master he accepted the inevitability of the final outcome but it should have been over by now, the small task force crushed. Revenge and vanity was unnecessarily protracting a stupid little war at the expense of some of their own men. A personal hatred was costing them lives. At this stage he would much prefer simply to wait, for if the task force was to attempt to rescue the prisoners they had no alternative but to advance and be wiped out. Meanwhile Kilewe continued to nibble. Ghalib saw the fanaticism he had noted so often before; never had it been so intense. Wisely he raised the glasses again.

They came out of a sun that balanced on the earth's rim like a huge reflector. Two indeterminate shapes cascaded strange auras as the light spun round them with the sky as a rose pink backcloth. The bonnets of the vehicles were in shadow and the rim of sun was impossible to face, sending fierce, fiery glares through the sand trails. They were travelling at speed.

"Get up the bloody ridge. Get those sentries back here

bloody quick." Thompson raced down the incline to climb the other side followed by Jimmy King who headed for the far end. They left one man to watch the rear.

The vehicles separated, leaving the sun to burst through between them to blind Thompson's men. The two sentries who had first seen them were racing back to the protection of the ridge and the third was coming in at a fast crouch from the east. Two of them were mown down just before they reached the ridge, machine gun fire coming from both now well separated vehicles.

After the third one had scrabbled down to safety Thompson gave the fire order and his men opened up.

King and Thompson fired at the wavering lumps shrouded by the scintillating halo of sight-searing light being used so effectively by drivers who lived with an eternal sun. Between bursts King bawled, "Jeeps. Reinforced to take that bleeding treatment." He had no sooner spoken than the jeeps veered again, closing as if practising a movement for silhouettes with rear stage lighting.

They fired at a confusion of shadows that blocked, then released sunlight at its most treacherous to make full use of swirling sand trails as the jeeps criss-crossed with well-practised moves. It was difficult to retaliate accurately when the air above the ridge was whining with bullets. Apart from the two Brens, manned by Thompson and King, the two platoons of men had nothing to offer back but rifle fire. They were up against mobile, evasive, distant and difficult targets. It was impossible to see if they had hit anyone. The jeeps were still careering, keeping a cunning distance.

The jeeps swung back into the sun then U-turned and fanned away from each other. Thompson and King opened up on the two blurs as the whole desert, it seemed, spurted into their faces. Two sustained bursts of automatic fire swept right along the ridge sending up sheets of sand, killing one man and wounding two. One simply fell forward over his rifle. Another dropped down the gulley, blood oozing from a bullet that had entered his mouth and exited through his cheek. The third was shot through the neck and was dying by the time he reached the bottom of the gulley.

Half-blinded by sand, the men ducked as the firing continued. Except for Thompson. He scooped at his eyes until he had some form of bloodshot vision just as King arched back, arms out, to crash down from the ridge, bringing his Bren part of the way with him. Thompson couldn't see properly but he saw enough. For a moment he just stared at the inert form of King lying on his back, legs up the slope.

Thompson's world stopped still. His old mate was lying down there. The pain in his eyes was forgotten. With a roar of anger he climbed on to the top of the ridge, fixed the Bren under his arm with iron hands and peered out for anything that moved. He could barely see. Shooting had started up from his own men again and somewhere in front of him he heard firing and could hear the rush of bullets. The fucking bastards. Jimmy. Oh, Christ. A shape bore down from the distance; he braced his legs, kept the barrel down and fired until the magazine was empty and then cursed profanely when he realised that it had only been half full. Ahead of him, somewhere in a massive patch of moving light and shade, the sun burst open and flame came leaping from the desert. If only he could see properly. There were shouts of triumph behind him and he guessed that one of the jeeps had gone up with its ammunition.

By now he was crouched on one knee but he could really see little. He scrambled back behind the ridge, felt rather than saw one of the men reload for him and take away the Bren. He didn't realise how close his head was to the barrel until the roar almost deafened him and an ejected round burned his cheek. *Jimmy*. He slid down the slope. Someone handed him a water bottle and he poured the precious fluid carefully into the palm of his hand and bathed eyes that felt full of hot cinders. On the ridge they were still firing and he must get back to help them. When he peered up, one of the men had recovered Jimmy King's Bren and was using it in controlled bursts. Then the firing faded and the silence was painful, full of false lull and suspicion. He must make the best of it. Jimmy was clearer now but still lying as he'd last seen him.

Thompson rose shakily; quite apart from his searing eyes, his wounded shoulder was playing hell. He willed himself to leave Jimmy until last. The living must come before the dead. The man who had been shot through the cheek was trying to fix a field dressing. Thompson cut the strips and stuck it down for him. "Okay?"

The wounded man said, "Two mouths. Double beer ration."

Thompson forced a grin. "You'll do. They'll patch you up when we get back." When? If. He had no need to check that the next man was dead. The other was practically dead. He was gurgling slowly, life fading away. The kindest thing to do would be to shoot him. There could be no recovery and he would never know. As hardened as Thompson was he found he couldn't do it. Not to one of his own. The man was unconscious, unaware of the pain. He put the man's displaced hat over his face and walked over to Jimmy King.

He couldn't describe the emotion he felt as he knelt beside his old friend but he had to turn his back on the rest of the men to hide it. Two days ago he was in jail and Jimmy was running a successful business empire. How had they got into a burning nightmare of desert, dead and wounded? The scorching sun was sinking, filling the gulley with strange patterns and colours, refracted light picking out the crystals in the sand like a bed of minute diamonds.

King's chest was moving. Thompson located the pulse, his own heart thumping. The bastard. The heartbeat was normal. Quickly and, for a rough man, delicately he ran his fingers over the body finding no mark. He wiped the sand from King's face, lifted the hair that had tumbled down over the forehead. A bruise had ruptured well above the left eye, already deep blue and red-streaked where the skin had broken. A rock must have flown up in his face.

Thompson straddled King then, his emotion rising, *"You bastard,"* he bawled. "You sodding bloody bastard." He slapped King's cheeks hard on either side. "Wake up you shyster. What will I tell Jeannie?"

Stuart Maxwell shook a clenched fist at the cloudless sky. The air was humming with missiles. He waved his Sten gun upwards then threw it down, the impact immediately discharging a round which startled Maxwell into jumping belatedly to one side. Sweat had clogged his beard and grit stuck to it like cement. "You see what you've done?" he bawled at the empty space he expected God to be. "You've landed me with a weapon tha' goes off on its own and has no bloody range at all." He was close to tears with the frustration of being unable to get close enough to the attacking enemy to make himself effective.

The raiders were keeping it at long range. With heavy machine guns they could afford to. They weren't showing the mobility that Thompson's raiders had. Instead they had found an outcrop to mount their guns and Maxwell had only the rifles that could accurately reach them.

So far no one was hurt but the gunfire was blistering with barely a pause. It was used to cover a group of four Somalis who sped to a nearer outcrop. There was satisfaction when one Somali was brought down before reaching cover. It was difficult to know what they intended to do. As far as Pietro Frascelli had been able to discern the small group were armed with machine pistols.

They found out when the first grenade landed short in front of them, bursting in their faces. Instinct made them duck belatedly but one man took shrapnel in the face and died instantly. Frascelli crawled frantically to where had packed the gun cotton and ammonal. It was safe from gun fire but this was a new danger. He pushed them as far under a rock as he could, scraping at the sand, breaking nails in an effort to get deeper.

Maxwell was too well trained to waste ammunition by firing at the grenade launchers. They were too well hidden, but he detailed his best marksman to shoot the first head to show itself. His inclination was to take his men over the top firing with everything they had. But he knew it to be wrong without knowing the alternative. What would Donovan do? Sod Donovan. Frascelli then? Frascelli was an explosives man; all he was waiting for was an opportunity to use his stuff to blast Kilewe to Kingdom Come. There was so much fire coming over that even squinting over the top was a hazard. Hazards he could contend with. The rim of sand was being scattered, the rock beneath it splintering into dangerous chips. Then he risked a look.

Another grenade was on its way. It was strange, like watching it in slow motion as it gained height, the setting sun behind them turning it into a small comet. The bastards must have grenade discharger cups. Shit. They'd gone out with the ark. Well, they were in the bloody ark right now and by the feel of it, it was on fire. Acting purely on reflex Maxwell rolled onto his back and as the grenade reached its culminating point he fired the Sten upwards from the hip. The grenade burst like a rocket, shrapnel screaming down while the men covered their heads, but by the time it reached the ground most of the steam had gone from it.

"You know what to do. Shoot the bloody things out've the bloody sky." With rifles? He had to be kidding. One Sten and one captured machine pistol amongst his group. There was nothing like the number of proper weapons. And Donovan had known it.

Suddenly the sky seemed full of grenades. The disadvantage of discharger cups was the elevation needed to get distance. They were coming over high and then dropping, the bursts being timed almost to perfection. There was absolutely no possibility of throwing them out before they exploded. Maxwell and Digger Williams did their best with automatics getting a couple of hits but the men with the rifles had a hopeless task. Grenades started to burst around them and the bowl was a sudden death trap. They were forced to cease fire as the first grenade exploded. Shrapnel was shrieking everywhere, the oppressive air full of choking dust.

Frascelli crouched against the pathetically inadequate refuge for his lethal charges protecting them with his body. If they went up, they all went up. Like a mother protecting her baby he huddled over the gap afraid to lie flat, for to do so would expose a gap in the rock crevice. Frascelli paid the price for his bravery. Amidst explosions and screams he felt an impact on his back like a knife being driven in and at the same time something red hot sliced his thigh. Still he didn't move, the agony mounting, breathing difficult. He tried to look round but they were in a fog of sand that moved in great rushes. Red, expanding blobs of fire spun through the mist every few seconds.

Maxwell skirted the rear perimeter of the depression, making use of the sand storm as cover, blaspheming vehemently all the way. He came scrambling out on the north side and ran crouched as fast as he could. His sten magazine was empty and he had not the time either to replace or reload it. The machine gun fire had quietened and he guessed that they were all watching the grenade blasts with glee on their fucking brown faces. He'd make the smile come out of their arses.

He circled away from the outcrop protecting the grenade launchers and approached at an angle. Part of their cover also protected him now. No shots were coming from the depression but someone was screaming in agony. A sound behind him made him swing round, a grenade in his hand. It was Digger Williams, the whole of his chest a mass of blood, a sickly grin on his face. "You don't think I'd let you run out on me, you pommy bastard?"

"Shit, Digger, you might'a been seen."

"You bloody invisible, sport?"

But they were moving forward all the time, the crude banter all that was left to them.

"This is near enough." Both men lay flat. Williams' face was screwed with pain as his chest touched the ground.

"Ready? Hold it for four?" If he was wrong about the timing they were dead.

Williams nodded, his face streaked. They each removed a grenade pin, released the lever and counted four seconds before throwing. The grenades landed in the outcrop on low trajectory, the bursts coming almost on impact. The two explosions were music to their ears and multiplied like an artillery barrage. Maxwell was on his feet as soon as it stopped, another grenade in his hand. "Come on, Dig." He glanced round to see Williams struggling up. Coming from the north side of the outcrop he was out of sight of the machine gun post and he jumped over the low rocks without hesitation.

There were two obviously dead and one dying. It was a gory mess. The machine gunners must have seen the explosion. Rapid shots came over and Maxwell dropped, realising that he had put himself on view. Where the hell was Digger? The Australian climbed slowly over the lowest rock as if in answer. Two machine pistols were there, one ruined, the other surprisingly in order. There was a rifle, stocks splintered, the grenade cup still attached.

He searched quickly and found two grenades that had miraculously survived by rolling under a small over hang. It was all there was. He had one more grenade on him and hoped it would fit the cup. It did. The machine gun fire eased, just an occasional burst to keep his head down. At least it took the heat off the boys in the depression.

The machine gun post was still too far away for a thrown grenade to reach it and there was no other cover for an approach. Maxwell pulled back the bolt of the operational rifle and giggled light-headedly. Incredibly a ballistite round had survived the eruption in the comparative safety of the breech. He risked a quick sighting of the machine gun post, sat behind a rock, rifle reversed, butt between his legs, trigger guard upwards. He pulled the pin from his grenade which he slipped into the discharger cup making certain the lever did not rise, placed the butt firmly on the ground holding the rifle in both hands. All he could now do was what Donovan had done, guess. But Donovan had at least had sights and ammunition to play with.

This extraordinary man, positive only in action, a law to himself, glared aggressively at the heavens once more as if challenging God when in fact, he was challening the doubt that would always be deep within himself. From this awkward position he pressed the trigger, there could be no squeezing it, and the grenade flew off. He went forward raising his head as far as he dared. The grenade fell short but was on course. There was no retaliatory fire. No fire at all. He'd got their bloody heads down by Jesus. He got down on his knees. "Digger, for Chrissake find another ballistite cartridge." His hands were pushing through the sand, searching frantically in fragments of blooded Somali clothing. "*Digger*. You dozey bastard." Sweating, rushing his search, Maxwell took time to look up.

Digger Williams did not hear nor would he again. He was face down over the rock both arms in front of him, a grenade slowly slipping from his right hand, his Kalaschnikov still in the other.

14

For a moment Maxwell was numbed. He saw the spread on the back of Digger's shirt. He must have a hole right through him. The thought was a safety valve in Maxwell's violent world. He wasn't sure how he felt. Digger had been a good bloke. An awkward Australian bastard, but a good bloke. Listlessly he saw the grenade fall and roll a little toward him. He reached, picked it up, looked at it. "Okay, Dig. I'll see that some of those bastards get it wi' yer best wishes." He got back to searching for a ballistite cartridge without success. They had all been blown to bits. Frustration built up again. The machine gunners had to be stopped.

Firing broke out as his search became wilder. He paused to listen. It wasn't coming his way. Rifle fire. And not much of it at that. The lads. He ignored caution and rushed to watch the machine gun post. The guns weren't on view. The bastards had pulled out. He clenched Digger's grenade tightly in anger. They were getting away and he could do damn all to stop them. The only thing that was chasing them was the red carpet of dripping sun creeping over the desert, cascading off outcrops, shadowing the depressions.

He stooped to ruffle Digger's hair. The dying Somali groaned. Hate-filled, Maxwell turned. The Somali was still spreadeagled face down. Maxwell was never sure whether he did it as revenge for Digger or to put the Somali out of his misery. He put a foot on the man's head and ground his face into the sand until the groaning stopped. He loosened the Kalaschnikov from Digger's fingers, picked up the other one and stepped from the outcrop. As he passed his dead friend he said, "Och, you were a fearless bastard." It never occurred to him that the words reflected them both. It was perhaps the only affinity they had really had. There was no time for burial, no time for anything except to get back and to kill as many Somalis as he could before they killed him.

Frascelli was being attended by one of the men when Maxwell reached the depression. Out of ten men, excluding Frascelli, there were six alive. Of those only four were virtually untouched. The two wounded were not too serious but, like Frascelli, Maxwell could not see how they could be used. They were casualties, leg and arm cases. He went round to inspect the makeshift medical treatment. One of the men had removed a grenade segment from Frascelli's back. It had gone in deep and downward but there had been sufficient above the skin to pull on. It had been a gamble that had come off. From the Italian's difficult breathing Maxwell supposed that at least one back rib was cracked. They had strapped him right round the chest which crudely dealt with both problems. The leg wound was longer, not so deep, but had affected a tendon and a muscle. The leg would not take his weight.

Maxwell helped positively with dressing the wounded. While he worked he was all right. Digger was dead and Frascelli immobilised. He went off to discover whether or not the thirty-eight set had survived.

Donovan's group fared better mainly because they had the ancient three-inch mortar which they were able to use from a sheltered position. When the attack came they lost one man who was too slow to respond but the rest kept down while Chianda and Donovan, who had barely got back, erected the mortar.

The Somalis used the same tactics as those who had raided Thompson; mobility, speed and firepower against the sun. While Donovan realised the impossibility of firing at fast, vaguely visible jeeps with a three-inch mortar he equally knew that he could blanket an area and change it without warning. He also had the advantage of smoke bombs he had not yet used. To save his men he ordered them not to return the fire. They were reasonably safe against machine guns as long as they kept down and let the mortar do the work.

Incredibly, while this was going on, Gerry Steinberg was working on the Rover, changing a wheel because he had found a gash in one of the tyres that might cause a blow-out at a critical time. His only concession to annoyance was to curse at having to work on his knees because of the shallowness of the gulley.

The mortars kept the jeeps at bay and Donovan decided to use his smoke bombs. He brought the range down to entice the jeeps nearer. With no wind he had to space them out and the smoke was slow to spread but there was the advantage of it dissipating very slowly. With six bombs he was able to create a very effective barrier making it impossible for any form of accurate firing from the jeeps. There was nothing so simple as a straight line of smoke from a weapon with as much play as a mortar. From the front it appeared that the slowly rolling cloud was continuous. In fact, it was overlapping leaving interspersed gaps like a simple maze.

"Colin, get the anti-tank up there." Donovan was standing, smoke bomb in hand, wondering whether he needed more. There was no sign of the jeeps but they could be heard somewhere behind the screen that lay like cloud glowing in sunlight. Vale did not move.

"COLIN. Get that bloody Boys up there."

Vale heaved the anti-tank rifle from the Rover. He automatically reached for a box of the .55 armour-piercing rounds. The gun was heavy. Thirty-six pounds. He climbed onto the top of the ridge and it would have made no difference to him had the machine guns been firing. If only he could clear his head. A numbness had been growing for weeks that needed unlocking; for some reason the last few hours had been almost intolerable.

He pushed the rifle forward on its bipod, carefully loaded the five-round magazine, lay down flat behind it. Its touch was reassuring, something once familiar. Yet it remained an instrument of death, would add to his sins if he used it.

A voice in his ear said, "Now listen. These bastards are bound to probe the screen or Kilewe will castrate them when they get back. At the first sign of a deepening shadow pump away. They're likely to try the trailing patches near the overlaps."

Vale turned to see Donovan lying by his side. He took sight through the aperture, drew back, lifted his glasses, wiped his eyes. "My sight's not what it was. The aperture's too near, misty."

"You've never missed a target in your life. And this old girl is the most accurate thing we've got. Concentrate."

Vale aimed again, lowered the butt from his shoulder. "It's not clear, I tell you."

Donovan glanced quickly at the smoke screen. It was gradually dissipating. A sudden burst of firing came through the smoke causing both men to duck down. "What the hell did you do, for Christ's sake? Nick the church silver?"

The sudden shots seemed to have cleared a fog in Vale's head for he said, "I stole, yes. To appease a baser instinct."

Donovan knew it was no time to pursue it, yet if he did not at this precise moment do so it would be lost forever. He needed Vale at his best and Vale needed someone to help him like never before. He took another urgent glance towards the screen, illuminated by what was left of the sun. "A man?"

Vale paled under the grime, his unshaved face suddenly coarser.

"A woman then? For Christ's sake! These bastards will be letting off."

Vale didn't answer, guilty in his silence, jawline jutting.

Donovan licked his lips. "Jesus, it must have been the Bishop's wife." He had spoken out of disgust for the whole situation. When Vale closed his eyes and his terribly cracked lips moved, Donovan was shaken. He hadn't really meant what he'd said, had wanted to stir Vale. He saw now that he'd hit near enough to the truth. He wanted to laugh. Out here in the desert, almost without water, being attacked by a well-armed enemy, and the chances of their own success, survival even, remote, Vale was worried about a bit on the side. "For Christ's sake, she must have wanted it. Be your bloody age."

Vale shook his head in anguish. "You don't understand. I betrayed my trust, a wonderful woman, a dear friend. And you think it funny. God help me."

Desperate, Donovan got to his knees. He waved his hands at the baking wilderness, the billowing smoke. "Look around you, you stupid bugger! Do you think it matters out here? Do you think God wants to punish the lot of us because you won't pull your finger out after knocking off a woman?"

"Why make it so cheap? It was never like that."

"Good for you, old friend. I never thought it was." Donovan heard an engine, tried to pinpoint it. "Listen, if you want salvation you bloody well earn it getting us off the hook. There's a jeep coming. Fix it."

Vale had his cheek resting on the butt. "Pat, I can't. I really can't."

"Then you shouldn't have come. You had no right to expect the rest of us to carry your burden for you. You know what to do. But to do it you've got to get back home, not get yourself and everybody else killed out here." Donovan turned to go back. One area of the screen that was breaking away needed more smoke. But it wasn't from there that the engine noise came. "If you let *me* down like you did your friend and his wife I'll blow your bloody head off." It was cruel, spontaneous, necessary. He had his legs down the slope when he heard the first shot. Vale's feet moved back six inches from the recoil leaving runnels where his toes had scraped.

Donovan kept his head above the ridge. The jeep was a faint outline drifting in and out of the wraiths of smoke. Vale fired again. And again. The engine noise died, there was a short silence followed by the frantic babble of frightened voices. *"Get up here quick. All of you,"* Donovan yelled, bringing up a machine pistol to his shoulder. "Keep your head down, Colin, for Christ'sake keep it down." He fired at the moving shapes, shouting, now screaming as the men joined him on the ridge.

The hidden second jeep returned fire but its elevation told its own story. Under sustained fire from the ridge the inevitable happened to a vehicle carrying so much ammunition; a box ignited at almost the same time as the petrol tank burst. The smoke screen reddened gorily at one point and flame and debris hurtled high above it.

When silence finally returned there was anti-climax in an unnatural stillness. The smoke screen was breaking up patchily to reveal the wreck of the jeep, charred bodies that no one cared to risk investigating. There was no sound or sight of the second jeep yet, strangely, few felt satisfaction. It was as if they all understood, as Donovan and Vale well understood, that Kilewe could have kept up the pressure with far more men had he wanted to. Kilewe, whatever his own losses, was a man who prolonged his pleasures.

Wearily, they sat around the gulley, three sentries still on duty. There could be no respite. Sparingly they sipped at their water. Donovan pushed back his hat. His skin felt as if it had been held too near to a fire. He hand wiped his face, turned to Vale who had brought back the Boys. "Good shooting, Colin." One or two of the men voiced consent. Steinberg was still prodding around the transport as if a shot hadn't been fired; a restless, yet conserved small bundle of persistent energy. Vale made no response to the compliments. He pulled out his Bible, now dirtied and soiled and wet around the edges, and went to bless the dead.

Donovan reached for the thirty-eight set. The news was grim. From the moment of crossing the border they had lost thirteen dead and there were four seriously enough injured to be of little use other than for reloading magazines. From a force of fifty-three they were effectively reduced to thirty-six. Kilewe had won his first battle; he had forced them to regroup, forced them into one contained unit, one area of advance. Donovan ordered them back, keeping his voice neutral.

His men lined the ridge again when all they wanted was more water and to lick their wounds. Lack of sleep was also beginning to tell. They covered the whole perimeter ready to supply covering fire to the widely-detouring platoons of Maxwell, Thompson and the recovered King. Even the transport had a weary look about it as it came in shadowy sight and was carefully identified in the dusk. Yet beneath the coatings of dirt and smut there was a pugnacious, bulldozing appearance that somehow suggested the attitude of some of the men. They came in, limping and lurching over the bad surface, creaking and rattling when close to, yet reflecting a draggletail kind of glory that stimulated those watching. These weren't defeated men returning but much mauled ones.

The dead had been brought back where it had been possible and lay in a covered heap in one of the Rovers where Vale gave them prayers. If they didn't get back before the heat of the next day they would be too high to carry and would have to be left. The wounded were cheerful, as wounded invariably are. But under the banter they were aware that time was important to them, that without proper medical attention, and with the present lack of hygiene, septicaemia and gangrene could set in. Gerry Steinberg's fingers were so dirt and oil-encrusted that he had to get Vale to check the dressings, and none had clean hands nor the water to wash them.

Those men not on duty had split into small groups as they lay back on the hot sand relishing the relatively cooling air. It was virtually thc last strcak of Royal bluc lying likc a ribbon in the west. A shielded Tilley lamp was suspended from the tailboard of one of the three-tonners to cast sufficient light to pick out shapes. The stars were up in their millions. Brown came shuffling up to join Donovan who was placing identity discs and small items from the dead in an empty ammunition chest.

"Hi, boss." Brown was still dressed like a native, his bow and quiver retrieved from Chianda. He squatted easily on his haunches. "Keep an eye on that gaggle over there."

Donovan didn't look up, trying to keep each dead man's items separated. "Trouble?"

"I would say so."

"Smithy said you would identify yourself if it became necessary."

Brown smiled. "I did that some time ago, boss."

"Almost from the beginning."

Croft had detached himself from the small group Brown had drawn attention to. He had one of the captured

Kalaschnikovs under his arm, his hand on the pistol grip. He picked his way through, a dark tall shape taking outline as he stood before Donovan and Brown who were still squatting. Behind him about six other mercenaries had risen and had fanned out, rifles ready.

"We're pulling out in one of the Rovers."

"The pace too hot for you?"

"The boys don't like the arms they've been landed with to fight machine guns."

"No one told me your terms were conditional. Maybe we should've supplied ice cream too."

"You bloody well know the odds are against us. Don't try to stop us."

"God forbid. What about the Princess and her friend over there? Terrified, hope dying, Kilewe degrading them?"

"That's their bad luck."

"It doesn't matter to you?"

"Kilewe can do what he likes with them. We've had a bellyful."

Maxwell had overheard the last two sentences and had picked up the gist. He jumped to his feet in sudden rage, Sten in hand. "You yellow-streaked rabble. You filthy deserting bastards. Ye'll leave over my dead body."

"If we have to. Don't lift that Sten or you'll stop one." Maxwell looked round. Six shadowy rifles were trained on him. He jumped forward and had Croft by the throat with one hand, hooking his Sten behind the neck with the other. The light was too bad, the figures too close together for anyone to risk a shot.

Donovan jumped to his feet. "Let *him go*."

"I'll kill the gutless bastard." Maxwell was squeezing the life from Croft with one powerful hand. Brown tried to pull Maxwell away but there was no way of releasing the hold, deep anger doubling strength. The men with the rifles were rushing forward to club Maxwell when Donovan yelled at the top of his voice, *"Sergeant Major, let him go."*

"Yessir." Maxwell stepped back, stood rigidly to attention before realising what he'd done, how he'd responded to a rank he had loved and still respected. By this time, not quite understanding what had happened, Thompson and King rushed forward to see Croft on his knees, breathing from a terrible rasp and clutching at his throat.

"This geezer looks as if 'e's throttling himself."

"Some of them want to go back home."

Thompson, who'd said nothing, wanted to continue what Maxwell had left off but Donovan stopped him with a gesture. "Let them go. We could never be sure of them."

"Then let them walk it." Thompson, determined to get them one way or another bent to take the still gasping Croft's machine pistol. He was puzzled by Maxwell who was coming out of a daze.

"What's the point? They'll return when our backs are turned." Donovan turned to the struggling Croft. "On your feet, you. Maxwell's right. You're yellow scum. You'll fight when the odds are with you."

"We'll want water." The croak was barely audible.

"You'll get nothing but your fair share. Where's Ossie Jenkins?"

They went over to the water trucks, by now the whole unit aware of what had happened. There were subdued boos and hisses, insults and threats but Croft and his men were unaffected; they wanted out. When they reached the truck Donovan found the floor of it wet. With sudden apprehension he jumped up, hurried forward to the one full water drum. He could *smell* water. Oh, Christ. Reaching it he rapped his knuckled on the side, the hollow ring turning his stomach. He tapped downwards. About a foot from the bottom the sound was more solid. "Bring that lamp, quick." Someone brought the Tilley. The light cast the dark stain around the drum. The seepage had stopped just below the bullet hole. As it was below the level of the gulley lip it could only have been a ricochet, probably off one of the stanchions holding the canvas canopy.

A foot of water left. Donovan did not try to work it out. They had all been too preoccupied by the need to survive for there to be recriminations. He turned to Croft at the tailboard. "You'll have to make do with what you've got."

Croft had the sense not to push it. He could feel the contempt around him. In spite of the ready rifles there were still many who would have taken them on but for the need to conserve themselves and their own resources.

Donovan changed position and saw the Somali prisoner

slumped, half hidden behind a drum. They had all been so occupied that he had completely slipped their minds. The poor wretch was dead, shot because no one had had the time to get him down from the truck. Donovan called out crisply, "Get this fellow off and put him with the other dead." It was not how he felt. The hunter had been caught up in something not of his making.

Donovan jumped down. "Gerry, give them the other three-tonner. And Jenkins, give them a crate of canned meat.

Steinberg looked at Croft, then at Donovan. "Have you told them that Kilewe will be waiting out there for them?"

"It wouldn't stop them."

Maxwell, playing a strange rôle, had not uttered a word since releasing Croft. He stood on the fringe of the group as if fathering them.

"Good riddance to them. Trash." Thompson's sudden amiability worried Croft.

Vale, Bible in hand, said to Donovan, "You're sending them into the valley of death."

Croft believed Vale; there was no reason for him to lie.

Donovan shrugged. He was tired and worried about the water and the remaining men who deserved much more of his concern than deserters. "It's their own choice. There's no way they can stay. For their own protection they'd better go through with it."

Maxwell, partially restored to his old aggressiveness, said, "They'd better not stay unless they watch their backs."

There was nothing to add. Donovan let them take their rifles but Croft did not get the machine pistol back. They were given some ammunition and Steinberg saw to it that they had a fair share of fuel. That was all there was to it. All seven men were silent as they boarded the truck, not because of the coarse hostility of some of the others but because they recognised that Colin Vale had spoken what he believed to be the truth. One thing they had learned about the oldies was that they seemed to understand the tactics of Hassan Kilewe. It should have registered before.

There was a grim silence as the truck drew away up the incline. It travelled without lights which would not be safe to use for some time.

Sensing the mood building up around him Donovan

spoke coolly for all to hear. *"Don't fire one single shot, any of you.* I know how you feel. It's tempting. But shots will pinpoint us. Kilewe is waiting but right now he can't be too sure whether we're all moving out. Don't tell him for the sake of shooting up that rabble."

When the truck had disappeared, the engine noise having died to the odd burst of revs, Donovan turned to address the men. It was clear that they were waiting for some kind of announcement. Reassurance was impossible. But these men had stayed at a time when they might have been caught up with Croft's emotions. Donovan was not to forget it.

"You can all count. We're down to twenty-nine men plus four injured who could've taken a cramped trip with Croft but elected not to. Perhaps they thought that Croft might have turfed them out after a while. And they could be right. But I'd like to think they stayed because they've got guts and want to see this thing through." Some of the men were smoking, showing the faintest of glows in cupped hands.

"You will have noticed that Kilewe over there doesn't seem too concerned about losses. They've lost more than we have but we'll never rescue the hostages by a straightforward attack. We simply haven't the numbers nor the arms."

Maxwell said, "You cleared the river bed. What's wrong wi' tha'? According to Brown and Chianda there's plenty of cover there."

"And a waiting Kilewe. That's where he'll expect us."

"That geezer'll have a gun behind every rock."

Thompson backed Jimmy King. "Kilewe could have taken us any time by now. He's settling an old grudge. The chopped off hand, the arm, the legs, the balls, the head. I'm not taking bets on which he's up to."

Donovan silenced them. "For most of us there's a night-long march. You'll all carry as much as you can stand with the exception of Brown and Chianda. They have extra to do the other end. I want to reach a point just north of Ober but there's no way we can go direct to it without being slaughtered. We'll have to go miles out of our way to avoid gun outposts and to hide the sound of our approach. We cannot use transport because he will hear it. When your feet are swelling and all you want to do is rest just bear in mind that to succeed we've got to be craftier than Kilewe. Get what rest you can before we move out." They would be with him all the way. Every one of them. To the end. Basic honesty prompted him to add more but he held back. There was no need. They knew that his doubts were no different from their own. Few might see the dawn and those that did might wish they never had. There was no way they could turn back, no method of checking a momentum that had brought them thus far. Yet this was no headlong rush to destruction. They would resist that to the very last.

Maxwell was coming to believe that these oldies had a positive disregard for their own lives. They didn't seem to mind if they died, as if they'd already decided that they were living on overtime. Yet they were far from old, had much in front of them. So what motivated them? What drove them to this lack of concern for themselves? Thompson he could understand, his alternative was prison, but the others had a choice. Two of them were wealthy, he'd discovered, so what the bloody hell were they doing out here looking like filthy tramps up for execution? Look at the Itie. Badly wounded he was at the moment, sitting with his back against the wheel of a truck reloading the Bren and Sten magazines and that bloody box of explosives never left his side, not even when he'd copped it. What had these men got for each other that formed such an exclusive club? Even the vicar had slammed the lead where it was needed at the right moment.

"Engines."

That was another thing. *Everyone* had learned to freeze into silence the moment the Zambian made pronouncements like that. Maxwell gave up wondering and concentrated on listening as they all were doing. Direction was difficult, the sound low and distant.

"Croft?"

Chianda shook his head. "Wrong direction, bwana. More than one truck." Chianda put his ear to the ground. "Several. South of Kilewe's village."

"Coming here?"

Chianda didn't reply at once. He lifted his head. "No. Some have stopped."

"They're preparing for us?"

"Maybe. Maybe we should leave here."

"We're going to anyway." Donovan raised his voice. "Can

everyone hear me? Now listen carefully. I can offer you no more sleep than last night. This is what we are going to do." Before he could continue there was the sound of rapid fire, subdued by distance and directionally distorted by space. And then a terrible scream that carried over the wilderness as it grew in terror.

15

In London, Smithy was catching what sleep he could. He had erected a camp bed in an office that had become his for the duration of the operation.

It was near enough to Sir Murray Field's office for the Military Intelligence man to be in constant touch with the M.I.6 chief. They were together now at eight thirty that evening.

The rumours of the task force had reached the banner headlines of the newspapers on Sir Murray Field's desk. As the Government had blatantly disclaimed all knowledge there could be no reason why a D notice should be issued to the press, and editors had seldom had such a bonanza of saleable speculation. That they might be putting men's lives in jeopardy came a distant second to printing their interpretation of the truth.

Smithy was mad at the ruthless way the carpet had been pulled from under the feet of the task force. He wasn't in any sense naïve, no intelligence man with his long experience could possibly be. But the rumours could have been squashed by positive Government announcement: they had only to say that the Kenyan Government had no knowledge of such a force. Instead they were so busy denying any part in such an attack that they left the possibility of a freelance force floating, as they had intended to do. Smithy's objection to this was that it openly alerted *official* Somali and Russian sources, who might be compelled to act on it at a time when it might have well suited them to close an eye to what was happening. The task force could well be confronted with a double danger. Smithy said as much to Sir Murray Field.

Sir Murray was not complacent. He had aged over the last two days, a fact that did not disturb Smithy; there were men in the desert ageing by the minute, what was left of them. Studying the latest report from Nairobi, Smithy said, "They've obviously taken a hammering. It doesn't look good."

Skeletal fingers trembled slightly as Sir Murray took back the decoded communique. The M.I.6 chief was having increasing difficulty in presenting an unflappable image. "It's worse than it looks."

Smithy sat down, alert to the ominous innuendo. "Oh?"

Sir Murray waved the paper. "These bulletins are coming in a shade too fast. They're a little too detailed."

"But the Kenyans have a good man out there."

"With a sideline view? These reports are coming in, it seems to me, almost as things happen. Number of dead. Wounded. Precisely stated. How can he know? No estimates, mark you. Facts. Even Kilewe can't be that accurate."

Smithy was disturbed. "You think the Kenyan agent has gone over?"

Sir Murray shook his head. "He wouldn't be so careless. My belief is he's dead. He probably has been for some time."

"Kilewe's sending his own bulletins?"

"It looks like it."

"Then *he's* been careless for you to arrive at that."

"If only that were true. No. He's done it deliberately. I'm

afraid, Smithy, that Hassan Kilewe suddenly wants us to know."

Smithy considered it uneasily. "If he's been sending messages all along he's set up his own position, the number of men."

"Precisely. It very much looks as if Kilewe has drawn us onto his sword. He wanted it to happen. Now he wants us to know that he has us by the throat."

"Poor bastards."

"Donovan's men?"

"Who else, for God's sake?"

"Keep your nerve, Smithy. Get them out of your system. They've walked into a carefully baited trap. It's better we forget them and start monetary negotiations. I thought you should know before I inform the Prime Minister."

"Is there nothing we can do for them?"

Sir Murray reached for his scrambler. "How can we? They don't officially exist."

"God help them."

"He's the only one who can. Unfortunately my direct lines don't extend that far."

Stella Donovan cuddled Jik, the Welsh terrier on her lap, and her tears quietly flowed. She buried her face in the dog's fur and the animal, sensitive to her distress, lifted his head to lick her ear. The television news had just finished. The whole country was in turmoil about the possibility of the Princess Anne kidnap. And now it was speculating on the rumours about a task force. Volunteers, for the Government had disclaimed all knowledge. The rumours were that this misguided bunch of patriots were being slaughtered.

Earlier telephone calls to the Ministry of Defence had been stonewalled. She was never able to raise the same official twice. Each one was evasive. Always the person who might know something more was not available. Her frustrations had mounted and with them fear.

Music was coming from the speaker but she had not the energy to switch off. A meaningless jumble of discords added confusion to her scrambled wits. "Oh, Pat. You fool," she moaned. And at the mention of the name the dog pricked his ears and looked around expectantly. "Oh, Pat, oh, Pat.

Come back to us. Please come back." It did not occur to her that she might be wrong. She knew that she was not. She was terrified at the strong possibility of losing him but a stronger terror reached out for concern of him, his plight at this moment. After all these years she was suffering it all again. It was worse now, life more precious, the resilience of youth no longer with her.

Jeannie King would have gone to her sister's and would have preferred to close the big London house. The only reason she hung on was in the hope of a call from Jimmy. Although he had said that he wouldn't be in touch for a few days you never knew your luck; he might phone.

For the first time in her life she was worried about him being missing. At other times she had been angry, hurt, she had threatened to walk out, but she sensed that this was different, that no woman was involved. There had been something in the way he had told her; something she hadn't detected before. And he loved her. After all these years, he really did love her. It gave her a glow she had not experienced for a very long time. Maybe he was growing up at last. It was high time. She watched and listened to the news. Now if Jimmy had got himself caught up in a force to rescue Princess Anne. *That* would be something. A knighthood, a medal, a visit to Buckingham Palace, all dressed up. She dreamed contentedly for a while. It was a wonderful dream. She sighed. It would never happen to them. Jimmy was too old to go chasing round the desert. All he could chase were young birds. The fool. Anyway, he couldn't harm a rabbit. Jeannie King dreamed away, worried yet proud that the Ministry of Defence had found need of Jimmy's services. One thing was for sure; wherever they had been tucked away for a few days he'd be surrounded by comfort. He wouldn't do without his comfort.

Dan Vermaak was in the lounge of the New Stanley Hotel in Nairobi. The place was crowded out with news reporters of every media from all over the world. Unlike the British Government the Kenyans had categorically denied any possibility of a task force passing through their territory. The more they denied it the more the rumours persisted. Vermaak was drinking an afterdinner South African sparkling Moselle. It was all he ever drank after dinner.

The *East African Standard* was resting on his knee so that he could read and drink at the same time. They had certainly clamped down on the press here all right, but skilful reporting could hint round a thing. He sipped the wine. He had not got the table to himself; there was hardly a spare seat in the hotel or any of the others. The noise level was as high as if there'd been an international meeting of the world press taking place. Almost every language floated round the room with the smoke and Vermaak felt out of place. Like the locals.

He read some more, not putting too much credence one way or the other on the task force denials. Who'd be crazy enough to do a thing like that? Who? He didn't have to think too long but the thought was prompted by the arms they'd found on the plane. He put down his glass. The boss? Surely not. No. And yet the boss had come up here on a strange mission for someone he had great respect for. He had wanted the arms smuggled through customs and by golly someone had done just that.

Concern hit Vermaak hard. The old fool. Why hadn't he said anything! His friend and pilot would have gone with him. For sure. Vermaak rustled through the pages. Where was it that this task force that didn't exist was supposed to be? He could not find mention of it. Mid Somalia was the nearest he got. In the middle of nowhere but heat and desert. He took his time to look round the room. There were enough reporters to keep him going for some time. They were supposed to be adept at winkling out the facts. The one nearest to him was an American; he had to start somewhere.

Hassan Kilewe was satisfied. He allowed himself a spartan meal. Appetite would come later. He had manoeuvred things his way at last. In London the British would be feeling sick with apprehension. They were just about smart enough to realise what he had done by now. They would, of course, deny the existence of that contemptible little task force out there. He would take a few prisoners and by the time he had finished with them he would be ready for certain Eastern cine camera crews, exclusive interviews, confessions from one or two of his better-preserved prisoners to prove to the world British Government complicity, hypocrisy. He could taste victory, not of battle so much as the all-round humiliation he would have imposed. Even then that would only be the start of it. He had already upped his demand to £15,000,000, payable half in sterling, half in American dollars.

Aref Ghalib entered the room to join Kilewe at the rough, wooden table. Ghalib observed the trace of satisfaction on Kilewe's usually unreadable face. He said, "We've lost many men. The marksmanship of the enemy is very high." Kilewe's expression did not change. "From now on we will lose few, ridicule the British and extort them."

Ghalib nodded. He had mentioned the losses as a matter of fact. "There are three prisoners still alive. One barely."

"Keep them. We will need them. And the strength that remains?"

"Twenty-nine fit men and four wounded."

Strangely it destroyed Kilewe's contentment. His eyes glared. "They should insult me so? *Twenty-nine?*"

"Might it not be better simply to kill them all quickly this time? Not play games?"

"I intend to, all of them but for a few. You should know that I don't play games, Aref. What I've done has well served its purpose. We have the goats tethered. It is time to put them down."

"That's all the water. Finished."

They had shared out the water as fairly as possible. From this point their entire ration was contained in their bottles. The Tilley lamp had been extinguished after the share-out. They were in total darkness, feeling the sweat turn cold as the evening air cooled.

"We leave the trucks behind with Gerry and the wounded."

On a reasonably flat stretch, Pietro Frascelli was practising on a pair of crude crutches that Steinberg had made from one of the arms' crates. They were rough, not at all well balanced and they had no crossbar. Frascelli himself had solved this by tying chunks of torn blankets round the top of the crutch to make them bearable under the armpits. He could move quite fast over short distances.

They loaded up. They had ammunition to carry, two men to a box. Donovan strapped on the tripod because it weighed forty-five pounds and was the heaviest part of the three mortar sections. Donovan refused to let Chianda carry anything but his Sten and spare ammunition. He wanted the Zambian to concentrate solely on his greater skills of bushcraft. Without him progress would be doubly perilous. To Chianda it was like picking up an old book he had not read for some time. After a few pages he was back in the story. He had already established a rapport with the brutal environment. Although they had no packs the grenade and ammunition boxes were of considerable weight and the mortar barrel baseplate and bombs had to be distributed.

The wounded were squatting by the transport, which was now reduced to two Range Rovers, the breakdown truck and one three-tonner. It was enough. With losses, more than enough.

They left camp in an untidy straggle of three shadowy columns. They had no need to be told to tread softly and they broke step to smother sound. As they started up the shallowest section of incline Steinberg could just distinguish King who had his Bren by the carrying handle. "Listen, you cockney crook, you owe me a bleddy dinner. I shall expect it when we get back."

"The best you've ever had you South African Ruaneck. Bleeding camel steak and sheeps' eyes, with curried coffee."

"Watch how you go."

"See you, cocker."

Steinberg risked raising his voice. "Look after them, Pat."

"Sure. Have a change of nappies ready."

The white smudge of Thompson's bandaged arm went past.

"Good luck, Tommy. Look after Colin."

"With my form and his prayers we can't lose."

It was many years since Steinberg had been so emotionally disturbed. He wanted to go with them but he had a job to do here. As the last man disappeared, as if passing beyond a dark curtain, Steinberg felt a hand on his shoulder. Frascelli had hobbled up. The Italian's voice wasn't quite steady as he said, "If it's any consolation to you, I feel the same. *And I fought against them.*"

They themselves had work to do. They returned to the depression and Donovan's Rover. The other three wounded watched them with interest. Their own lives lay in the hands of these men and those who had left.

If the air had seemed cooler with the sinking of the sun, the illusion passed quickly once they began to move. The close humidity of the night was stifling as they trudged away from the direction of Ober Uen. Some began to stumble, the ammunition boxes almost impossibly heavier now they were on the march. Behind him Donovan heard the groans and grumbles, the quiet blaspheming and he was satisfied.

With what they had to cope with the men couldn't fall asleep. Walking, straining their muscles, complaining, kept them awake.

Maxwell, heading the column next to Donovan, understood the need to keep moving. As Donovan was carrying the tripod he had volunteered to take the barrel weighing forty-four pounds and one canister of bombs in addition to his Sten, just to show Donovan's limitations. He knew Donovan was under strain, that his back was playing up; he would have given anything to hear him complain. Maxwell moved silently and grimly.

Bill Brown travelled light. All he carried was a Sten, his bow and arrows and two canisters of mortar bombs. He preferred the Somali wraps to European tropical dress even though they stank. He had got used to the smell, had endured it all before. He closed his mind to the walking, the thirst, the swelling tongue. Physically, he and Chianda had used up more energy than any of them and that meant loss of body water. He was able to anchor his sight on the dim shape ahead and close his mind to everything else, leaving the tiniest of escape hatches to receive danger warnings.

Ahead of them all Chianda progressed at a lope slow enough for the rest. It was really *too* slow for him but he understood the problem and was grateful that he had not been overloaded. He resented the desert as well as accepting it. Trails were more difficult to follow with hard rock immediately beneath. There was a lack of smell because there was an absence of anything that grew or moved. In his home country he could read almost at a glance whether the signs of crushed grass indicated that a lion had dragged its prey or perhaps a water buck had slept there. Here there were no lion, water buck, not even grass. So he had to rely on other signs; it was difficult at night. Direction was no problem, it never had been. Yet the strangest thing of all about this strange war they were waging was being at the head of a bunch of white men when, if he survived this, he would be going back to fight them. And in the contradiction to those thoughts came the realisation that nothing felt so natural as being with Bwana Menya, who had not changed, and Bwana M'futi, who had.

Jimmy King, halfway down the column, was feeling his age. He carried his Bren and a canister of mortar bombs. Two spare Bren barrels, useful for quick changing when the others were overheated, were strapped to his back. His legs were like lead, but his cockney humour burst out here and there and earned him a few grins. No one noticed the strain behind the effort. If Jeannie could see him now!

Thompson and Vale brought up the rear so that the columns were topped and tailed by veterans. They had fallen slightly behind the others, realised the dangers and were striving to close the gap. One of the reasons for the lapse was the awkward weight of the anti-tank rifle on Vale's shoulder. It was too heavy to carry any distance by its carrying handle and the hard metal bit into Vale's narrow shoulders. He had used it, he considered it his. So he suffered as he'd intended that he should.

Several times Thompson tried to take it from him but Vale refused, pointing out his friend's badly-wounded shoulder. Well, it wasn't *bad*. But by Christ it hurt if he moved it too suddenly. At the moment there was a deep throbbing beneath a creeping numbness. It needed cauterising, as all the wounds did, but there was no chance of that. He still carried his Bren in his good hand and he'd got one of the lads to strap a bomb container to his back. He carried a grenade in each pocket.

Vale said, "I didn't realise you were in prison. I would have visited you."

Thompson was caught off guard. "We're lagging, Colin. Can you lengthen your stride?"

"Does it embarrass you so much?"

"It's not the sort of thing you send out change of address cards about."

"You told Pat and Jimmy. Why not me?"

"I didn't tell them. They had long ears, read the papers." Thompson dropped his voice lower as they began to catch the others up. The effort increased the throbbing in his shoulder.

"Was it something terrible?"

Thompson was irritated. Colin was a friend but he was also a clergyman and the last thing Thompson wanted was a confessional with a cleric. He bit back a sharp retort when he realised that for one of the few times on this bloodlust jaunt, Colin's mind was not on himself. It was a minor miracle.

"I caught my wife on the job and knocked her off in a fit of temper."

"You killed her?"

"She'd been deceiving me from the moment we were married."

"It made you kill her?" Vale was incredulous.

"Cut it out, Colin."

"My dear fellow. You poor, poor man."

Thompson didn't answer. Even for Colin's sake there was nothing more he was prepared to say. He had no need. When he risked a glimpse a little later Vale seemed to have shrunk into his shell again. Worse. He was muttering. Thompson wondered what the hell he had said. But they had caught up, there were immediate dangers to think about. Out of a sense of guilt he could not understand he said, "You sure you don't want a break from that bloody Boys?" Vale didn't answer; he hadn't heard. He was gazing ahead, keeping up with the rest, but that was all he was doing. It was doubtful, just then, if he knew where he was or if he was conscious of the unbearable humidity.

Among the men all that mattered was to keep one foot moving in front of the other, monotonously, eternally. Their crusted faces were breaking pattern, new rivulets running through the sand layers as the sweat pumped with the effort of their young bodies. Every so often, as a controlled drill, they all stopped, changed loads or changed the grip to their other hands. Starting off again was murder. Their feet were swollen, their bodies alternately hot and cold. When it came to it they would rather suffer the agonies of carrying the heavy loads when they were dog-tired than to run out of ammunition when they might most need it. Above all one thing kept them going. These old bastards just kept at it whatever came up. They were comparatively slow but they knew how to pace themselves. And they hadn't forgotten how to shoot straight. They seemed to communicate that they knew what they were doing and that did not mean the technical data of the twenty-third lesson of the Bren gun. Better to be in their hands than someone like Maxwell's; he was respected more as a trigger-happy fearless bastard.

"It's crude, man, but it should work. With luck." Steinberg studied the rope fixed to the steering wheel and anchored to the near side door handle. "What will be more difficult is the offside. I can't tie it to the door handle because I've bleddy well got to get out." He sat in the driver's seat of Donovan's Rover. The door was open and Frascelli leant against the frame, supported on his good leg. When he changed position he winced as the broken ribs squeezed his lungs like nutcrackers.

"You could perhaps loop it under the clutch pedal." Even that hurt.

"No. I've got to use it. Same with the accelerator."

"The brake, then."

"I'm thinking about it. I'll need that too at first but maybe I can give it a final pull before getting out."

Steinberg climbed down and Frascelli lowered himself to the ground to lean against the wheel. Steinberg disappeared and Frascelli could hear him rattling around in the back of the three-tonner. They were working in the dark. The other three wounded men had been helped into sleeping bags and were fast asleep, the only ones in the task force to enjoy the luxury.

Steinberg came back with a roll of bandage, a hammer and some nails. With a wide strip of bandage over the pedal he found that he could tack the ends of the composite floor of the cab to keep the pedal down. There might be better ways but as long as it held it would do.

"We should get down to arithmetic, Gerald."

Steinberg smiled. "Are Italians always so polite? Has it occurred to you that we might have the privilege of dying together? Anyway, arithmetic is not my line."

"A banker who cannot do arithmetic?"

"That's shrewd calculation, observance, interpretation. Acumen, if you like. But it ain't arithmetic."

"Then we'll do some calculations together."

"Look, you do it while I check these bits and pieces."

"*Together*, Gerry. I must check the length of the fuses with your mileage estimates."

Steinberg acquiesced. "Keep the weight off your leg while I sort out the empty fuel drums. Got enough explosive?"

With all the night before them they could afford to detour provided they could stand the strain and they could resist the urge to drink the little water they had left. Fear, itself a stimulant, helped keep them awake, alert to sound.

They rested for a while, posted sentries. Donovan would not allow smoking. He slipped off his load, relishing the relief. He refused offers to help him with the tripod. Its unaccustomed weight was crucifying him but he had always believed in leadership by example. His refusal to change over meant that Maxwell was landed with the barrel too, for the ex-para would have died rather than allow Donovan to score over him.

After the all too short rest they moved off again, as silently as the loads would allow them, still cutting west away from their final objective. It was the worst part. Walking away, knowing that they had to loop back.

Nor was there sleep for Hassan Kilewe and Aref Ghalib. They were, however, able to enjoy their restlessness in moderate comfort and they had plenty of food and water. Every building was manned. The area of the river bed, best suited for an advance on the stronghold, was covered by machine guns concealed behind carefully pre-selected rock outcrops and in the river basin itself. Any one of these posts could easily wipe out the whole task force if it showed itself.

Around the stronghold alone were well over a hundred men, all heavily armed and behind cover. In the wadi about two and a half miles north-east of the stronghold were reserves with transport and animal stock, the life-blood of any desert community. There was sufficient food and water for both men and animals.

Restless guards were still stationed round the hut that had housed the women prisoners. Inside were Croft and two others that Kilewe had picked up from the escaping Rover. One man, tortured beyond endurance, was barely alive. Croft and the other one had suffered agonies but were still in one piece. Because of the time factor, Aref Ghalib had been forced to obtain the information on the task force's strength quickly, and therefore most brutally.

Croft had long since ceased to regret deserting. His thoughts had overflowed into a tortuous numbness that tried to exclude the constant pain. His only concentration was in striving to shut out life itself; anything that would bring a measure of relief and oblivion would do that in acceptable form. Croft had carried his cowardice into the web of his misery and his suffering was thereby multiplied by weakness and self-pity. When the door opened he whimpered.

Two guards cut him loose, handling him roughly. Croft showed no dignity, no pride. The most unfortunate thing that had happened to him was that Maxwell had not been allowed to finish the job of throttling him.

They took him out into the middle of the square. Kilewe stood in the walled entrance to his villa opposite the church. The old jail was further down. Roughly midway, a big stake had been driven into the ground. Croft, eyes wide with fear, could just make out the shape of it and the white waistband of Kilewe.

The stake was old. Croft could smell it, his senses at fever pitch. It had been used many times before; the central hole was not newly made. It was as if the stake itself was warning him of its part in former terrors. Croft screamed. Screams had been heard before. They excited no one. He struggled as he was lashed to the stake. When he was bound his legs would not hold him and he began to slip down the pole. They pushed him upright again and held his head up by his short hair. Someone slipped a noose over his head and tightened it round his neck.

Croft nearly passed out with fright. Soon he realised he could still breathe and that he was now alone, his guards having left him without a word. Lights were suddenly switched on from the side of the jail. He had to close his eyes tight as twin beams spotlighted him. An engine started, a jeep moved to his left. Through closed lids he could feel the lights full on him as he was caught squarely in the beams. He turned his head away from the glare, opened his eyes. Now he could see the frail figure of Kilewe much more clearly as he, too, was caught on the fringe of the beams. Bleak eyes locked on his own and he saw no hope. None. He found himself crying. His knees sagged and the garotte fastened to the top of the stake tightened round his throat until he gagged. In sudden terror he pushed himself up to ease the noose and was choking as he turned his head frantically from side to side to loosen it.

Croft survived his crisis under watchful eyes. His heart was pounding from terror, his whole body quivering. Oh, Christ, in the hut he had wanted to die, now he craved to live. If his legs could hold him. For how long? His knees were quivering. His only hope lay in Donovan's success. He would have to bear it as long as he could and pray to the God that looney Vale prayed to. It had not done *him* much good.

Kilewe watched dispassionately. These British were soft. The man was crying again. He gave a signal and the lights went out, not out of compassion for Croft but because he wanted to save batteries. There would be a time for the lights. When he had shredded the enemy, he would use Croft to illustrate to the paltry remnants what was to happen to them and the women prisoners. They would have time for fear and time for pain. It would be good for the morale of his men, and a warning to them too. Kilewe did not consider himself at risk in the open gateway. Too many posts surrounded the whole area. There would be no danger until the first shots and they would merely signal the beginning of the end. Of all things only two were completely predictable.

Somewhere in the desert was a hopeless little force that had come to rescue the English women. To do that they had to come to Kilewe; there was no other course. That was one. The second was his certain victory, finance for what he wanted, and power.

16

THE DESERT WAS empty of all life but themselves. The sky went on for ever, the rare sight of the Plough and the Southern Cross at its northern and southern extremities. For the rest, the black void was crushed with stars as if God had trampled all over them. The Milky Way was an infinite, overcrowded mass of layers, awesome to the naked eye, stupefying through ordinary binoculars. Donovan had used the glasses in an effort to keep awake.

This was the last rest before taking up final positions. The men were falling asleep as soon as they sat, some before they had removed the weapons from their shoulders. He could not blame them. They had enjoyed little sleep on the plane out, the following night had been taken up with travelling, and now they'd spent another sleepless night, much more arduous than the others. It was one o'clock in the morning and at last reasonably cool. The pattern had changed again.

Now the heat came from within, from unrelenting exertion.

Donovan hated driving them the last leg, dreaded the thought of rising to his own feet. Jimmy King had been right in London; they were beyond it. Over the hill. He felt feverish and when he looked at the nearby huddled shape that was Jimmy he could see that he, too, had reached the end.

Donovan didn't think he would ever get up again. Their objective had lost meaning. The mind, the body could only take so much. At their age they were mad to have tried it. It was over. Finished. Having used all the excuses he could find for giving in he turned to the man next to him. Maxwell had his hat off, was wiping grit from his eyes. He had one hand on the mortar barrel by his side. He had become Donovan's spur. Punishment and inducement at the same time.

"Come on, Max." Somehow Donovan levered himself to his knees. He went dizzy, held on. "Come on, Jimmy. Colin. Tommy." His voice croaked. It didn't matter. They all croaked. "That you, Brown?" He couldn't stomach the thought of the tripod again. Oh, Jesus. But Chianda had lifted it for him, holding the harness open for him to slip his arms through. Chianda, perhaps the oldest and certainly the least exhausted among them. Chianda, who knew him better than he knew himself.

It took Donovan all his time to keep upright. He had to lean slightly forward or topple backwards. While the others climbed to their feet with obvious effort, complaints were subdued by the mere fact that Donovan was asking of them nothing more than he and his friends could do. Some of them were well aware that he was more than twice their age. It made awkwardness difficult for them.

They travelled for another forty-five minutes. No one spoke during that last lap. There was simply the sound of feet, of creaking harness, the clatter of weapons as men sometimes staggered against each other. Donovan widened the three columns to prevent repetition of this. No one had the strength to dissent.

The moment of magic happened when Chianda halted to hold up an arm. He led them into a small fissure about knee high. There was room to spread out, to lay down to rest. For the moment it was ideal; a refuge where they could remove their loads and gain respite.

As the rest of them dropped down Donovan remained standing, finding an unsteady balance that somehow kept him on his feet. "This is fine for the men but the mortar will be out of range."

Chianda understood. "We'll need to go more than a mile, bwana. I'll take the tripod."

A mile. God. He'd never make it. Donovan almost let him have the tripod then.

He didn't know how he would ever get moving again. He looked down at the slumped heap that was Maxwell and shook his head once more. "On your feet, Max. Unless you want your men wiped out we must move the mortar."

Maxwell didn't say a word. He climbed up full of a burning resentment far worse than the day they'd met in London. He kicked at the man with the baseplate. "We'll need some bombs."

Jimmy King left his Bren behind and went with them, taking four cases. Chianda took four and so did Brown, who also took over the baseplate to prevent a scene with the exhausted mercenary who had been carrying it. Donovan and Maxwell took two cases each. It was more than enough, almost certainly more than they would get an opportunity to use.

Maxwell arranged a password with the sentries and threatened them if they fell asleep. The five men started out, sustained by the fact that they would return empty handed. Donovan had taken a compass bearing, the luminous dial bright in the darkness. He knew little about the last stretch. He recalled the immense relief of shedding the tripod for the last time, of the clang as it hit the ground.

They sat in the open desert without the protection of a depression or outcrop. There was none. The fissure was the only cover for some distance except for south of where they sat, towards the river bed and Kilewe's men. Somehow they got the mortar mounted and pointing in the rough direction Chianda had indicated. Donovan pushed them further into unpacking the bombs, laying them in rows beside the mortar. In the darkness it was impossible to see which were smoke or high explosive. It was a cardinal sin for a mortar team to have the bombs mixed up or even together. Here, it no longer mattered. He inserted maximum charges in the tailfins of all the bombs.

Chianda had disappeared before the bombs were laid out. It wasn't until it was time to return to the fissure that his absence was noticed. Donovan decided to wait, even though he had the compass. To try to find their way back to the fissure at night in so featureless a terrain was more than any of them were prepared to do. They could be hopelessly lost within seconds.

None of them heard Chianda return. The first they knew was a whispered password from out of the air, followed by a shape that rose from the ground. He set the estimated mortar range he had just risked his life to obtain and had to peer with eyes almost touching the sights to read the figures. Even a cupped match would stand out like a beacon.

They went back to the fissure. The sharp sound of a rifle bolt came from the gloom and Maxwell rapped out the password followed by a vehement demand to be told why a bullet hadn't already been up someone's spout.

Most of the men were just heaped about the fissure. Somehow Donovan had to rouse them for their own sakes. Maxwell did it for him, roughly, sometimes brutally. They synchronised watches once more. Brown hoisted his quiver onto his back, made certain an automatic pistol and his knife were in his waistband. A grenade was in each pocket of his shorts under the native robe. Chianda, still dressed as a Somali, checked his panga, pushed it back in its broad and battered scabbard. He wouldn't part with his Sten. He took his boots and socks off, preferring, from now on, to work in bare feet. The two men left the fissure.

For the moment there was nothing for the rest of them to do but be prepared. Jimmy King had his back to the wall, his hands clasped behind his head, his hat off, gazing reflectively up at the stars. "I could have been on my bleeding yacht looking up at that lot. Drinking champers and stuffing king-sized prawns. So I'm landed with you bloody shower, no bloody water and liquid bloody bully. Anyone got a toothpick?"

Thompson was checking his Bren as he did at almost every spare moment. He kept an extra magazine near him and made sure he was near a box of ammunition. His only thought just then was that he could do with more magazines to save time reloading. His shoulder was a furnace.

Maxwell was checking his Sten but he did so automatically. He hated Donovan's guts for not caving in but respected him at the same time. It was a respect he would never voice.

Vale was the only man who had no inclination to sleep and showed no physical sign of the arduous journey. Of all the men he had been the most likely to crack, yet he had been the least complaining. Since talking to Thompson he had gone completely within himself. The fact that Thompson had been moved to kill his wife tortured him. He saw himself too clearly as the other man. It could have been him. He could not read his Bible in the dark but he held it close to his chest. The Boys anti-tank rifle was by his side and he gave no indication of the massive bruises and ruptured skin on his bony shoulders. It was doubtful if he felt the pain.

They had thought walking was the worst part. Now it was waiting. Fatigue demanded that they close their eyes; fear prompted them to keep them open. Self-preservation was an uncertain winner. Only action could completely revitalise their energies, only danger could stimulate their senses. Positioning in the fissure was worked out, firepower distributed. They all had grenades.

Out in the desert Brown and Chianda moved fast and noiselessly. The young S.A.S. man and the old African warrior had made a superb team, understanding between them rarely having to be voiced.

They were making straight for Kilewe's stronghold, travelling due south, a direction Kilewe could hardly have anticipated yet still had covered. The time was three o'clock.

The two men were half walking, half jogging. There was enough surface sand to deaden the sound of their advance but it was an asset more to Brown than Chianda, who could walk on gravel as silently as he could cover grass. Both men had thrown off tiredness with the ease of discarding a cigarette stub. Their lives depended on complete awareness. They covered the desert like ghosts, somehow managing to half crouch without unduly straining.

In mid stride Chianda suddenly grabbed Brown's arm and stopped. After the land mine episode Brown had learned neither to be surprised nor to query such an action. He stopped a mere half second after Chianda. They sank to the ground without a word or further gesture. Chianda lay down, peering into the black screen ahead, nostrils dilating, body absolutely still. They were close enough to each other for Brown to observe his colleague. Moonglow and stars gave faint luminosity to the dull yellow stretch ahead.

Brown could see nothing. Chianda had the tremendous advantage of in-built radar. With a brief motion of his hand Chianda signalled Brown to stay still as he himself began to crawl forward, pushing his panga scabbard round to his back to prevent drag, and keeping his Sten in his right hand.

They had got the empty petrol drum onto the back of the Rover without difficulty. What had caused a problem was the opening which had been too small to take packs of ammonal with their gun cotton centre plugs and fuses. Steinberg had sweated for hours enlarging the aperture with inadequate tools, the hollow clanging waking the wounded and carrying across the desert.

Steinberg's wrists were throbbing, his fingers clawed, by the time he finally broke through the tough metal. The very crudeness of the result offended his sense of perfectionism, but Frascelli was satisfied and it was his opinion that mattered. Once the drum was on the back Steinberg helped Frascelli up, well aware of the Italian's suffering. Once on the back Frascelli was able to prop himself against the supports, avoiding pressure on his back and using one crutch to keep the weight off his injured leg. Steinberg got up to help him.

They crammed in everything they could spare; battered wheel discs, ammunition, grenades, a couple of spare mortar bombs, two of the Kalaschnikovs left behind due to lack of ammunition. And, layer by layer, Frascelli packed an ammonal block with gun cotton insert into which was placed a detonator and from which trailed the carefully measured fuse wire outside the drum.

There was a good deal of room in the drum. Steinberg removed the spare wheel, jerked off the tyre and, with a hacksaw, cut it into chunks. They had most of the night. They needed it. After cramming the rubber at various levels in the drum they filled it with every loose piece of metal they could find, including sawn door panels from the Rover. As they worked, the rising petrol fumes were at times almost overpowering. Step by step, foot by foot, layer by layer, they filled the drum tightly, finally padding the top and empty side spaces with material from sleeping bags the deserters had left behind.

As ammonal took the least line of resistance, Frascelli finally hammered on a wheel disk he had kept back, to close the aperture. As a bomb it was the most primitive ever. As a lethal weapon it had yet to be proved. They climbed down exhausted, having worked non-stop for several hours.

Donovan left Thompson in charge, much to Maxwell's annoyance, but Donovan wanted tough nerves not insensitive heroics. It was absolutely essential that nobody made a move until the right moment and that required judgment Maxwell had shown no signs of possessing. Maxwell would have gone over the top with a banshee scream and would have killed until he dropped. Donovan wanted the girls out and knew that he could not do that by force of arms. He took a careful compass bearing before setting out for the mortar post. He had refused to let anyone come with him, knowing he was setting himself up in a suicidal situation.

He felt lost without Chianda, missing the Zambian's sense of direction. It was eerie with no one else. Vast. Unfriendly. Unyielding. He reached the site, picking out the brooding form of the mounted mortar, incongruous in the open desert but offering him strange comfort.

He took up lonely vigil by the baseplate and rested his arms on his knees. He made careful note of the time. Could solitude ever be more complete?

From a prone position Chianda saw the outcrop and, with more careful scrutiny, the barrel protruding from it. There would be at least two men behind the rock. Perhaps three. Two he could tackle. He considered it very quickly. On the flanks, somewhere, would be other outposts. Within hearing range. He had not expected a post so far out, having anticipated that fire power would be concentrated much nearer the stronghold so that destruction of the task force would be a simple formality.

Chianda pushed himself further back until the outcrop had disappeared. Even then he crawled some way before rising to progress at a running crouch. He was only a few feet away before Brown saw him. They lay side by side heads close together. "Machine gun. No talking. Maybe two, three men. You go this way. I go that." The finger drew a pincer movement in the sand but Brown understood without seeing: "We meet at back."

"How far?"

"Seventy-five yards, maybe. Others around. No shooting."

Brown patted his bow, Chianda looked doubtful. Brown whispered. "We could miss each other at the rear."

"I find you."

They separated and moved off. Skilled though he was, Brown could not match the natural bushcraft of Chianda, so to advance silently he had to slow down. He had difficulty in locating the outcrop and was wondering whether he had flanked it too much. Then he saw the gun barrel like a cigar from the craggy face of rock. He kept on past the post, cutting in when he considered it safe. By now used to Chianda rising from nowhere he noticed that the Zambian had not gone too far in.

They met, closed heads. "Three. You take one on left. I take other two." Chianda withdrew his panga. They crept nearer.

Brown withdrew an arrow, raised the small bow. He indicated that Chianda should creep in closer. He fitted the arrow. It had been some time since he had used a bow. He saw Chianda approach, leaving his own field of view free. Chianda had stopped. Brown could barely see him. He sensed the Zambian was looking towards him. He fired, immediately moving forward. He didn't hear the soft thud of the arrow but Chianda did and had already chopped at the neck of his nearest man as both had suddenly stirred to see why the third had fallen over the gun.

The first and second men never knew what hit them. The third came fast out of a state of somnolence, immediately thinking his comrade had fallen asleep across the gun and changing his mind at the sound of the panga hacking away the life of his other comrade. He came to his full senses in the time it took for both Chianda and Brown to reach him. He rose to defend himself, his mouth open to scream a warning which died with him. It was problematical which had killed him, Brown's knife or Chianda's panga. It was Brown who eased him to the ground.

They stayed long enough to ensure all three men were dead. They resisted the temptation to take the machine gun because it was too heavy for the part they had to play. Brown removed the breech block and kept it.

They continued on some distance, until they heard subdued voices. One of the greatest difficulties of discipline was to stop men talking after many hours of silence. A whisper, through boredom, could betray. The armed might was Kilewe's but the game of nerves, so far, had gone Donovan's way.

They sank down as they did at every suggestion of danger and a long, prodding finger from Chianda pointed forward to a dark mushroom shape, beyond which they could hear someone whimpering. They glanced at each other. It sounded like a man. Someone deranged. The sound was muted by distance, sometimes barely audible, sometimes not at all. A cry for mercy reached them on a note approaching a scream and that cry had been in English.

Lying flat they tried to ignore the mixed sounds of terror and pain coming from the centre of the stronghold. The guttural voices of whispered dialogue were nearer to them, seemingly from the direction of the hut. When Brown strained his eyes he could pick out two squatting sentries either side of the hut. There were certain to be others on the far side and also facing them, outlines hidden against the dark shape of the hut itself. There was something unnatural about the whole background silence as if the place was just waiting to erupt. And there was something quite ridiculous about sentries so openly on view, even allowing for the fact that no force of size could get within sight of them without the risk of annihilation.

This was the moment of truth. Chianda drew his panga again and Brown his knife. In his other hand was the machine gun's breech block. They must get nearer. Both checked the time before moving.

Donovan checked his watch again. Ten minutes. He huddled, as if cold. There was psychological safety in numbers. Alone, the whole weight of his responsibility was open to inspection. For the next few minutes there was nothing to distract him from his own conscience. Whatever the outcome, people were going to die and he was going to start the process. Whatever material he might have expected to find here it was not this. Agony of mind was a private thing and helped none of those who suffered it. There was no finer example than Colin Vale. The degree of crime was a personal thing too. Vale had committed adultery with the wife of a dear friend. To Vale it was a monstrous, self-destructive sin. What then was the holocaust Donovan himself was about to start? He had gone soft. And thanked God for it. Solitude produced strange thoughts, ghosts, fears.

Two minutes. His gaze swung over the dim shape of the bombs around him. He prayed that Chianda's directional sense in sighting the mortar would not let him down now. Maximum range two thousand eight hundred yards. The figure had stuck in his head all these years.

One minute. Donovan rose with the first bomb in his hand. It seemed heavier than before. Fifty seconds. His hands were sweating. Thirty. If they sweated much more the bloody bomb would slip. Fifteen. Was he holding smoke or high explosive? Five. What the hell did it matter? Zero. He dropped the first bomb in, immediately reaching for another. And another. And another. Blast after blast in his ears.

It seemed no time at all before the first bomb went off. Then there was a short gap before the next explosion, and he guessed, as he still worked away, that the second had not gone off. The third registered only dully in his mind and he supposed that it must have been a smoke bomb. There could be nothing more confusing than an unpredictable mixture of smoke and H.E.

Donovan worked at a very fast rate, his splayed feet never moving as he dropped each bomb then bent for the next. He had got five bombs into the air before the first one landed, a high standard for a man out of practice and working alone. His back ached somewhere around the lumbar region, but it was now something he barely noticed, his one aim to get off as many bombs as he could in the time he had.

The sound of explosions was interspersed only by brief lulls due to a smoke bomb or perhaps a dud. Once there was a high whine as a tailfin flew and the bomb swished as it somersaulted to fall short. He was thankful not to be in a forward O.P. A new sound reached him and he hesitated fractionally. The cry of terrified animals came wafting across the desert in an untidy sound of varying volume. But it was clear, unmistakable. Still working, he glanced involuntarily at the baseplate. Had it sunk? Had the barrel moved? There was no time to find out. The whole idea was to make the animals panic but he was certain that he could hear cries of pain. Were the bombs falling short?

He got a grip on himself, forced tears back. The barrel became a misty well into which he continued to place the bombs, knowing there was no way back. Shit. Alarms, yes. Cruel but essential. To kill and maim was different. There were faint human screams, too, now emerging from the general uproar.

A third sound. Movement underlying the screams, the squeals, the agonised roars. Animals on the move. If most of the bombs had landed right he had left the animals one way to go, directly opposite to the explosions and spreading smoke at their rear.

He was getting more bombs off than he had expected to do. Smoke traces from the barrel would not be picked up at night but anyone with night glasses should find him.

They did and retaliated in savage form. Donovan dropped flat at the first volley of bullets. The firing was wild and from a distance but there was so much of it that he could not raise his head. He lay flat, the air alive above him. He started to crawl away, even then having the sense to check compass direction, when a mortar opened up against him. The first warning was the high-pitched whistle of a bomb that fell far short. Smaller calibre than his own three-inch. The comparison registered quite professionally. The sudden burst of light had seared his eyes.

Taking a chance he crab-crawled, keeping his head low, knowing it was a matter of time before the mortars put down a blanket as he had done. A bomb burst on the fringe of the site and he waited before rising to run for his life. Distance at this time was far more important than direction. Keeping down he ran as fast as he possibly could through a hail of bullets and bomb blasts creeping disconcertingly nearer.

Bent double, breathing was difficult. Concentration was around the mortar site and he had gained distance from it. Machine gun fire was sparser, he must be near the fringe though the whines passing close were still no comfort. Nor was the sudden, multi-dimensional roar that burst out behind him like a volcanic eruption. He wasn't sure whether it was blast or the need to survive that hurled him to the ground as shrapnel shrieked in every direction from the repetitive red blasts at his rear. All he could do was to lie there, hands over head as if they would protect him.

As Donovan had placed his first bomb in the mortar barrel Steinberg and Frascelli were taking a semi-circular route in the two Rovers to approach the stronghold from the south. Frascelli was seated sideways behind his wheel to ease the pain of his wounded leg and somehow he managed to keep his back from the seat rest. His makeshift crutches and a rifle rested against the passenger seat.

Steinberg drove as if he were on a day's outing. Hat correctly placed, face like a wrinkled prune, eyes quietly concentrating, he whistled softly to himself Suikerbossie. They were working on time factor alone, the noise of Donovan's distant bombs lost beneath the sound of their own engines, it was conceivable that at any moment they might be fired upon. It was their joint, calculated opinion that that would only happen if they misjudged the distance. Kilewe would want a certainty not a doubtful long shot. He could wait, must already have heard the engines.

When Steinberg slowed Frascelli, behind him, guessed they had entered the danger zone. Steinberg pulled up and switched off. Frascelli stopped a few yards behind and climbed out with difficulty reaching for his crutches and the rifle. He peered towards Ober Uen not sure whether or not he could see anything.

Inside the other cab Steinberg was tying one side of the steering wheel to the nearside inner door handle. He pulled tightly on the rope making sure it was stretched and that the knots were firm. He then tied the other side to the brake pedal, not so satisfied with this arrangement and relying mainly on the first. He opened the offside door, depressed the accelerator and tacked it down with the folded bandage and nails. He went to the rear.

Frascelli said, "Are you certain we are pointing in the right direction?"

Steinberg, hands on hips, stared into the darkness. "As

right as it can be, man. I can just make out the white smudge of that bleddy wall round the villa." He smiled. "Want to take it all the way to be sure?"

"Help me up." Frascelli climbed onto the back of the Rover. His leg was a furnace from knee to hip. He patted the petrol drum almost with affection. He sniffed around the top. The fumes had evaporated. What was left in the drum was now sealed in. "You want to switch on first?"

"Okay." Steinberg switched on, came back. "Have you allowed a few seconds for me to help you down?"

"Not, they're instantaneous fuses."

Steinberg chuckled.

Frascelli lit a fuse match low down. "Are you always so relaxed under pressure?"

"Always. It's hanging around with nothing to worry me that knots my guts. I don't see you biting your nails either."

Frascelli had lit two of the fuse wires trailing from the drum before Steinberg had finished speaking. He now lit the remaining two, immediately lowering himself to the tailboard. Once he was down Steinberg didn't wait. He jumped into the cab, depressed the clutch, moved the gear lever into second. He pulled the handbrake as far as it would go, releasing it fractionally as he raised the clutch pedal. The Rover strained forward uncertainly. Steinberg switched on the lights to full beam, took the handbrake off all the way, kept his hands away from the steering wheel and his foot clear of the accelerator. She rolled and rumbled, the wheel tried to turn but the ropes held it. There was nothing more he could do. He opened the door, jumped out, swinging the door shut with a bang as he went. He fell and rolled and grazed his knees, swearing softly. By the time he reached his feet Frascelli, who had started to hobble forward before the Rover had moved, reached him.

The two men stood watching. The Rover careered across the desert her lights shooting up and down, cutting the darkness with startling effect, brilliant white against the black. In the distance the outmost fringe of pale reflection showed on the walls of the old jail and, to the right, Kilewe's villa, wraith-like glimpses.

"It'll be interesting to find out what they make of that."

"Most interesting."

Steinberg glanced at Frascelli. "Do you feel up to a walk?"

"Why not? It's a beautiful night."

"Sure you can manage?"

"A little way. Will you carry my rifle?"

"Sure. We ought to see it."

They started out. Frascelli moving quite fast on the crutches, hiding from Steinberg the spreading pain.

Steinberg said, "I can see the fizzing of the fuse wires."

"Do not worry. Kilewe's men cannot."

"The old girl's travelling well."

Way beyond the stronghold was the faint drum of a stampede. They had just missed Donovan's mortar fire but above the distant sound of the panicking herd, they could hear machine gun fire and small explosions, even pick out the distant sight of the flashes. When Donovan's mortar sight went up they stopped, spellbound and worried. Then firing broke out on their side of the stronghold.

17

CHIANDA AND BROWN had eased round to the north-west side of the guarded hut. They had taken their time, checking foot by foot, covering each other as they went. They had heard Donovan's onslaught, the machine gun fire and the final massive explosion which worried them. Close to the ground the drumming of the herd was frighteningly loud and coming their way. They could hear the cries of the animals.

Beyond the far end of the stronghold twin headlights were cutting across the desert towards them, dipping and rising at every bump, shortening on the ground then scything through the sky. The two men nudged each other with controlled excitement. The bloody great monstrosity was on course. Kilewe's men opened up and now the firing was acute but ragged none of it coming towards them. In spite of the heavy fire the lights came on then there was one only, nearer, probing, lurching terribly as the tyres were ripped apart. But still coming. There would never be a better time. Brown grasped the breech block, pulled his arm back and let fly.

The breech block clanged on the iron roof of the hut, rolled down it with a clatter. The guards rose as a man, machine pistols swinging round to face the danger. The three heavy machine gunners detailed to cover the hut opened fire without giving the sentries opportunity to clear. Kilewe had ordered them to blanket fire at the first sign of an attempted break-in. One sentry flung himself sideways to crawl away to a reasonable position of safety from where he screamed abuse at colleagues who had almost killed him. The other sentires were killed almost instantly. The trap Kilewe had set backfired as the machine gunners were puzzled by the absence of return fire and no sight of the enemy. To add to their consternation a solitary headlamp was wavering behind them and then it too went out and the return of darkness was overpowering. They continued to fire for a while, aware that there was firing behind them interspersed with the unrelenting sound of an engine. Above it all were the repeated screams of the man tied to the pole as he realised that he was fully open to stray shots. The screams turned to insane, piercing shrieks punctuated only by the need for breath.

At an angle beyond the hut Brown and Chianda were pushing themselves into the sand, grinding bodies and faces into it as the firing swept over them. Behind, the herd was steadily drumming towards them.

The gunners maintained a prolonged series of bursts until the hut started to shred, great chunks of adobe falling away, clumps of straw hanging out in patches. It wasn't until they received a screeching order to cease fire from Kilewe himself that they eased back, wondering what had gone wrong.

Meanwhile the Rover, riding on its front rims, bonnet shot away, radiator burst with water and steam hissing into the night, what had been left of the windscreen smashed and the back of the cab a colander of holes, struggled on as if it had not been touched. It was about forty yards from the nearest building, its speed slowed to a bare crawl due to the absence of front tyres.

From the shelter of the thick ramparts on top of the villa Kilewe and Ghalib had belatedly guessed its purpose but could do nothing more than was being done. When it eventually limped to a halt, twenty yards from the old jail they ordered men forward to defuse it, pulling back gun outposts that might be obliterated if it blew up.

The Rover was canted wearily. The drum of explosive had been pierced many times but the ammonal had been missed. Dozens of bullets were lodged in the body work, the seats, the back of the cab. It blew up before the small nervous team got to it and before some of the gunners reached safety. The Rover was literally blown to bits, its parts scattering over a wide area, the noise a prolonged roar, explosion following explosion.

As the petrol caught it shot into the air a myriad of sepsrate tassels of flame that cascaded down in awesome beauty, dropping slowly to spread across the desert and drip, bloodlike, into the shallow crater where the Rover had been. The air was a frightening mass of shrieking metal, of disintegrating mortar bombs and grenades. One side of the old jail had a hole blown through and a corner of the building began to collapse. Somalis ran in terror to escape or be caught by blast and flying shreds of metal. Blood started to join the flames and nearby bodies began to incinerate.

Chianda and Brown had raised their heads following Kilewe's cease fire. They could not believe their eyes at the magnificence of Frascelli's bomb. Almost too late they had to rise, regardless of the dangers, as the herd came up behind them and suddenly veered, swinging away from the frightening sound and spectacle at the other end of the square.

The camels had come first. Some were hobbled, rearing pathetically at the new danger, trying to separate tethered legs. Some fell, to cause more confusion, and rose awkwardly to continue bellowing. Behind them came hundreds of goats, heads down in terror, veering as the camels had before quite reaching the hut. And behind the goats came the terrified sheep, bunched, following the others until the whole north end of the village was blocked with a mass of struggling animals, piling into each other in wild efforts to escape and so increasing their terror and confusion.

Machine gun posts were overrun, Somalis fled from the path of the animals. Some attempted to drive them back but it was hopeless. Visibility was extremely poor and the onslaught continued. Somalis still manning posts dared not fire for risk of hitting comrades but, above all, the acute need of the desert dweller for his animals prevented them from shooting. Without the animals they had nothing. It would be like cutting their own throats, their lifeline. Herders and reserve troops coming in from behind were trying to restore control over the stock. It was a hopeless task and their guttural shouts could be heard mingled with the bleats and squeals. The only light was from the aftermath of Frascelli's bomb and that was at the other end, throwing shadows, strange reflections. From the general crescendo came Croft's demented screams, Kilewe shrieking orders that could not be obeyed and the cries of the many wounded.

If they were noticed at all it was impossible to identify Brown and Chianda as they dodged through the congestion, sometimes literally brushing shoulders with Somalis desperately trying to quieten a herd that had now broken into two main channels. They reached the gateway to the villa and were almost opposite Croft.

Deranged, he had been hit in several places and it was incredible that he was still alive. His voice had become hoarse with screaming. He was so reduced that his only comfort was the sound of his own terror; his only reassurance that he lived while a nightmare raged all around him.

Both Brown and Chianda could see his struggling shape. The sound of him was impossible for anyone to miss. Brown stepped across the open gateway, saw the Somali guards who had withdrawn quickly inside when the bomb had gone off. He was glad now of his Somali garb. Stopping the other side, he backed to the wall, glanced across at the indistinct shape that was Chianda, sensed the unspoken signal and both men stepped through the gate.

The guards had machine pistols unslung but had no chance to use them. As before, one died by the panga, one by the knife. The problem was not in killing them but in keeping them upright and to stop their machine pistols clattering to the ground. They dragged the Somalis outside. Removing the machine pistols, Brown and Chianda allowed the bodies to slump. Brown took one of the Kalaschnikovs, removing magazine and breech of the other; Chianda still preferred his Sten.

There was more movement near the villa now. Someone was screeching from the roof and men were emerging into the square to try to retrieve the situation, to check on the dead and wounded and the damage. The fires at the south end were dying, shadows shortening, figures difficult to see beyond short distances. Brown and Chianda stepped inside the entrance pillars again as the guards might have done. They looked round the courtyard. Two more sentries were posted beyond the grotesquely rising flagpole. The guards were indistinct, dirty smudges against a white wall. The villa showed no lights. In the far corner of the yard was the dark shape of a vehicle.

Brown drew an arrow. It was not far but visibility was poor, the walls shutting out what little light had erupted from the petrol fires. The vast importance of the shot made him nervous. He lowered the bow. Chianda had crept away from him, nearer to the other two sentries but not near enough to raise suspicion. None of them were any more than shadows. Brown raised his bow again. He shut out the wails, the cries, the shouts and near pandemonium going on outside, fastened onto a blotch and released the arrow.

Chianda heard it go home. There was a gasp of pain but the Zambian was already moving in, bare feet silent. The sentry fell forward. The machine pistol clattered to the ground. The other sentry, greatly unsettled by the commotion beyond the walls made worse by being unable to see what was happening, ignored his stricken fellow and swung up his machine pistol. Chianda, moving fast, released the panga like a throw knife. By the time he reached him the sentry was on his knees grasping the panga protruding from his stomach, the machine pistols resting between his thighs.

Brown reached the side of the other sentry who was juddering but not quite dead. Both arrow head and the poison behind it were doing their deadly work quietly. Chianda had to finish his unfortunate victim off and they dragged the bodies to a corner of the yard. With their guns held at the ready Brown and Chianda flanked the door in a street-fighting stance and Brown leaned forward to open it.

When Donovan regained his feet from the blast of his own mortar site being blown to bits, he ran hard. While he had lain flat self-preservation coupled with calm disposition had dictated that he check his compass. He reached a point when he realised he had missed the base.

Being lost in the desert was soul destroying. Then he heard again what they were all to hear that night, the hoofbeat of the mixed herd, soft but clear, heading for familiar ground and the smell of water at the well. He listened carefully, decided their direction and set off at a fast jogtrot, lungs bursting, craving water, the machine pistol a dead weight.

In the fissure they all heard the battle of the mortars and the machine gun fire. The noise of it alerted every man to full readiness. When the site went up Thompson, King and Vale could not hide their concern for Donovan. Even Maxwell showed remorse. The herd was on the move and, by the sound of it, going the right way. But Thompson insisted on waiting a little longer for Donovan, the spectacle of his blown up mortar base still visible.

Finally King dug Thompson in the ribs. "We'll 'ave to go, cocker. He'd have wanted it. Anyway that bugger's indestructible." Thompson nodded. "What chances now of joining you in London?"

They advanced from the fissure in one long line abreast, well separated, making it more difficult for gunners. They jogged along heading for the animal sounds, arms ready, thirsts almost unbearable, the little water left slopping hollowly in their bottles. They were converging on the herd, amazed by the size of it, when Frascelli's bomb went off and they realised just how close they were.

Frascelli and Steinberg had suffered torment as the Rover rolled near to the stronghold. They had never considered that it would get so close, that it might endanger the very people they had come to save. They had banked on it being fired upon and stopped. The most they had hoped for was some destruction of outer terrorist posts and a massive distraction. From the prone position from where they watched the result was almost too good.

In the light from the flames they had seen the damage to the old jail wall and terrorists streaming from it. In a short time the area seemed clear. Eventually the fireglow dropped, vision reduced. Being south of the makeshift bomb its noise had covered the sound of the herd which they now picked up again. In the comparative silence they guessed that the Somalis would be regrouping and they knew that with or without Donovan the pathetic little main force would be on the move.

Steinberg scratched the back of his head. "I have an idea. You may not care for it."

The very casualness of the South African warned Frascelli. "I think I know what you have in mind."

"It could be suicidal."

"But it would help the others."

"You married?"

Frascelli inclined his head. "Happily. I would not be but for Pat Donovan."

"It's not too good a motive for sacrifice, Pietro."

"It's good enough. To repay a debt. To finish all square. What reason have you?"

Both men were watching the last hungry lick of flames along the sand crust. They could just hear some of the dying and the wounded and above that Croft's piercing shrieks. "Boredom. The lack of real love." He turned his head like a sparrow. "Would you believe I've enjoyed myself here?"

"You are not even armed."

"I wouldn't know what to do with a gun. A spanner's different. Anyway, there are many ways to skin a cat."

"Then we had better do it." Frascelli climbed up, hobbled to the back of the Rover. Steinberg did not question it when the Italian asked him to help him up. Once there, Frascelli took four ammonal blocks, plugged them with gun cotton, fused them, crimping the metal ends over short lengths of fuse wire with his teeth. He wasn't sure whether Steinberg could see him. "Did you know hot breath could set off a detonator?"

"That's why I was holding mine."

They climbed into the cab, smiling. Steinberg started up. "Comfortable?"

Frascelli eased his leg. "With you driving how can I not be?"

They were still smiling as they drove off. Steinberg said,

"I'd better give it the full treatment to be convincing." He switched on the lights to full beam. The stronghold, the dying chaos came into focus.

"Keep your head down, Pietro. And be ready to dive."

Dive? With this leg? "You too, my friend."

"I'm so bleddy short arsed I can barely see above the dashboard."

The rule had been set for good humour. If they were going out it would be with a smile.

The herd was strugging over a great distance by the time Donovan reached its fringe. The animals were congesting around the stronghold struggling and blocking each other and then veering west. At the moment he was mainly occupied in trying to keep his feet while cutting through the herd and avoiding all tall shapes and the voices of the striving Somalis. As long as he didn't get too close to one he was reasonably safe. He was panting hard.

Seeing the hut he made for it, breaking loose at last, quickly noting the damage to the hut close up and tripping over one of the dead sentries. It was too good an opportunity. He crammed the ready-made turban on his head, stripped off and donned the Somali clothes. He dragged the naked body into the sagging hut, almost falling against Croft's two comrades, now dead, riddled by bullets. He went outside. With the herd around there'd be little risk of fire but the animals were thinning out by the sound of it, stragglers bleatingly trying to catch up with the rest.

Back against the wall he listened to the confusion. Frascelli's bomb had been magnificent. But he could sense, too, the beginning of a return to order. Panic had undoubtedly been caused, was still thinly under the surface, but the Somalis were collecting their wounded, slowly responding to the screeched orders from the villa roof. Donovan had always considered that Kilewe would be in the villa. What was needed was another shot of panic before things settled down against them. He openly crossed the square towards the villa wondering just how far away was his main force.

He went through the entrance, stood with back to the wall. He could see little but the dark shape of the radio van.

He stepped cautiously across the yard to find the untidy heaps of the two sentries. The wall entrance was suddenly reflecting a pale wavering light and above Croft's screams was the unlikely sound of an approaching motor engine.

Frascelli propped his crutches against the dashboard. He groped for one of the ammonal blocks, fuse matches ready. Steinberg, hands steadily on wheel, gave him a quick glance. "What're you going to do with that?"

Frascelli shrugged. "I don't know. Use it as a grenade given the opportunity. It might frighten them."

Startled Somalis were coming into their beams. Some were being dragged from the square. They were looking up towards the Rover, dazzled by its lights. One or two fired and ran. Steinberg was quick to seize on the signs of terror. *"Hold on."* He accelerated hard and blasted the horn.

The effect was incredible. It needed one man to start the panic. Suddenly those nearest were racing hard down the square, preventing anyone further down from firing. The wounded lay waving arms, screaming, remembering vividly the bomb that had injured them. Central to the scene the demented Croft was still on his feet.

Steinberg yelled, "We've sold them the idea. They're shit scared." They careered towards the square, clearing the whole area as they went. Another truck bomb. The panic spread fast.

"Stop by the prison."

Steinberg did not question Frascelli. They had to stop somewhere before their huge bluff petered out. He pulled up with a skid, appalled by the near sight of Croft who was less than half a man. There was nothing he could do for him yet. He dived out, racing round the rear to the other door to help Frascelli out. The blazing headlights were helping, throwing them in shadow while illuminating the front. It seemed that every terrorist had dived for cover waiting for the new bomb to explode.

"In here."

The old jail offered immediate cover. Steinberg took Frascelli's rifle, saw him fumbling as he dropped one of the ammonal blocks. They were relying on the building being empty with the Rover just outside and the gaping hole in the wall a vivid reminder of what the last bomb had done.

In the temporary safety of the jail Frascelli lit a fuse match. It hissed almost like a sparkler, casting its uncertain light, burning much longer than an ordinary match. Both men searched about them, Frascelli wobbling on his crutches. He traced the two pale barely discernible blobs against the far wall and he said, "I thought I glimpsed one of you peering round the doorway. Ladies." He managed a slight bow, ignoring the pain for the moment. "We apologise for taking so long."

The fuse match cast the shadows under his cheek bones, showed the great strain, the grime, the dried sweat. But the dark eyes were bright, expression reduced by effort to polite enquiry. Steinberg was more explicit. *"Jesus Christ!"* And hurried forward, taking the match from Frascelli who lit another.

While Steinberg crossed the rubble, Frascelli lit three fuses, went to the door and tossed the blocks into the cab. The Somalis were belatedly getting down to firing at it. He called out, "We had better get through the hole in the wall quickly."

Donovan went up limestone steps at the end of the corridor. He passed several doors on the way, hearing snatches of Somali from behind them. The outside walls of the villa were undoubtedly lined with Kilewe's men waiting with machine pistols at the windows. They must have been totally bewildered as part of the herd thundered under their noses. Frightened stragglers were still coming.

A door faced him. He levelled his Kalaschnikov, opened the door quickly and stepped onto the roof. Reflected light from the advancing headlamps cast sufficient glow to pick out three white-clad figures, one holding a machine pistol on the other two. Before he could glance either side of him, a muzzle prodded him in the back and a voice in Swahili told him to keep still and to drop his gun. He recognised the language without fully understanding the demand.

He kept still, then said clearly, "Your Swahili was always a disgrace, Chianda."

Chianda came round, his grin huge. Quickly he recovered, kept his voice down, approvingly eyed the garb Donovan had put on. Brown, who had heard, did not make the mistake of turning round. Softly he said, "We've got mastermind and his oppo. Our passports out."

Chianda remained by the door while Donovan approached. He had never seen Kilewe; he experienced mild disappointment. The man with him possessed much more the aura of a leader. "Does he speak Arabic?"

"He understands it, Guv."

"You did well, you two."

"We're not out yet."

"No."

The Rover had pulled up opposite and the Somalis had started to fire at it. Donovan walked over to the other side of the roof. Steinberg and Frascelli were already in the jail by the time he got there. The lights were full on Croft who had ruptured his throat, his cries reduced to a soul-rending croak. What the hell was the Rover doing there? And where were Thompson and his men?

The headlamps were blown out. Donovan went back. "I suppose Croft was put there to show what would happen to us."

"It didn't get too far, did it, Guv?"

"Tell him to order his men to cease fire."

Brown translated. Kilewe remained silent, hatred riddling through him, burning, consuming.

"Time's running out. Dawn isn't far off." Donovan raised his machine pistol and killed Aref Ghalib with a short burst.

Brown said conversationally, "I'd have done that for you, Guv. I know how you feel about it."

"Now ask him."

Kilewe did not flinch. Donovan ripped the turban from Kilewe's head and tied his arms behind his back with it. The ammonal charges went off at that moment. At the other side of the roof, the small group were protected from the enormous blast. The noise was worse than the damage. The explosive took the line of least resistance and found plenty of escape. But visually and acoustically it was frightening, parts of the Rover flying through the air. The Somalis did not wait to draw comparisons. The north end was again in disarray. They fled into the face of the approaching Thompson and his men who had made full use of the confusion and who now opened up with everything they had.

There was desultory return fire. Most of it was wild,

spontaneously designed to provide time to escape. The rout was aided by the lack of cohesion of the escapers. They merely fled in every direction without a semblance of co-ordination, missing the lashing tongues of Kilewe and Ghalib on whom they utterly relied. Totally bewildered, out-manoeuvred, tactically outclassed, seemingly surrounded by enormous resources of arms and men, deserted by leaders who had first misled and then betrayed them, they ran into the desert in every direction, defeated and demoralised.

And from out of the sound of fleeing, of the ragged one-sided battle, came a voice from across the square. "If anyone is bleddy listening, there's a jeep down here and we're pushing off. The ladies are in bad shape."

Donovan felt like weeping. Brown was grinning savagely hoping Kilewe would make a move. Donovan bawled. "Keep going south, Gerry. We'll be right behind you."

A cheer came from Steinberg and Frascelli in reply and in recognition of the raggle taggle force that entered the north end like discarded ghosts. They could not see them all but they could hear the aggressive Maxwell swearing loudly that he'd been deprived of satisfaction. Steinberg called out to identify himself, to explain. Donovan, Brown and Chianda called down from the roof. Cheers went up all around. Thompson became recognisable, smoking Bren under his good arm, finger still on the trigger. And then, incredibly, Vale appeared, his anti-tank rifle cutting into his shoulder. He advanced alone like a military saint offering himself as a sacrifice but there was no one left to destroy him. He stopped in front of Croft, appalled by what he saw yet protected from much of it by the darkness.

Vale put down the Boys. Croft was somehow still upright but with no knowledge of what was happening. In the stuper of pain, of derangement, he had at last found a courage he could not find before. Vale's thoughts went outside himself. And there they stayed. Sickened by Croft's suffering, knowing that nothing could save him, he put out a hand to the lacerated forehead and gave a quiet blessing, transmitting compassion in a strong emotional wave. He closed his eyes and as he did so, Croft's head fell forward, checked by the noose. Croft was free at last. Vale finished his prayer then turned, leaving the anti-tank rifle in the middle of the square where it remained. His absolution was far from complete but it was at last on the way.

From somewhere behind him a cracked voice started to sing: "Oh, my old man's a dustman, 'e wears a dustman's hat."

They found lamps. They found dead and wounded; there was nothing they could do for either. When the terrorists returned they would have to care for their own. They found, too, signs of the most repulsive torture and a little of its results. Brown found the block of fused ammonal which Frascelli had dropped before driving off with Steinberg and the girls. And they discovered the arms dump in the church.

They filled water bottles from the deserted well and then they prepared to get back to base to pick up their own transport. With the radio van available nobody intended to walk. To pick up Somali transport from the depression would be too dangerous, pushing luck too far.

There were twenty-eight in total. Twenty-seven task force and a shrunken Hassan Kilewe. He was their insurance. The radio van was not designed to carry twenty-eight men, but the springs had been strengthened to take the heavy radio equipment. Somehow they got in. Fortified by success, relieved thirsts, their spirits were high. Some cramped into the front. Some climbed onto the roof lying flat and clinging tenuously to the edges. Others mounted the banks of equipment to stretch out on top of them. The remainder were pressed into the narrow channel between the two rows of equipment and suffered the compressed heat and drastic loss of air. In this boiler-room discomfort they sang and joked. Before they set off Brown ran back to the church, lit the ammonal fuse and tossed the block into the ammunition dump. He raced back to the van, thumped the side, then mounted the rear step, clinging precariously to the open door as they moved off. The biggest, most devastating and colourful bang of the night almost blew them out of the desert but by then they were far enough away to survive.

Dawn had broken by the time they reached base. They loaded the three-tonner with the remainder of the fuel. Donovan led with the truck with Hassan Kilewe tied to a back support, surrounded by most of the task force.

Donovan passed no comment when he noticed how many men were suddenly armed with machine pistols instead of rifles. The small convoy moved off, the sun juggling on the haze of the eastern horizon. The whole mood of the force had changed but Donovan knew that it was not over. They had still to get out.

Amongst the mercenaries he had found a radio operator but was reluctant to use him for fear of attracting officialdom. He had no idea whether the set radioband was monitored by the Somalis or the Russians or not. He had decided to continue without radio contact while everything went well.

By mid morning he had cause to change his mind. As they drew level with Mogadhu, track troop carriers appeared on their left. Armoured cars flanked them. They were some distance away but the sand streamers were like approaching storm clouds. Donovan made up his mind. He stopped, went back to the radio van, wrote out a message and instructed the operator to transmit continuously.

The huge aerial was cranked up. The transmission began. "This is the Volunteer Task Force calling Nairobi from Somalia. Relay to those concerned the following message: "Terrorists routed. Hostages, worse for wear but uninjured. Convoy consists of advance jeep with freed hostages. Arrange to meet with helicopter and doctor. Also have doctor and ambulance copter at border for own wounded. Approximate arrival point one degree latitude, forty-one degrees five minutes longitude. Spotter aircraft should locate and adjust copter pick-up as necessary south of Lorian Swamps. Somali authorities showing greatest co-operation and help in escorting us to border. This help of great value, their restraint over our entry magnificent. Their protection essential with terrorists loose. Present position west of Mogadishu. Estimated time of arrival, mid afternoon."

The military convoy had been closing gradually, close enough now to show pennants on the carriers. About half an hour later the convoy straightened and began to run parallel. There was a lusty cheer from the three-tonner and the radio van which had closed in.

Ahead, a speck appeared at almost ground level heading towards them at fantastic speed until it appeared that a twin-engined jet was using the desert as a massive runway. At zero feet it soomed up above their heads and banked towards the west, coming round in a tight circle. Miles ahead Gerry Steinberg had already identified it as his personal jet, had waved frantically. On the flight deck Dan Vermaak came back on course, took note of the double military string, shot ahead of Donovan's convoy, waggled his wings and gave her full power as he saw two MIGs hiding in front of a raw sun. He was too old a hand for that. Hadn't they all been? He radio'd the convoy's position, returned to zero feet and headed for the border filling in authority with more exact information.

The raggle taggle force was coming home.

Five miles from the border the military escort drew back. From the troops in the carriers came a solitary hand wave which gained momentum until the troops were openly standing and waving. It made the task force feel good. They knew the acknowledgment was in no way for what they stood for or even for the rescue, which would not appeal to a system opposed to theirs, but for what they had achieved in a military sense against all odds. They were the waves of soldiers for other soldiers.

Two miles from the border Gerry Steinberg was waiting alone with his jeep. Donovan stopped, asked Chianda to stay seated and stepped out to meet the South African. "Where're the others?"

"Taken out by 'copter. I came back to wait for you."

"The girls okay?"

"Not molested but not exactly nurtured either. They'll recover."

"There's something on your mind."

"Is Kilewe with you?"

"In the back."

"What will you do with him?"

"Hand him over." Donovan saw where it was leading. He stepped away to wave the radio van through. It rumbled past, the men calling madly at Steinberg through the open rear doors.

"I told you I'd let you know when I wanted a gun, Pat."

"Execution is not the answer."

"You hand him over and they'll have to hand him back. Lend it to me or I'll borrow one of the others."

Donovan handed it over. They walked to the back of the truck. The mercenaries grinned and waved at Steinberg.

"Get him down."

The grins changed. They bundled Kilewe from the back. He stood under the white hot sun, his hatred now clearly maniacal, yet he made no attempt to move.

Steinberg said, "You didn't change your ways much. You were transparent, Kilewe. You hadn't changed a tactic. Did you think the tortured remnants of one of our own men would stop us? Or did you believe that we'd all be in the bag? We made rings round you, you bastard. You were destroyed by your own vanity."

Chianda had climbed out quietly to translate into Swahili. Kilewe gave no sign that he understood. His dark eyes were blazing.

Steinberg said, "What you did to Croft wasn't as bad as what you did to my brother. I'll treat you better." He emptied the magazine into Kilewe, still firing as the Somali hit the ground.

The only surprise any of them felt was that it should be Steinberg who finished the job. Steinberg, who had not carried a firearm throughout.

Sir Murray Field stirred his coffee.

"Good show. I knew they would do it."

"Really, sir!" Smithy, though quietly incensed, kept his observation pointedly dry.

Sir Murray was unruffled. The greatest weight of all time had been taken from his shoulders.

"Didn't I say they knew the form?"

It was too despicable to warrant reply.

"We'd better tell their wives. They're in for a shock. Get them down to the airport and fly in Mrs. Frascelli from Rome as our guest. Oh, and Smithy, keep the homecoming quiet. No fuss. Don't let anyone know which flight they are on. Make sure that all the task force fly in to London. I'm sure Her Majesty and the Duke will want a word but behind the scenes. We can transport Steinberg and Frascelli to their homelands afterwards. And that damned terrorist, that Chianda fellow."

"I'm sure Chianda will enjoy taking you for everything he can. And so he should. As for the other two I doubt that they need free hospitality of the standard you might provide. Still, you must think it a pity that we can't claim credit for all this." Smithy hesitated, then continued with considerable satisfaction. "One thing you might have forgotten—Thompson's immediate parole."

The plane arrived early evening, an unscheduled flight. It touched down as it had flown, softly, beautifully, providing comfort to men who, in four short days, had forgotten the meaning of the word. The plane, engines whining, taxied to the prearranged spot. The steps were wheeled forward. The door opened and, after the entry of two officials, the task force came out to crowd the platform, an odd, unlikely assortment in a variety of clothing that had been provided by a relenting Kenyan Government. It was in order if one won.

The diplomatic bickering over territorial invasion was for the politicians. The Somalian Government had come out with dignity, having picked up the remnants of Kilewe's terrorists; the British Government with some disgrace. Why hadn't *they* sponsored the task force and provided them with what they should have had? But the British themselves prospered by the respect gained by a few veterans all of whom, since their return, had claimed that they were well beyond it.

When the dust had settled some few weeks later, at a private audience at Windsor, the Queen bestowed decorations to a handful of men in the presence of her family. It was a happy occasion, and a reunion of a fistful of heroes, only slightly marred later by one of them trying to sell his award on the open market.